LIGHTS OF AURORA

Book Three of
The Stone Legacy Series

Theresa DaLayne

CHAPTER ONE

Zanya

The scent of dried herbs and fresh rain poured through the open window.

For the rest of her life, with every whiff of sage or wet earth, Zanya would remember Contessa's quaint home in Moscow and the shock of that day— of losing Jayden.

She might as well have been gone when he needed her most. Zanya could still see Jayden's bright blue eyes staring back at her while he struggled to hold Sarian off long enough for them all to escape.

She could have saved him if she'd been more focused, more experienced with her abilities. Instead she'd done exactly what Contessa thought they'd do all along. Failed. She couldn't even heal Jayden. Instead she froze under the pressure.

A tear slipped down her cheek, and she tightened her fists while staring down at Jayden's body.

Someone had to care for him. Even though his spirit had been torn from this world, he deserved his last rites.

Zanya dragged the sheet that covered his body over his face.

Their mission to retrieve his soul could also fail, and the boy she'd first met in the orphanage could be ripped out of her life, leaving an empty hole of memories and regret.

She crouched beside Jayden, placed a kiss on his shrouded forehead, and whispered in his ear. "Hang on. I'm coming for you." She curled her fingers around the cotton sheet. "I'll get you back." Her voice caught in her throat, and she choked back a flood of tears.

Arwan placed his hand on her shoulder. She looked up at him and saw empathy in his gaze. "We will get him back." The silky tone of his voice usually comforted her, but not now. Not until Jayden was back, alive and safe. It would happen somehow. She'd make sure of it.

Zanya forced herself to stand. The fabric of her canary-yellow ball gown swooshed with the movement, a badge of blood smeared across the front. Jayden's blood. Somehow that made it worse.

First she needed to get out of her ridiculous dress. She wouldn't be able to hike through the caves of Naj Tunich in a gown.

Renato's dress shoes tapped over the floor as he approached from behind. "I'm calling Peter." He dialed a number on his phone, stealing the occasional glance at Contessa from the corner of his eye. "I hope he is still at the hotel."

"Make sure you don't tell Tara where we're going," Zanya said. "She'll freak out."

"As she should. This mission of yours may as well be a suicide attempt." He frowned. "The king of the underworld will never allow you to leave there alive." Renato walked outside to Contessa's front step without another word.

He was probably right, but she couldn't turn her back on Jayden when he needed her the most. Suicide mission or not, she was going after him.

Hawa moaned, tearing Zanya's attention away from her thoughts. Hawa lay on Contessa's couch with her leg elevated on a stack of pillows. The break was bad, but she wasn't crying anymore. That was a good sign—even if Contessa had only healed Hawa to make her shut up. The red-haired witch even had the audacity to say that aloud.

Renato walked back inside, the corners of his mouth sloped into an even deeper frown. "Peter did not react well to our plans. He insists on going with the two of you. He's coming here right now."

"No, he can't come with us. Tara will already be pissed at me for taking off without telling her. I can't take Peter too."

"Then you should depart as quickly as possible." Renato rested a hand on Arwan's shoulder. "I know you will take good care of her."

Determination sparked in Arwan's eyes. Zanya didn't doubt what Renato said was true. He would protect her, no matter the cost.

Zanya bit her lip. She was touched that he cared so much, but he was risking his life now too.

The cab took nearly an hour to arrive. While the

taxi waited by the curb, Zanya stood on Contessa's doorstep. She and Arwan would drive straight to the airport, but first he'd have to come out of Contessa's house. No doubt Renato was giving him every precaution to take before their journey.

She gazed lifelessly at the mud-crusted rims and the fogged taxi light while her mind wandered between realms.

Whispers yanked her out of her thoughts.

You will never recover him. You are a failure, just as your mother was. But I have plans for you, and soon you will be mine.

She turned and peered over her shoulder, expecting to see someone there—someone she would promptly punch in the face for being such an asshole. But she was alone on the steps.

Was she seriously going crazy?

The blare of the taxi's horn made her jump. It must be the stress, or the fact she had barely slept for the last few days. Deprivation played tricks on the mind.

Renato's voice became louder as he and Arwan walked toward the open door. He handed Arwan a credit card and some cash before they shook hands. The lines on her uncle's face deepened when he turned to her and pulled her into a hug. As he cradled her against his tailored suit, the rich scent of tobacco surrounded her. All of her life she had wished for someone to care about her the way Renato did, though she'd only known him for a short time. Still, his embrace was enough to make her hesitant to say good-bye.

"You must make it out of this journey alive," he

said in a raspy whisper. "Even if you do not succeed in retrieving Jayden's spirit, please—" he held her tighter, "—return unharmed."

Zanya nodded and forced a smile. "I'm not planning on dying anytime soon. The stone needs me."

His grip loosened, and he looked down at her, his familiar brown eyes filled with a mixture of despair and pride. "The stone is not the only one who needs you, Zanya."

His fear was well founded. She was about to walk straight to the gates of hell with no knowledge of what to expect.

"Now go. Go, and come home safely."

"Make sure to tell Tara…" Her throat ached. Leaving her best friend behind was something she'd sworn she'd never do. Not in the orphanage. Not after they were taken away from that place. Not ever. Now she was going against every oath she'd ever made to herself—and to Tara.

Zanya reached into her bag and grabbed the pendant Cualli, the middleworld goddess, had given her. The pendant was a gift and an omen of support, and usually it calmed Zanya.

Arwan lifted a duffle bag from the floor. He traced his fingers down her cheek, holding her gaze until she finally allowed a hint of a true smile to break through. His touch was all he could give to comfort her. Showing him it had worked, even a little, was the least she could do in return. After all, he insisted on going with her, and there was nothing she could do to repay that.

The cab's horn blared again. Zanya jumped and

glared at the taxi. "You'd think he'd be happy to just sit there with the meter running."

Arwan shook Renato's hand one last time. Her feet were rooted to the ground, contemplating one last hug. When she glanced at her uncle, her eyes stung with more tears. He must have noticed her hesitation. Maybe even understood it.

With a soft smile, Zanya walked straight to the cab without any more good-byes.

***

After grabbing some clothes off the rack of a sporting goods store, Zanya continued into the dressing room and checked herself in the mirror, horrified at her reflection. Wet, limp hair stuck to her cheeks and neck. A huge bloodstain spread over the front of her once-beautiful gown, which was now smeared with mud and torn in several places. Her cheeks were burned from the biting cold, and her nose was so red she could pass for Rudolph.

She sighed and worked at removing the pins and ties from her hair until it finally came undone, and then used one of the ties to lock it in a bun. The next thing would be to get out of her dress and change into something warm and dry.

Zanya craned her neck as she fumbled with the strings laced down the back of her gown. The damn thing was threaded so tight there was no way she could do it herself.

Zanya sighed. *Perfect.*

She grabbed the dressing room curtain and pulled it aside. "Arwan?"

"Hm?" He lifted his head from his hand where it was rested, his eyes half-glazed over with sleep. Her shoulders slumped forward. The poor guy was exhausted. She couldn't blame him. He'd been through a lot these last few days. They all had.

"I just…" She pointed to her back. "I need some help with this corset thing." The man sitting two chairs to the left of Arwan gawked at her. Zanya made double sure the curtain hid the stain on her dress.

Arwan stood and eased toward her. "Turn around."

She noticed more people shopping and several men slumped in the rows of chairs in the waiting area. "Uh, no. Come inside." The fact she had to ask for help undressing was humiliating enough. There was no way she'd let him undo this thing with everyone around.

He opened the curtain and slipped in, then secured it behind him. He rested his hands on her waist. "Turn around."

She did and stood with her back straight, watching his reflection in the mirror while he worked at to loosen her bodice.

The pressure around her ribcage eased, and she drew in a deep breath. "Thank you. That thing was killing me."

The air caressed her skin as the damp corset slowly opened, exposing the curves of her back. She crossed her arms over her chest to prevent the top half of the gown from falling off completely.

Arwan worked to unlace the last of the silk ribbon. His fingers brushed against her lower back, spreading warmth up her spine. She studied him in the mirror. He was soaked and miserable, yet he hadn't complained—not even once. "You should go get changed. I can handle it from here."

He rested his hands on her shoulders, and his gaze slid over her bare back.

Besides riding together in the taxi, they hadn't spent more than a few moments alone since London. The longing she had carried all this time now suddenly overwhelmed her.

He placed a kiss on the curve of her shoulder. Her eyes fluttered shut, and she gripped her dress tighter, tilting her head to the side and exposing her neck.

"Arwan." This wasn't really the best place, never mind the fact she probably smelled like wet dog.

He hooked her elbow and gently spun her around. When they stood face to face, it was clear her heart was no longer hers. It belonged to him completely, and even though they'd only met recently, it seemed as if they'd known each other for a lifetime.

Whatever drew them to each other—whatever made her promise herself to him so completely— they had a bond that would never be broken. And even though it surprised her, she'd made that promise with all of her heart.

He cradled her face. "If anything happened to you..." His jaw flexed. She wanted to press her fingers against his chest and run her hands along the curves of his shoulders, but if she let go of her gown, it would fall to the floor.

He brushed his thumb along her lips, and his

gaze flickered to them. *"Si algo te hubiera pasado…me hubiera roto el corazón."*

Her chest fluttered. She really, really needed to learn Spanish. Regardless of what he said, hearing him whisper like that made her weak in the knees.

He pulled her close and kissed her, one arm wrapped around her waist, the other caressing her cheek. The light in her chest—the mark of her heritage and power—flickered on and filled her with the cold energy it always brought.

She pried her arms free and wrapped them around his neck. With the top of her gown pinned between their bodies, the sides of the corset fell open, exposing the curves of her waist. He ran his hands along the length of her bare back before resting them on her hips.

The light in her chest brightened, and electricity sparked over her skin. His lips curved into a smile, causing them both to pause.

He pulled away just enough to look her in the eyes. "Your heart's racing. I can hear it."

She ran her fingers through his hair and drew him closer, into another kiss. He held her with a tenderness he hadn't shown before.

Her light dimmed as a new type of passion took over.

She didn't just want him, she wanted his heart, forever.

"Ahem." A woman on the other side of the curtain cleared her throat, sounding annoyed. Zanya pulled away and looked down. At the bottom of the curtain, she saw the foot of a store employee tapping impatiently. "Is everything all right in there, or do I need to call security?"

Zanya's cheeks blazed with heat. "Everything's fine."

Arwan clearly wore a crooked grin. "Maybe we should finish getting our supplies." He slipped out of the dressing room to speak to the woman waiting outside. His tone was apologetic while he explained Zanya's wardrobe malfunction.

The time is getting closer now, a voice whispered in her mind.

She shut her eyes and tried to block it out. The light in her chest grew warm rather than cold, making her stomach gurgle with a sick heat.

Prepare to rule under me.

Zanya squinted her eyes shut.

You are mine. Don't ever believe differently.

The whispers started after she'd claimed the ancient Mayan relic and taken it back from Sarian. She suspected this voice was his, reaching through the only link they shared and using one of the few things she loved to drive her mad.

After spending more than she could comprehend at the sporting goods store, Zanya and Arwan loaded all of their new supplies into two hiking packs. With Cualli's pendant hanging around her neck, Zanya unzipped the front pocket and transferred the very last and most important item.

Her stone.

The only pocket big enough to accommodate the large oval stone was the main compartment. Funny enough, though it was large, it wasn't heavy. Perhaps a magical quality she hadn't noticed before.

The stone's energy scraped against her skin, raw

and sharp from Sarian's partial hold. He may have broken the spell set upon the stone at its creation that made it obey only the guardian, but it still recognized her.

Unfortunately, unlike when she'd bonded with it, her stone no longer spoke to her. It was quiet. Too quiet.

Its colors morphed and pulsed, transforming from its normal hues of white and blue to deep violet and brown. Its polluted energy burned her skin as if she were handling a hot coal. She wanted to flinch away, but ground her teeth and cradled the stone closer. She had to prove it was home, where it belonged. Luckily she could heal after her brief encounters with the stone.

"Are you ready?" Arwan stood and slung his pack over his shoulder.

She rubbed her temples, then blinked to clear her vision.

"What's wrong?"

"I just have a headache and…" She considered telling him about the whispers but that would only worry him. If she got some rest, her mind would be stronger and maybe more capable of fending off the mental attacks. She stood and slipped on her backpack. "Never mind. It's not important. Let's go."

CHAPTER TWO

Hunkered down in a window seat, Zanya jumped when her phone buzzed in her pocket. She hid it from the flight attendant patrolling the aisle as she read the message from Tara.

Tara: Renato just got back with Hawa. How could you not tell me you're leaving?

A heavy weight settled in Zanya's stomach.

"Excuse me, ma'am." Zanya's raised her gaze to the brunette flight attendant smiling down at her. "All cell phones need to be powered down in preparation for takeoff, please. You'll be allowed to turn them back on when we land in Guatemala."

"Oh, sorry." She'd have to answer Tara once they landed. Plus, she had no idea what to say. *"You're totally right, I'm a jerk?"* That wouldn't exactly help things.

The flight attendant moved on when Zanya tucked her phone away. She rested her head on Arwan's shoulder and sighed. "Tara's mad. You think she'll forgive me?"

Arwan kissed the top of her head. "Of course. You're her best friend. She'll understand."

She wanted to believe him.

Half an hour after takeoff, the Fasten Seat Belt sign finally pinged off. Zanya unbuckled, reached under the chair, and pulled out a small leather book from her pack. Renato had "borrowed" it from Contessa's shelves and apparently thought it was important enough that she needed to read it on the flight.

The front cover was engraved with a giant tree inside a circle. There were three levels inside the circle. The first danced above the branches, the second lingered in the middle, and the last—most ominous of worlds—was trapped beneath the tree's enormous roots, deep underground.

The title on the first page of the book read *Yaxche and Xibalba.*

She had read about both of these in the scribe journals from Renato's library. A smile tugged at her lips. She missed that house. It had only taken a few weeks for her to feel at home there.

Zanya turned her attention back to the book. Yaxche was the tree of life that spanned from the heavens to the middleworld and down to the underworld. Long ago, the Maya had understood that the earth spun on an axis. The ancient enchanted tree was that axis. It secured the planet in place and connected all three worlds. Yaxche was not only earth's stabilizer, but a portal, and Zanya suspected they would have to eventually travel through the massive trunk to find Houn, the god of death.

"Hey." She tilted the book toward Arwan. "Do you know much about Yaxche?" When he didn't respond, she looked up and saw he was asleep. Zanya lowered the book into her lap. Some rest would do him good. She yawned. Maybe it would do her some good, too.

She tucked the book under her leg and crossed her arms, then laid her head on Arwan's shoulder. He drew in a deep, sleepy breath and pressed his cheek against her head. As she rested, her mind drifted into semi-consciousness.

A voice wove through her exhausted mind.

You will be mine, whether by force or compliance. Make no mistake.

She shuddered at the snaky hiss of Sarian's words. Her dream state deepened, paired with an image of Tara's bright hazel eyes.

"How could you leave without telling me?" The broken tone of her friend's voice stabbed at her.

Another image formed behind her lids. A book— the one Zanya had first seen in a dream, then again in her vision when Sarian had broken the obedience spell. Its pages flipped faster and faster until they stopped. Blood seeped from the yellowed parchment.

The image of Renato shaking his head as he stood on the patio in Victorian London.

Sarian in his beastly form fighting against Arwan, who moved with almost inhuman speed and accuracy.

"He does not need help." Renato's gaze finally

met hers, and the depth of sadness in his eyes nearly took her breath away. "Arwan is not who you think he is."

Zanya opened her eyes and sat up, rubbing her face. "What the hell was that?" She clutched Cualli's pendant, running her fingers over the smooth curves until her heartbeat returned to normal.

With her three crutches—her stone, her music, and Cualli's pendant—she hadn't had a panic attack in months. But Sarian had clearly broken into her mind and didn't intend on leaving. Her night terrors—more accurately, Sarian's blatant intrusions into her dreams—had always been isolated to a deep sleep. Now they were everywhere. His hold on her stone had taken its toll, and unless she figured out a way to stop him, his invasions would undoubtedly become much worse.

***

Arwan

Arwan watched out the bus window as trees and small village huts flew past. He and Zanya had been traveling for almost two hours on a route that would bring them to the entrance of the caves.

He frowned at the dark circles casting deep shadows under Zanya's eyes. She must not have gotten any sleep on the plane. Perhaps she was ill, though that was unlikely for a guardian with the ability to heal. Like Peter, her healing powers made her nearly immune to middleworld sickness.

Still, she hadn't been acting normally over the last few days. Headaches and lethargy were obvious signs something had happened that she didn't want to tell him about. Something more serious than her concern over Tara or her heartache over Jayden.

He too carried worry in his heart, and just like Zanya was doing to him now, he hadn't told her the entire truth either.

Maybe it was just a matter of time for them both.

The bus slowed to a stop, delivering them to their destination. They had taken the route to the back entrance of the caves, surrounded by dense jungle and heavy overgrowth.

The government authorities had restricted tourist access to the front side of the caves years ago, but the area would still be crawling with photographers and small-time archeologists, all of whom would have a watchful eye on the glyphs, and thus anyone going in or out.

Arwan checked his watch. There was still about two hours before sundown. They both needed their strength to hike, especially because it wasn't Zanya's strongest skill. He'd packed energy bars in her bag, though he had no idea how long they'd be stuck in the cave.

A cave his mother had once crawled out from.

A cave he wished he could forget.

He pictured the drawings hung on his bedroom wall at home. His mother's face was calming and somehow torturous at the same time. But he wouldn't forget her. She was the reason he still lived, while his father was the reason she had been ripped from his life when he was just a boy.

Zanya massaged small circles over her temples, her eyes closed and her skin visibly clammy.

He brushed his hand against her leg. "Are you sure you're all right?"

She drew in her bottom lip and sat back in her seat. "I'm fine. Just tired."

The single door at the front of the bus screeched open. They had a long journey ahead, and he had to be mentally prepared for whatever was to come. "We're up." He grabbed his bag while Zanya stood, and followed her down the aisle and outside, onto the dusty ground.

It was the wet season, but there hadn't been rain in weeks. The earth was cracked and the air was dry. Many of the locals probably suspected the gods were angry. Telltale signs proved his suspicion true as they strode down the wide dirt road between huts and small bakeries selling freshly made flatbread. Offerings lay scattered along the ground, some in basins, and others lying in beds of banana leaves. What was left of the river lazily flowed downstream, over shiny pebbles and old stumps that hung on to the compacted silt.

The town had changed since he'd last visited. Boxy televisions were propped in the corner of several outdoor market stalls, and many of the villagers had cell phones pressed to their ears. It was as if the life had been drained from the rich culture of their Maya descendants, all of whom had nearly forgotten the honor and greatness of their history. Instead of building great cities, they wove blankets, carved colorful trinkets, and sold small statues of the abandoned temples, once the pride of their nation.

At least this village was one of the few without Catholic churches towering over the ruins. Instead of Christmas, this small community still celebrated winter solstice—and had, since Arwan could remember.

The shortest day of the year marked the beginning of longer days, but more importantly for Riyata, the time in which bonds of the soul were made. He felt it coming, deep in his bones. All the years he had observed the solstice, celebration the coming season. It was the only surviving link to his lineage that he'd kept as part of his life.

A statue of the rain deity, Chaac, stood in the center of the town with offerings scattered around him. Basins of fresh water lay near the statue's feet, and hand-strung beads hung from the lightning ax gripped in Chaac's hand.

Some still believed.

An elderly woman sat beside the statue with a wicker basket nestled in her lap, begging for scraps of food. Her meek frame was buried under layers of tattered clothes and a shroud of fabric draped over her hair.

Arwan paused beside her. The painted markings on her hands and forehead meant she was a village elder. When he was part of the community, elders were respected.

He reached in his bag and found an energy bar. If giving it to her meant he'd go hungry, so be it.

He broke away from Zanya and walked toward the woman. Her wrinkled face turned up as he approached, and her gaze followed him down when he crouched beside her.

The emptiness in her eyes told of extended neglect and hunger. He placed the food in her basket. He hadn't spoken his native tongue in such a long time, but she was a Maya villager from the old tribe—probably one of the last—and most likely didn't understand anything but Yucatan. Shame weighed on his shoulders. He hung his head, all but having forgotten how to greet her properly.

Her shaky hands reached out and rested on his forearm. His heart weighed heavy to see his people begging on the street. To find her begging beside a statue of Chaac was worse. It was a common practice among beggars to sit beside a statue of a deity in hope those withholding charity would feel guilty and be more compelled to give.

It had come to that.

The people's hearts had turned cold.

He stood and glanced back at Zanya waiting for him on the far side of the dirt road. Her head was hung, her gaze cast to the ground. It was obvious she understood the elder's situation was grim.

Arwan gave the woman the respect she deserved by resting his hand on top of her head, wishing her well on her journey through the underworld, to the heavens, once she passed. It probably wouldn't be long.

She stilled, and her eyes slowly shut. She understood what was happening.

He was telling her good-bye.

As he stood, he dropped a few coins in her basket—as much as he could spare. Perhaps she could buy food, or a good night's rest in a suitable bed.

Arwan walked back to Zanya's side. She took his hand. Her warmth was the only remaining link he had to mankind.

"That was really nice of you," she said with a gentle smile. Her gaze moved to the woman. "It's so sad." She squeezed his hand.

He checked his watch. "We have about an hour to be in town. Let's get something to eat before we start the hike."

She sighed. "Hiking. Right. I wish I knew where I was going, I could have transported ahead."

"But you don't, and I would really rather you stay close. Just in case." He draped his arm over her shoulder. She had no idea how badly he needed to be close to her, though he still couldn't explain why. When he'd met her, he hadn't expected the connection would be so strong. The bond wasn't just physical but something tangible that linked them together. He just hoped what was soon to come wouldn't tear them apart.

***

Zanya

The uneven ground pushed against the bottom of Zanya's feet as she followed Arwan over the game path that stretched from the village's eastern border of the jungle. At least that's what Arwan had told her. She couldn't tell east from west if her life depended on it.

"How much longer do we have?" She took a few quick steps to catch up to him.

He tipped his face toward the sky. A bead of sweat ran down his temple. "We have about three miles to go, but the terrain's going to get more difficult." He examined the thick foliage on either side of the trail.

She grabbed her water bottle from the side pocket of her backpack and gulped down half of her supply.

Arwan's eyes narrowed as he came to a complete stop.

Zanya swallowed the rest of her mouthful and poured some into her palm. She patted the back of her neck and fanned at her damp skin. "What's wrong?"

He pressed his finger to his lips as his gaze darted through the trees.

Zanya froze. The only sounds were the distant screeches of monkeys and a few birds in the branches above them—typical jungle soundtrack.

After a moment, he finally spoke. "I thought I heard something. Let's keep going."

"Okay. But what did you think you heard?" She slipped her water bottle back in her backpack and tried to keep up.

"There are a lot of things we need to be careful of. You aren't used to being out here, so I'm just being cautious."

She glanced around. "Cautious of what?"

"I'm not trying to scare you." He guided her over a sudden incline in the path.

"I won't get freaked out. I promise." A promise

she'd probably break in about five seconds, but she needed to know what they were dealing with. They'd hiked together in Belize, but back then they'd traveled on well-known paths the tribes had used to collect water and visit each other. Now they were on a barely discernible game trail in the middle of nowhere—totally different story.

He exhaled. "Tigers, elephants, snakes…" He paused and turned toward the greenery.

He sensed something was out there. That much was clear.

His grip slid from her hand up to her wrist.

His focus intensified by the second. "Go. Walk ahead of me."

"Why?" She gripped his arm.

"So I can keep an eye on you."

She walked ahead, her senses tuned to every noise, every twig that snapped in the trees, every chirping bird—

Zanya paused. The birds. They'd all gone quiet. Something had spooked them, and she had a feeling that whatever it was, it was still close by.

CHAPTER THREE

The twilight skies were streaked with hues of red and pink when Zanya followed Arwan out of the canopy of trees. An area bare of foliage lay straight ahead. They were supposed to make it to the mouth of the cave by nightfall, but considering they hadn't reached it yet—probably thanks to her short stride—that was probably not going to happen.

"What are we going to do?"

Arwan dropped his pack on the ground. "We need to make camp. It's almost dark, and we need to collect firewood. This is a good spot for us to spend the night."

Zanya groaned. "I figured as much." They didn't have any real shelter, and there were more bugs than she could fathom, all of them probably waiting for her to doze off so they could crawl over her face. She cringed. "What if it rains? We'll get soaked."

"It hasn't rained in weeks, and I doubt it will rain tonight. The skies are too clear."

"Oh. Right." She'd have to learn how to look for

signs like that. She rolled her shoulders and let the pack hit the ground with a *thud*. Throbbing pain pulsed through her neck and upper back. "Ugh." She reached across her chest and massaged the knot.

"I'll gather firewood. You can get out your sleeping bag and—" He pointed to some rocks near the path. "If you can gather some stones and make a circle for a fire pit that would be helpful." He unzipped his hoodie and tossed it beside his backpack, revealing the muscles packed under his T-shirt.

Heat spread through her body, and she cleared her throat. "Sure, no problem."

"I won't be gone for long. Yell if anything happens. I won't be far."

She bit her lip in an attempt to suppress a smile. "Thanks for being so worried about me."

He examined her with a quirky grin. The kind of grin that made her heart skip a beat and her breath hitch. "You're the guardian. You don't need me around to protect you. You just think you do."

An hour later, the sun was all but gone by the time Zanya finished organizing the stones into a circle. She wiped her dusty hands on her pants and unzipped her bag and then spotted Arwan's pack. He hadn't returned with the firewood yet. He must have been gathering enough for the whole night.

It would be helpful if she got his sleeping bag out, too. He'd have to build the fire when he returned—God knows she had no clue how to do it.

Twigs cracked behind her, and Zanya spun and fell back on her butt, her palms pressed against the warm earth. She scanned the tree line. Too bad it was dark and she couldn't see anything but a thick wall of foliage.

"Arwan?" Her voice came out in a squeak. She cleared her throat and slowly stood, her focus never leaving the jungle. "Arwan?" Another crack sounded from in the trees. Zanya scanned the branches until she spotted a huge white owl perched on a branch just above her.

She exhaled and rested her hand on her chest. A smile crept over her lips. "Oh thank God. It's just an owl." The creature looked down at her inquisitively, rotating its head from side to side. It was beautiful. Large, with caramel-brown feathers outlining its heart-shaped face. The moonlight shimmered against the bird's feathers.

It hopped toward her down the branch, seemingly unafraid. Though out here, it probably didn't have any reason to fear people. Zanya stepped closer, her focus on the bird's almond-shaped eyes that analyzed her every move.

She smacked her lips and extended her hand, rubbing the tips of her fingers together. "Hey, beautiful. What are you doing here?" Her voice turned to a soft coo as she waited for it to move closer. "Don't worry, I won't hurt you."

More twigs snapped behind her and she turned, sure she'd see Arwan walking toward her with a huge stack of wood piled in his arms.

There was only darkness and silence.

Zanya dropped her hand to her side, her eyes wide. A soft growl radiated through the night. She stepped back, her senses on high alert.

She gripped the wicker emblem hung around her neck, and for the first time since London, her stone spoke to her.

Its whispers morphed to static. A spike of adrenaline tore through her. She rushed to her backpack and ripped open the zipper.

With the stone cupped in her hands, she shifted away from the cluster of bushes in front of her. Her breath stalled when her gaze met a pair of pale yellow eyes peering at her from the foliage.

She tried to speak, but her voice was trapped somewhere in her chest. Her stone, scalding scalded the tender skin on her palms. The large cat's gaze moved down to the pulsing orb in her chest, then to the light that radiated from her stone. It bared its teeth and then relaxed, smoothing the wrinkles in its snout. The animal cocked its head. Its small, perked ears made it look as if it were curious.

"Good job on the fire pit." Zanya spun around and jumped to her feet. Arwan must have seen her panicked expression because he immediately dropped the firewood and ran to her side. "What happened?"

She pointed to the bushes where the large cat had stood just a moment ago. Now only shadows loomed in the empty space. Arwan must have scared it away. "There was a—wait!" She spun and pointed to the branch where the owl was perched, but the bird, too, was no longer there. "First it was a—it was right there!" She turned back to the bushes and surveyed the empty space. "It was some kind of cat. Maybe a cheetah or something. It had spots."

Arwan grabbed her wrist and pulled her closer. "Where?"

"There." She pointed to the empty space where small plants lay crushed into the soil by the beast's paw.

"What else?"

"An owl. It was *huge*." She pointed to the tree. "Right there. It was all white with some caramel feathers on its face and dark eyes." She drew in a sharp breath. "What if the big cat comes back? Maybe we should sleep in the trees or something." She gathered her sleeping bag off the ground and hugged it against her chest. She wasn't Steve freakin' Irwin. She didn't jump on gators or tame snakes. She certainly didn't sit face-to-face with a predator that considered her a snack.

"Sleeping in a tree isn't a good idea."

"What? Why?" She clung tighter to her sleeping bag while she scanned the jungle. "At least it would keep us off the ground."

"Because it was a jaguar, and they drag their prey into the trees to eat. At least normal jaguars do."

Her eyes widened. "What do you mean 'normal'?"

"'Normal' as in middleworld."

"Middleworld? You don't think they're from here?"

The possibility that the jaguar wasn't from this realm seemed ten times worse than it being just an ordinary jaguar on the hunt. Especially after being attacked by the demon from the caves near Renato's house, and then the gargoyle-like beasts on the beach. Suddenly facing a regular big cat didn't seem so bad. "Well, how do you know it was a jaguar? It could have been a cheetah, right? Or a lynx or something. Something totally middleworld." She swallowed.

"Cheetahs don't live in this area, and the jaguar has been stalking us since we wandered into its territory. But I don't think it wants to hurt us."

"And how did you come to that conclusion?"

"Because if it did, you'd be dead."

***

Arwan started the fire like an old pro. It was too risky to catch something and cook it. The smell of fresh meat would tempt not only the jaguar, but also other predators in the area.

He sat beside Zanya on his sleeping bag, and pulled up his legs, resting one forearm on his knee while using the other hand to poke at the glowing logs with a stick. "As long as we keep the fire going, we should be safe."

"*Should* be safe?"

"I'm sleeping beside you just in case. Don't worry." He tilted his face toward the treetops. "Noises from the other animals will let us know if something is close. The monkeys are good for that."

Zanya unwrapped an energy bar and took a bite. "Freakin' monkeys better be on high alert or we're screwed."

Arwan let out a chuckle. The flames rose and fell, casting shadows over his face. The jungle atmosphere suited him. He seemed at home.

She sat back and admired the millions of tiny white orbs speckling the night heavens. The sky wasn't black, rather a deep shade of royal blue. "Look up."

He followed her prompt, and a faint smile spread his lips. A sad smile—the same kind that graced his face whenever he spoke about his mom.

After a moment of silence, he let out a deep breath. "The cave is only a few miles away."

She covered her mouth through a deep yawn. Man, she was tired. "Well, that's good, right?"

He poked at the fire again, causing flames to waver and dance. "Are you sure you want to go through with this?"

She crinkled her brow. "What do you mean *am I sure*?"

He stared intensely into the embers. "Once we enter the caves, we can't turn back. We will need to go through the appropriate channels in order to enter. There are no shortcuts. No free passes."

She had to be brave. Not for herself, but for her friend. "Jayden only has two days left. If we don't get his soul from Houn by then, we won't get it back. We have to keep going."

"If that's what you want."

Maybe he was scared. She didn't blame him. She was too. But she couldn't put her own fear ahead of saving Jay. He wouldn't turn his back on her, and she couldn't do that to him. Even when he'd left her in the orphanage, he'd thought he would go back to her. That they would be together again. She didn't love him in that way. Not anymore. She loved Jayden like she loved Tara. That was enough.

Arwan lay down and stared up at the sky. His features were solemn.

He wasn't the only one with weight on his shoulders. The dream she'd had about Arwan on the plane was something she needed to address. She hadn't found the right moment to bring the two-ton elephant into the room, but no moment would seem right for something like this.

She gathered her hair and pulled it over her shoulder, playing with strands between her fingers. It was all she could do not to seem obviously nervous. "Renato made a comment I can't stop thinking about." When he didn't react, she continued. "He said you aren't who I think you are."

Arwan's jaw ticked. "He said that?"

Zanya observed his tense shoulders. He was hiding something, and she had a right to know what it was. "Renato isn't the only person who told me."

Arwan looked at her. "What do you mean?"

"Sarian said the same thing. He said you and him aren't very different. I just thought he was trying to manipulate me."

"And you believe him?"

"You're not giving me a reason not to." The truth was, she didn't know what to believe. If he insisted on staying silent, she'd have all the more reason to pry.

"I guess you can believe whatever you want." He turned his attention to the fire, poking at the burning embers with a stick.

"That's not fair."

"Fair or not, that's all I can tell you."

"That's all you *will* tell me, you mean."

"Stop prying, Zanya."

"Or what?"

He stood and stared down at her. "Or you may find something out that you really don't want to know."

She pushed to her feet, holding his gaze. "I have a right to know."

He fisted his hands, his chest heaving with every breath. He paced to the other side of the fire. "I knew eventually it would come to this."

Zanya wrapped her fingers around Cualli's medallion as anxiety bubbled in her chest. "Come to what?"

The flames slashed at the air as his piercing gaze bored a hole in her heart. "Are you sure you want to ask me this? Because if you ask, you have to be sure you want to know the answer."

In reality, she wasn't so sure. His sudden change in demeanor was so unlike him, and that kind of one-eighty could only be caused by something serious. She shifted her weight. "You're starting to scare me."

Anguish washed over his handsome features.

She couldn't bear seeing him with such a tortured expression for a second longer. She moved beside him and laid her hands on either side of his face. He shut his eyes. The despair radiating from his touch was nearly unbearable.

She understood his longing. She had desired so much in her life—relief, acceptance, courage, peace—and never received any of it. Until she'd met Renato and the others. Being told she was precious was more of a reward than she could have ever hoped for. So she'd give him the acceptance he longed for. She'd give it to him without any more questions or accusations.

Whatever he was hiding wasn't worth tearing him apart to find out. Not over the word of Sarian. Not even over the word of Renato.

"Listen to me. I won't push you to tell me anything you don't want to. I don't know what could possibly be so bad—"

"Will you still want me?" His voice was ragged.

She furrowed her brow. "What?"

"Just…please." He buried his fingers in her hair and pressed his forehead against hers. "Tell me you will still want me, no matter who I am."

She sensed his anger, fear, agony—all radiating through his touch and the desperation in his tone.

"Please believe me. I would never do anything to hurt you. *No puedo vivir sin tu amor.*"

She pushed a strand of hair out of his face and brushed her thumb over his eyebrow. "You know, you've got to start translating for me."

She waited for him to crack a smirk. When it failed to come, she kissed him anyway. The fire warmed her back while a chorus of sounds echoed around them. The jungle was deafening at night, but in that moment, his touch drowned out the noises.

He slid his arms around her and crushed her against his chest. She squeaked, and then melted into him, twisting her fingers in his T-shirt, finding solid muscle underneath. She couldn't help but push under the material to explore.

His skin was warm, and her fingers brushed

against a thin line of hair trailing down his stomach. She followed it until it vanished beneath the buckle of his pants. His chest expanded with a sharp inhale. The subtle fluttering in her stomach exploded into a fierce energy radiating through her body.

His lips slid to the corner of her mouth and down her jaw. She tilted her head back toward the night sky while his mouth ran over her neck.

He pulled away, nearly panting. "Zanya—"

"No." She rose on her tippy-toes and kissed him again. She wouldn't have him try to talk reason into her. Not now, when they were finally alone.

When dawn broke, they would risk their lives. This could be their last chance to be together if it all fell apart.

She spread her hands across his back and trailed them over his shoulders. His fingers dug into her hips and he broke their kiss again. "Heavens help me," he whispered in a raspy breath. "Zanya, please."

She shifted her weight. "What's wrong?"

He shook his head.

"Don't you…" The thought of saying it aloud made her blush. Maybe he *didn't* want to move forward, though his kiss said otherwise. She hung her head. How could she have been so wrong?

He hooked his fingers under her chin. "I can't. It wouldn't be fair."

"Fair? What are you talking about?" She bit her lip, trying not to notice the electrical current that spread over her skin from his touch. What the heck was wrong with her? She'd never acted like this before—wanted anyone so much.

He brushed his finger along her cheek. "Please, trust me."

She paused, realizing she'd moved her hands under his shirt, and was resting her hands against his solid muscle. The mental haze slowly faded. Being this into him was a little scary.

Zanya slowly pulled away and pressed her hands against her sides. Maybe it was the fresh jungle air, or maybe it was just that they were headed into the unknown the next day. Whatever drew her to him was relentless. Her head spun, and she rested her fingertips on her temple. It was as if something had taken her over. Something with an insatiable need.

She blinked away clouded vision and forced a soft smile. He was right. Waiting was better. She'd sworn she'd take it slow. He'd promised he'd wait. Not push. Not pressure her. And he hadn't. Not even a little. There was nothing wrong with taking things one step at a time.

Except suddenly she wanted to leap.

CHAPTER FOUR

Arwan

Two miles to go before they reached the caves. That gave Arwan just two miles to make Zanya smile. She'd been forlorn all morning. Perhaps because of what happened the night before. Of course she would be upset. He'd rejected her, but not because he didn't want her. Certainly that wasn't the case. If she had pushed, even a little more, he might not have shown the willpower he had.

He watched her, so quiet and despondent. "Do you need a break?" It was a legitimate question, but a part of him just wanted to see if she'd answer.

She shook her head.

Not quite the response he'd hoped for. "We're making good progress. At this pace we will arrive in less than an hour."

Zanya glanced at her watch. "Good. We don't have a lot of time to waste."

Her tone was cold, distant, and so unlike her.

He'd hurt her feelings, though not intentionally. They had no other option than to slow down. That, or they would have done something she might later regret.

Especially after today.

"We should skip lunch," she called over her shoulder. "The less we stop, the quicker we'll get there."

The tension in his muscles wound tighter. Each passing minute meant they were growing closer—closer to the caves, closer to the underworld, and worse, closer to Zanya finally knowing the truth.

He was the only one who could get her past the gate. It was the reason he'd volunteered to escort her, and though he hated the idea of her going at all, if she went alone, she'd never be able to get through, and that would crush her.

"I think we should take a short break. You need to keep up your strength."

"I told you. I'm not hungry." She squirmed under the weight of her pack while pushing forward, fighting against the pull of the load on her back.

She was angry, but that didn't make her invincible. "You clearly need a break, Zanya."

"Would you stop being so fussy? I'm a big girl, Arwan, and I know when I'm tired." She continued walking with more determination.

He squared his jaw and caught up in a few long strides. He grabbed the nylon handle of her backpack and yanked, stopping her mid-step. Her arms flailed as she fought to keep her balance, and she spun around to face him. He didn't expect to fall victim to the bitterness that poured from behind her eyes.

She balled her fists. "What?"

"What's wrong with you?"

"You know…" She pursed her lips. "Never mind. Let's just go. We don't have time for this." She turned and stalked back up the trail. A few moments later she glanced over her shoulder and noticed he hadn't moved. She stopped. "What are you doing?"

"I was fine with giving you space, but if you're upset with me, you need to tell me why."

She scoffed and faced him. "You've got to be kidding."

"You're angry."

"Oh, really?" She threw her hands in the air. "That's a very astute observation. Anything else, or can we go now?"

"Is it because of last night? Zanya, please. I just didn't want to—"

"Yeah, you made that much really, *really* clear." She crossed her arms and hung her head, digging into the soil with the toe of her shoe.

He let out a long exhale. "You didn't let me finish." She waved her hand, as if saying *go ahead*. He cleared his throat. "Trust me. I wanted to." He slowly closed the space between them. "But you have to understand that I need you to be sure, and you can't be sure. Not yet." He trailed his fingers down her arm.

She jerked away. "Don't—" She glanced up at his face. "Don't touch me."

He stepped back. "You don't want me to touch

you?"

"I…" She looked away. "I do, but…"

He gathered her in his arms and hugged her close. She didn't respond at first. But soon she uncrossed her arms, slid them around him, and rested her head against his chest.

"Why are you trying to torture me?"

He pulled back and stared into her face. "What are you talking about?"

"You keep…" She stepped back and extended her hand, then let it scale the length of his body. "…looking like *that*. And when you kiss me, I swear, it feels like you really want me, you know? And I don't know what the hell is wrong with me. I can't seem to control this feeling." She shook her hands out as if they were cramped, then rested them on her hips and hung her head.

A grin pushed through. He couldn't help it.

Her head bobbed up and her lips parted. "Well, I'm glad you're so amused. Ugh. I should have known better than to tell you." She covered her face with her hands. "This is so humiliating."

He let out a laugh and wrapped his arms around her again. "It's all right, Zanya. I'm so sorry you're suffering like this. But if it makes you feel any better, it's not your fault."

She uncovered her face. "What do you mean?"

He couldn't stop grinning. "It's the solstice that's making you…imbalanced." He hooked his thumbs around the straps of his backpack. "I remember when my first real solstice hit me."

"Wait. What do you mean? What hit you?"

"Think of it as a rite of passage. When a Riyata

reaches maturity, their abilities take hold. You just turned eighteen, so it makes sense you're going through this now. Plus you recently bonded with your stone, and you've been using your powers more. That's good, but it creates…side effects. Your inner ability is being awakened by the pull of the energy of the solstice lights."

"Lights?" The word came out in a squeak.

He let out another laugh. "It'll go away after the solstice is over. For now, just know that you're not abnormal. And…" He laced his fingers with hers and grinned. "I hope you don't stop touching me altogether. *Extrañaria tus caricias.*"

Her breath hitched. "That's another thing. You have to stop doing that."

"Doing what?"

"Saying stuff in Spanish that I don't understand. It's bad enough with you looking at me the way you do, but then you say those things and…it's just not fair."

Warmth spread through his chest. He had no idea he affected her so deeply. If he were honest with himself, it was endearing. He couldn't help teasing her further. "And if I were to translate, *mi mariposa*?"

"Arwan…"

"*Mi Vida.*"

"You're so mean."

"*Mi corazón.*"

"I swear. I'll get you back."

"I doubt it, *mi cielo.*"

"You…" She pointed at him, an escaped smile winning over her attempt to appear stern. With her finger pressed against his chest, she dropped her head and stared up at him through feathered eyelashes. Her smile bloomed.

Mission accomplished.

CHAPTER FIVE

Zanya

Finally the caves were in sight. Good thing, because it meant Zanya could finally break the awkward silence. Her humiliation and raw need for some alone time had prevented her from saying a word for the last hour.

Yes, Arwan had handled her little predicament with class—but still. Your libido being ramped into overdrive *was* abnormal, no matter how much he wanted to claim otherwise.

She still had a lot to learn about being Riyata, and this was definitely a curve ball. Especially when it was caused by a force completely out of her control or understanding. Worse, she had no idea when these feelings would calm down, or at least lend her a little sanity. Plus, even though she hated to admit it, Arwan was right. She couldn't be sure. Not yet. Not until she learned exactly what Renato was referring to and what was eating away at Arwan so deeply, that he refused to talk about. For now, she'd have to be satisfied with finding something legitimate to discuss so the topic didn't come up again.

God, please don't let the topic come up again. Her cheeks flushed.

"Do you want to set up camp here or go straight into the caves?" She focused on the terrain ahead, doing her best to keep her distance—even if they camped out again, jaguar lurking in the jungle or not.

"We need to keep moving," Arwan replied from behind her. The texture of the earth changed under her feet as they drew closer to the entrance. The ground, once spongy and cushioned with layers of fallen leaves and soil, had hardened to dry, compressed dirt. The shadow of the towering mountain face cooled the air and sent a chill over Zanya's skin. It wasn't just the temperature that made her shiver, but the dark energy that grew stronger with every step.

She was able to ignore it until the light in her chest flickered on by itself, and her stone responded to the energy with a burst of panic.

Zanya stopped and clenched her hand over her stomach. She peered into the gaping mouth of the mountain. "This place is freaking me out."

Arwan stopped beside her. "We're about to enter the gate to the underworld. I'm not surprised."

She should have expected as much, but she never thought the cave would carry so much power. A pool of saliva collected under her tongue. "So, do we just go in?"

"I guess we don't have a choice."

"Right." She swallowed. "Okay. Let's do this." She pulled out the most gung-ho tone she could muster, then shifted the weight of her pack, drew in a cleansing breath, and took a step forward.

The atmosphere shuddered, and a vicious energy forced her to her knees. She clawed at her chest, every breath burning her lungs.

Arwan grabbed her around the waist and pulled her to her feet. She clung to him, working hard to regain her balance. It was as if they had walked into some kind of barrier. One she didn't react well to. His clenched jaw and stiff brow told her he sensed the change, too.

"Let's just keep going," she said between her teeth. It took a few yards, but she was finally able to shake the effects and stand on her own.

As they stepped into the darkness of the cave, Zanya brightened the light in her chest to guide them. A wavering glow, like that of a candle, cast over the rock walls.

The textured surface of the caves was a canvas for ancient drawings. Zanya examined the crude figure of a man in a headdress. Speckles of blood dripped from the blade of a knife, which protruded through the man's tongue clear to the other side.

Zanya narrowed her eyes and rested her hand against the cold surface of the rock. "What the hell?"

"Bloodletting. It's a common practice among the Maya during religious rituals."

"Jesus." She peered at the surrounding images of women with pierced breasts, and children—she took a step back, allowing her fingers to slip away from the stone. "Why didn't they just kill a goat or something? This is barbaric."

"Human blood appeases the gods. Animal blood is inadequate. It's considered an insult."

She scanned the painted walls and realized there were drawings all around them. "Let's just get out of here." The cave's raw power scraped at her nerves. Another chill ran over her skin. "These people were monsters."

"These people are our ancestors."

"Those *people*," she jabbed her finger at the paintings "may be our ancestors, but we're nothing like them. They were obviously evil or they wouldn't be killing kids to summon rain. It's stupid to think that would work anyway. It's just sick." She turned and threw her pack on the ground.

Arwan didn't reply. Probably because there was nothing to say in their defense. How he could even remotely side with that kind of religious practice?

Killing people to please higher powers. What kind of god would require that? Not any *she* chose to revere, that's for sure.

Arwan set his pack beside hers and pulled out a bottle of water and an energy bar. "You should eat something before we move on." He cracked open his water and drank it down all at once. "I don't know when we'll have a chance to eat or drink again."

Zanya removed her stone from her pack and cradled it in her hands. Its colors morphed from dark blue to violet. She frowned and rested it against her chest. "I know you're freaked out. Just try to stay calm. We won't be here long."

He leaned toward her. "You're talking to it?"

"Yeah. It understands me. But it's scared." She ran her fingers over its hot surface. Her skin scalded with red blisters and then healed. She was getting used to the pain and the relief that soon followed. Too bad she hadn't had that ability back at the orphanage. Zanya clenched her jaw. "You know, it's just like Sarian to do something like this. He breaks the obedience spell with that book, and instead of just doing whatever he has planned, he drags it out. I mean…" She slumped her shoulders forward, aching from the weight of her pack. "I don't know what he's up to, but it's typical for him. He gets off on watching people suffer."

"Which is why we need to keep going."

"Yeah, I know."

"We can't take our packs with us."

Her head bobbed up. "What? Why?"

Arwan zipped his pack closed and shoved it against the wall. "We won't be able to bring them through the portal."

"Oh." But her stone was large and too awkward to carry in her hands. She had to figure out a way to take it and not have it weigh her down. After a moment in deep thought, she raised it to eye level. "I bet you'd be awesome as a river pebble." Arwan continued to watch her, but she didn't mind. He was curious, and for once, it was nice to know something he didn't.

She cradled the stone against her chest and closed her eyes, focused on holding the image of a river pebble clearly in her mind. A soft plume of power rippled through her body, and when she opened her eyes, her stone had changed to a smooth, oval rock nestled in the palm of her hand. Though it retained its color and light, it was much more portable.

She closed her fingers around its hot surface, causing her skin to scream. Zanya ignored the pain and focused on calming down the stone with deep, cleansing breaths.

"How did you do that?"

"It's called transformation. It's an ability I read about in one of Renato's books." She opened her hand to the stone. Its colors slowly returned to white and blue. "I practiced it at home a few times with some things from my mom's old vanity. Cool, huh?"

"It must be strange to feel the stone's thoughts and emotions like you do."

"A little, but in a way it's been a part of me my entire life." Back in the orphanage, she'd dreamed about the stone again and again. She was drawn to it. Linked to it. No matter how much danger there was around her, she always sought it out. Of course, Sarian had managed to step in the way each and every time, but she'd never stopped searching until she found it.

She slipped the stone into the front pocket of her sweater. "Okay. I think I'm ready."

Arwan propped her bag against the rock wall. "We'll leave our supplies here and get them when we come out."

The air chilled as they traveled deeper into the caves. The narrow passage they were following finally opened into a grand cavern. Stalactites hung from the roof of the chamber, giving off an eerie amber glow. The angles of each formation guided droplets of moisture to their points until the drops slipped to the stone ground, filling the space with soft patters and drips.

In the corner sat a stone altar. Zanya crept toward it over the slick ground. As she drew closer, the light in her chest allowed her to better see the slab. Her heart dropped.

A small stack of bones was piled on either side of the sacrificial altar with a stone bowl rested on top.

The bones could only belong to a child.

Zanya's stomach slithered. "This is wrong." The words caught in her throat.

Arwan slipped his fingers between hers, reassuring her with his touch. "I know."

They stood side by side in a mutual moment of silence for the tiny victims.

"You were right," he said in a low growl. "They *were* monsters."

Carved markings on the altar's base caught her attention. She took a hesitant step closer, peering at the symbols. "What is this?" Zanya stooped to see them more clearly, as they were dusty and discolored with age. She brushed her fingers over the glyphs. Each carving seemed to represent a word, like the logograms she'd learned about in ancient history class in the orphanage. "What does this say? Can you read them?"

Arwan crouched beside her and analyzed the markings. "This is a sacrificial portal." His gaze rose to the stone bowl fused to the top of the altar.

"Child sacrifices were used to gain access to the underworld when those trying to enter didn't belong."

"What do you mean, 'belong'?"

"Blood analysis isn't as new as science likes us to believe." He stood and rested his hands on the rim of the stone bowl. He dragged his fingers along it, then paused over a sharpened edge. It was still darkened with bloodstains from the last sacrifice. "Those who are at least part underworlder are required to give a blood offering before they are allowed to pass. It's the only way to cross without a life being given in exchange."

Bile churned in her stomach. Everything about this place was dark. The energy of the cave, the weird glowing stalactites hanging from the ceiling, the altar, and the bones. The metallic stink of blood still hung in the air.

"This is too weird. We need to keep moving." She couldn't stand being near the remains for another second. Not when the faces of the innocent children rose through the folds of her imagination. Their tiny bodies must have struggled, knowing what was about to happen, while grown men forced them to lie down.

She had once read that being offered as a sacrifice was an honor, and often times the elder shaman would give women and children a message to deliver to the gods before they were killed.

A shiver ran down the back of her arms. What a horrible, unnecessary way to die.

She stepped back. "How do we get to the portal?"

"This *is* the portal." He turned to face her, his gaze piercing, intense, and unsettling. "Tell me you'll always want me." His words came out in a soft plea.

"What?" She shifted her weight.

His grip tightened over the stone bowl. "Please, just tell me that after this, you'll still want me." His eyebrows arched, as did the panic tearing through her.

Before she could reply, Arwan pressed his wrist against the bowl and slid it across the sharpened rim. His skin sliced open, and his blood began to flow.

CHAPTER SIX

Arwan

Zanya's scream tore into him. He pumped his hand to encourage the flow of more blood, knelt beside the stone bowl, and laid his wound over the altar. His shoulders slumped forward as blood trickled into the offering bowl.

He'd sworn he would never go back to his old life. He'd made an oath to leave that world behind and fight against every soul that dwelled in the shadows—every force responsible for causing pain. Now he was going to break that promise for her, even though he may lose her in the process.

Zanya clenched her hands on his shoulders. "What did you do?"

He hung his head as low as he could, wishing he could disappear completely. In that moment, his honor had been stripped away. Shame hung like a heavy cloud over his soul, mocking the years he'd spent hiding the truth and forgetting his ancestry. It had all been for nothing.

As his blood filled the cracks of the aged rock, the atmosphere of the cavern shuddered. He wrapped one arm around Zanya's waist and pressed his forehead against her belly as if already begging for forgiveness. But there was no time for that now. He had to hold on to her or she would be lost in the transport.

A cyclone ripped through the cave. Zanya screamed and grabbed on to him as she fought against the blast. Darkness consumed them, snuffing out any guidance Zanya's light produced.

His vision blurred. Only the warmth of Zanya's body kept him grounded. He clenched his jaw while they were sent to the gate, where worse terror awaited.

The wind died in an instant and slapped them down on the cold stone of the isolated cave—the other side of the portal.

The gate to the underworld.

He struggled to push to his feet, but he had no strength left to support his effort. Zanya's breaths grew louder until her warm hands cradled his cheeks. He opened his eyes, barely able to see past the pain blurring his vision.

She grabbed his hand. "Hold on!" Her voice was frantic. "I'm going to heal you." Warmth seeped into his wrist from her trembling fingers, and his wound knitted together. She rested her hand over his chest, and he relaxed his muscles as the heat from her body poured over him.

The darkness inside of him thrashed through his gut, curling him into a ball on the floor. He'd managed to keep from changing all these years by staying near the goodness of Riyata, and far from the powers beneath. Crossing through the portal, they were now trapped beside the gate to the underworld. He had to control his darker half, and quickly, or risk it emerging from inside him.

Zanya's heat was gone, leaving him frozen on the ground. The chilled air prickled his skin, making it impossible to concentrate. He opened his eyes and peered at Zanya through blurred vision, just long enough to see her expression turn to horror.

She leapt to her feet. Her footsteps dragged over the ground with each backward step. "What just happened? You tell me right now what just happened!" Her screech bounced off the stone walls. "Your eyes are black. Completely black!"

He struggled to sit, concentrating to cage the force within him. He'd nearly forgotten how powerful it was.

He didn't want her to be afraid of him, but the hope she would still want him had faded at the sound of her trembling voice.

It took everything he had, but finally he was able to see clearly, which meant his eyes had returned to normal. For now.

He gathered the courage to meet her gaze, wishing had never come to this damned place. Now he would never be with her like before. Before she learned who he really was.

Zanya stood at least ten feet away; her hands were tucked under her chin while she took more backward steps.

"Zanya—" His voice was cracked and raw.

"Where are we?" she said in a soft whisper.

"What happened to you?"

He wanted to answer her questions, but each one was more difficult than the last. He'd start with the first and work his way to the second—if he could just stand. With an upward heave, he pushed to his feet.

Zanya flinched.

The anguish in his heart deepened. "I'm not going to hurt you." He gripped his ribs, aching from the impact with the stone ground. "Please stop trying to get away from me."

She shook her head. Strands of wild hair hung around her face. "*You.*" That single word carried more accusation than he could stand.

He straightened his posture, still holding his side. "I got us through."

"By giving *your* blood."

He turned his head and examined the placid cave lake yards away. The mirrored surface reflected the light from the glittering clusters of rocks overhead, glowing like amber stars.

"You better tell me what the hell is going on, and I mean *right* now."

It wouldn't be that simple. In order to get through the gate, she'd have to trust him. If he told her everything, there was no way she would.

"We need to pass through the gate to enter the underworld, Zanya."

Her eyebrows pushed together and she let out an exasperated breath. "So you're just going to pretend like nothing happened? Like you didn't just slit your own wrist!" She raked flyaways out of her face and then rubbed her heaving chest.

She hadn't suffered an anxiety attack in a while, but if anything was going to set it off, this was certainly worthy. He stepped toward her and rested his hands on her arms.

"Listen to me. Now that we've crossed from the middleworld to the gate, we need to pass through."

"Why aren't you answering me?" She pulled away from him and squared her jaw. He recognized that look. She wasn't going to back down. "You've been lying to me." It was a matter-of-fact statement, and there was no truthful way to respond. Not at the moment at least.

"I never lied to you, and I swear I'll tell you everything when we get out of the caves."

"*No*. You said you would tell me if I wanted to know." She hugged herself, now shivering. "I want to know."

"We can't do this right now, and if you'd just listen to me for a moment, you'd understand why."

She continued the facade of being fearless, but he could see she was freezing cold and on the edge of breaking down. Every muscle in his body ached to hold her and ease her shaking, like he'd done at the coffin house in London, when she still wanted him. He could almost feel the warmth of her bare skin from the dressing room just a day ago—something he'd be lucky to experience ever again.

Her silence dragged on another moment before she hung her head, and her shoulders dropped. "It's not like I have much of a choice now, so *fine*."

His gaze flickered from her to the lake, dread spreading deep to his bones. "The water is the portal." He swallowed and braced himself for her reaction.

"The water? I thought the blood…" Her gaze flickered to his wrists.

"It was, to the Mayan underworld realm."

Zanya carefully analyzed their surroundings. "So…we're…"

"No longer in the middleworld."

Zanya's expression turned frantic. "And that…" She looked at the lake.

"Is the entryway to the underworld."

She sucked in a ragged gasp. "We have to swim? We'll die from the cold. You know that, right? It's suicide."

He clenched his fists. "Exactly."

"*What?*"

"We have to drown. Water is the portal. It always has been. Only the dead can enter the underworld. We have to die to get through. It's the only way."

She inched away from the water, staring into the murky depths. "No." She glanced at him. "I can't…" She rushed to the farthest wall, where she frantically pried her fingers between every seam in the stone. "There has to be a way out of here." With every word, her voice rose in pitch until it cracked as she searched more of the cave wall.

"I asked if you were sure you wanted to continue. I told you there was no way out."

She spun, opening and closing her fists. Electricity sparked over her skin, and the light in her chest flickered to life. But its color was dark, and deep shadows crawled over her face—the same kind of shadows he would expect to see on someone from his native realm.

Zanya took a bold step forward. "You did *not* tell me we would have to drown in a freezing-cold lake to get there." A bead of sweat ran down her temple and her lips parted. She clutched her chest. "Wha—"

She dropped to her knees and doubled over on the ground. Arwan hauled her up and cradled her against his chest. Something was wrong. Maybe Sarian's hold on the stone was affecting her. In that case, her situation was worse than he thought.

Her body trembled, silence weighing heavy in the air. He'd do anything to make her unafraid, but death was so profound, and it brought even the most courageous men to their knees.

"If you want to get Jayden back, this is what we have to do. We can't go back the way we came. The water is the only way out."

With her forehead rested on his shoulder, she shook her head. "I can't." She twisted her fingers into the front of his shirt. "I'm scared."

"I know." It spent every ounce of willpower he had not to kiss her softly. "It won't last." He buried his face in her hair. "It just takes a second, then it's over."

He scooped her into his arms and stepped toward the gate. She clung to him tighter as he walked into the lake.

The freezing water flooded his shoes. His feet immediately tingled with frostbite, and his muscles recoiled from the chill of the water inching up his body. His lips quivered.

The still surface rippled, and the amber glow of

the rocks reflected off the silken waves, absorbing the color, painting the lake scarlet.

When the water touched Zanya's skin, she gasped and clung tighter to his neck. He paused for a moment. If there were only another way. "It will feel like you're dying…" He took a moment to contemplate his words. "And you will be. But we're beyond the middleworld now, and death means something different here. Once we leave the underworld, we'll return to the middleworld unharmed." His words didn't seem to offer her any solace, though he could do little to remedy that.

It would be better to get this over with as quickly as he could. She would fight. It was human instinct to run from death.

Heavens help him.

He'd have to hold her under.

CHAPTER SEVEN

Zanya

The water crawled over Zanya's shoulders and up her neck. Her entire body succumbed to numbness, overwhelming her with panic. "I can't do this." She slashed at the water in a desperate effort to get back to solid land.

Arwan tightened his grip around her.

She searched his face. "Let go of me, Arwan." Her voice trembled, though she tried not to let it show. His eyes saddened. With a powerful lunge, she struggled to break free, but his grip was like iron. "Let me go!" The water turned white, churning from her pounding fists.

"Zanya!" The tone of his voice shocked her. Her muscles went rigid. She'd never heard him shout in anger before. He pulled her back to his chest. "Wrap your legs around me." Her toes couldn't touch the bottom anymore. His legs pumped, holding both of them above the surface. "Please. I'm freezing." His quivering lips were tinted blue.

Hot tears filled her eyes and stung her skin when they slipped down her cheeks. Shit. She really had to do this. "You're sure we'll be okay when it's over?" As much as she loved Jayden, she didn't want to sacrifice ever seeing Renato again. Her memory of her uncle's pleading tone when he begged her not to go jabbed at her heart. If she didn't get out of this, he'd be crushed. And Tara. "Oh my God." Her eyes widened. "I never called Tara. What if we don't make it out? What if I never see her again?"

"You will." He hugged her closer. "But we have to drown, not freeze to death. So wrap your legs around me and I'll hold you the entire time."

She swallowed, more tears slipping down her face. "Promise?"

He nodded, and then kissed her. His mouth was the only warmth and the only comfort to be found. So rather than running away from her yearning, she dove into it. Hopefully the warmth of his lips would distract her until it was too late to turn back.

She wrapped her legs around his waist and her arms around his neck. Her hands were numb, but she could still feel the texture of his hair as she ran her fingers through it. He dragged his hands up her back and hooked them over her shoulders, locking her against him.

Arwan brushed his lips against hers. His hot breath made her skin tingle and her heart race. She parted her lips and deepened their kiss, running her tongue over his mouth. He tasted like earth and herbs; hot and tantalizing. Before she could take in her next breath, they were underwater.

Instinctively, she locked her breath into her lungs. Arwan pulled away from their kiss and she forced open her eyes.

The water was so cold she could barely manage, but she had to see him. He watched her with a mask of serenity as if nothing were wrong. As if they weren't submerging themselves into a black hole of death.

The light from her chest wavered over his face, dancing shadows over his features. He blinked slowly, and tiny air bubbles escaped his nose and rose toward the surface.

Her hair floated around them. The sight was almost beautiful, until her lungs began to burn.

She swallowed the urge to pull in a breath. The urge intensified, and the need to find air gripped her throat. She wriggled, and squinted toward the surface. A surface that was no longer there. They had sunk down what must have been a hundred feet, away from any hope or chance of escape.

Panic streaked through her while instinct and logic battled inside her. She didn't want to die.

Not even if it didn't last.

Not like this.

Arwan's fingers dug into her shoulders as they sank into the darkness.

Finally, the need to breathe was too much to bear. She parted her lips, and water flooded her lungs.

Bright lights tore through her closed eyelids. Zanya coughed and sputtered water from her nose and throat. She rolled to her side and clawed at the scalding stone beneath her while her frozen body jerked back to life.

She was still shivering, and the sudden change in temperature made her head spin. Her palms burned from pressing against the sun-beaten ground.

She pried open her eyes as chanting from what sounded like thousands of people drummed in her ears.

Then it hit her. The stench. Bitter and noxious in the intense heat, it burned her throat like venom. It was the same scent Sarian carried. Now it was obvious why. After he'd roamed the underworld, the stink of the place clung to him.

She pushed herself off the ground, peering at waves of people jumping in place, all of them with their backs facing her. Her vision blurred, stacking the scene two and then three times over itself before her sight finally settled in the middle.

She swayed like a drunkard as she stared at an entire city of people gathered in that very spot. None of them had on more than a simple loincloth to cover their genitals. It couldn't have been much of a shield against the elements.

Stone ruins littered the cracked ground, but none of them offered shade from the unrelenting sun.

Air had never been so hot.

She shielded her eyes and squinted to the top of a great temple. The air danced, making the structure shimmer like a mirage.

She slowly drew her gaze up to the sky, and realized it wasn't a sky at all, but soil with coils of roots writhing above them. The realm seemed endless, and whatever sun was there, however it existed in such a place, scorched everything below it.

There was no doubt. She stood under Yaxche, the tree of life.

The people chanted in unison, bobbing on the balls of their feet with their fingers stretched toward the sky.

She tore her attention away from the scene and searched for Arwan, but he was nowhere to be seen. There weren't many places to hide, except behind a few sun-scorched boulders or maybe one of the ruins, though he couldn't have gotten far without her noticing.

A chorus of shouts rose from the crowd. Her attention darted back to the peak of the temple where something resembling a man stood with his hand raised in the air, blood coating his forearm.

A human heart throbbed in his clenched hand.

Zanya stumbled back and fell to the ground with a slap. Her eyes widened. The sacrifice…it couldn't be Arwan. She shook her head, willing herself to believe it wasn't true. She would find him. They would get Jayden's soul back and then hightail it out of there. That was the plan. As long as he was still alive.

Drums pounded all around her, and the crowd continued to chant and dance. Another sacrifice had been made. The roar of the people was deafening. She did her best to block them out while she collected her thoughts.

She crawled along the dusty ground in search of somewhere to hide and a place to scout for Arwan. She squatted beside a large rock but didn't dare to touch it. The rock would scald her, and she had no idea if her healing ability would work here—or if any of her abilities would, for that matter.

Dust that was once caked mud between her fingers flaked off and fell to the ground. Her skin, already burned underneath, was now an angry red. The sting in her eyes worsened when she squinted at the far sides of the city. There were no hills. No trees. No shelter of any kind. Just more temples, all smaller than the one in front of her.

Was it possible Arwan hadn't made it through? He had kept some serious secrets from her already. What if one of them meant the difference between life and death?

The shouts from the crowd fell silent. She froze. The quiet hissing of their breaths were the only noises, as if they were all standing like statues, watching her.

A single drum pounded in a slow, rhythmic beat. She didn't want to look—maybe because she knew what she would find. But she didn't have much choice. She lifted her head to find thousands of people watching her with bloodshot eyes.

She slowly stood. There was no use trying to pretend she was safe. She was an unwelcome guest in the first layer of hell, and everyone knew it.

The unforgiving sun scorched their faces. Strips of flesh hung from their necks and foreheads. Boils bloated their skin, oozing liquid and pus. No wonder the underworld's stench was so vile. Death and rot loomed in the unrelenting heat, only magnifying the stink of their infected wounds.

They were all seething, their teeth bared from under dry, cracked lips. They looked as though they hadn't had a drink in years.

They looked thirsty.

So thirsty.

Up hundreds of narrow stone steps, on the peak of the temple stood a man, his bony index finger pointing directly at her. The skin on his arm was stripped away, and his esophagus showed through a gaping hole in his throat. His entire bottom jaw was completely gone.

Zanya clutched her chest. There was nothing she could do. She definitely couldn't run. Not if there was even a possibility of leaving Arwan behind. Who was she kidding? There was no way out even if she did run. She'd probably just die in the—

Zanya froze. She *was* dead. Her gaze slowly dropped to her hands, outstretched in front of her with her fingers spread. Even with her skin red and tender, they looked normal enough. Like *her* hands. Her normal, everyday hands. Tendons and veins buried under skin. Long, thin fingers. A scar on her left thumb from where she'd cut herself in the kitchen when she was a kid. Was that how the hands of a dead person looked? Just like normal hands?

The tempo of the drum grew faster, and Zanya's attention was pulled back to the scene in front of her. She searched the peak of the temple, but whoever, or whatever, had been there was gone.

The people turned back toward the temple and parted like the Red Sea as the creature glided across the ground toward her. Blood coated one of his arms, dripping from what was left of his fingertips, leaving a trail of gore upon the ground.

The chants were too low to understand at first. Zanya strained her ears to figure out what they were saying. The entire city mumbled in unison to the beat of the drum until the chants grew louder, and the word they repeated was clear enough to make out.

Houn. Houn. Houn.

They repeated his name in a low, ominous tone as if trying to provoke him. This was the deity they had come to see.

The bearer of souls.

Houn reached out to Zanya with his bloodstained hand. A thick drop of scarlet plumped on the curve of his knuckle and swelled until it fell to the dusty earth. Zanya swallowed.

Standing eye-to-eye with a god was a lot like standing eye-to-eye with your worst nightmare. Maybe she should have been used to it by now, but Houn's tattered body and foggy eyes turned her stomach and stalled her breath.

Physically he wasn't much larger than she was, but what he represented made him seem ten feet tall. His power radiated over her, the weight of his energy nearly pushing her back.

Houn slowly dropped his hand. He hadn't spoken a word. She figured he couldn't with no jaw, though by now anything seemed possible.

He turned and looked at the top of the temple, and she noticed the leather sack strapped to his back. *There* was where he carried the souls.

Houn pointed to the top of the Mayan ruin. A man appeared behind the altar with a book. She immediately recognized the shine of his tailored suit and the gloss of his black hair. After everything, she shouldn't have been surprised Sarian had followed her to the underworld. The anticipation of *why* made her hands tremble.

Her light burst to life, churning with white and blue. A cool rush of relief washed through her. Her powers were intact, which meant she might have a chance of getting out of here as planned.

Sarian opened a large book and ran his hands over the pages. His lips moved, though she couldn't hear what he was saying. When Sarian's eyes met hers, a sick heat crawled through her veins, and dark hues of violet blotted the light that shined from her chest. The dark magic Sarian conjured coiled around her, tearing the strength from her legs. She clung to the boulder, scorching her skin.

Sarian descended the stone altar, following the path of Houn to where she stood. The closer he got, the weaker Zanya became. The rest of her limbs shook with fatigue, and she sank to the ground. Her head bowed, and a pair of shined dress shoes appeared before her knees.

Her gaze swept up his creased slacks and stopped on a two-button jacket. His skin was completely intact. Her lips twisted at the sight of Sarian leering down at her with a heinous grin, leaning on his brass cane.

Houn bowed and backed away, as if giving allowance to the general of the realm.

Sarian took Zanya's hand with an iron grip. She struggled to pull away, but he pinched her fingers together, making small circles over her skin with his thumb.

She wanted to scream, though it would be useless. Sarian tugged up on her hand, leading her to her feet. She stood with shaky legs, forced to lean on him for support. His eyes morphed through shades of purple and black.

He was enjoying this. That much was obvious by the way he held his head high, his chest pushed out and chin tipped up. "You are in my kingdom now, young guardian. There is no safe haven for you here."

While he led her down the stone path, his fingers snaked over hers. He flashed a serpentine smile and paused at the temple's base. The sick heat in her chest wrapped around her lungs.

"I had no doubt you would eventually make the right decision, my queen."

CHAPTER EIGHT

Zanya's next step landed her shoe into something wet. She slowly lowered her gaze to the river of blood flowing down the steps.

Her heart raced.

"It has been a long road to get here, has it not?" Sarian escorted her up the stairs, practically dragging her the entire way. When they reached the top of the temple, Zanya's legs throbbed from the climb. The heat intensified, blistering her cheeks and forehead.

"This place is a wasteland." He surveyed the dead, cracked land. "Its true potential has long been wasted by a king who prefers to stay hidden in the deepest layer of the underworld, mourning a son who rejects his throne." He drew in a deep breath and exhaled. "But no longer. I will resurrect this kingdom as my own." He flipped the pages of the book. "But first, I must cleanse it of the unworthy."

Zanya's hatred for him grew so fierce she would kill him herself if she were able. If only she had the strength.

Sarian clicked his tongue. "Now that's not very becoming, Guardian. You shouldn't have such thoughts about your future king."

Zanya sucked in a breath. Could he hear her thoughts or somehow see into her mind? What else did he know?

He leaned in so close to her, his breath washed over her ear. "Everything, my dear. I know absolutely everything." He placed an unwanted kiss on her cheek. "I was going to force you into obedience when I first broke the spell." His lips brushed against her jaw. Bile rose in her throat. "But listening to all of your thoughts and fantasies about that boy was too enjoyable. All of the *thoughts* you have about him." He gripped Zanya's wrist so tight, the delicate bones ground together. She gritted her teeth. "The *dreams* you have about him. I could do those things to you."

She turned her head and spit in his face.

He flinched back, his lips pressed tightly together. He raised his hand as though he was going to strike her, but paused and curled his fingers into a fist. He wiped the streak of saliva from his cheek, his features turning to stone. "Very well." He turned to the enormous book propped on the altar. "The Popol Vuh." He practically cooed the words. He ran his hand over the pages. Etched in faded ink on the pages were the same kinds of markings she'd seen on the stone altar in the cave. He read the first few words, and the markings glowed with life.

Zanya's stomach lurched as he continued to read aloud. With every word that passed through his lips, her limbs grew heavier and harder to move.

The thousands of people raised their hands toward the sky, chanting in unison. Their words slurred and morphed into white noise.

Sarian reached into her pocket and removed the stone. Its light shuddered, and Zanya's heart tore open when her stone streaked with panic. "You wouldn't accept my proposition willingly. Perhaps you will reconsider now that you see all you could reign over once you belong to me. By my order, the stone will strip you of your abilities—at least until I see you are willing to obey my commands." She struggled to keep standing. Sarian yanked her against his chest. He narrowed his eyes. "You can either accept your fate and live, or I can release you to the will of the underworld and you can die a slow, agonizing death."

Zanya curled her lip and summoned every bit of her energy, then grabbed his hand and wrestled him for her stone. He threw her against the altar, where the blood from the last sacrifice had already dried and turned to dust. "Stupid girl!" She blinked when bits of soil fell onto her cheeks and eyelashes from the roots slithering above them.

His eyes narrowed as they locked on the pendant around Zanya's neck. A scowl arched his lip. "You believe the heaven deities can help you now?" He grabbed Cualli's emblem, tore it from her neck, and threw it to the ground. "You are mine now. They have no power here." He towered over her, glaring as if he hated everything about her. "*I own you.*"

He cradled the stone close to his mouth and read from the book. The moment the words passed through his lips, her stone flashed with purple. The sickness crawling through her veins burst with such intense heat, as if she'd been set on fire. The dark energy clamped around her heart.

Zanya's muscles locked. He extended his hand and trailed his fingers over her cheek. She slapped him away, but it didn't seem to faze him. He trailed his hand down her neck to her bust line, and stopped just as his finger caught the lace of her tank top. Her powers were gone, and instead his dark force pulsed through her.

"Now. Let us watch the cleansing of your new kingdom."

Zanya didn't reply, partly out of fear, though mostly out of resentment. Sarian grabbed hold of her hand and rested her open palm on his cheek. He dragged his lips over her wrist, inhaling her scent. His eyes closed, and his throat visibly tensed with sexual desire, making her want to gag. "Remember." He opened his eyes and stared into her face. "Your abilities are chained, and if I so choose, you will be just another corpse lying at the bottom of the temple. I suggest you exercise some sense and do as you are told, young guardian."

Zanya swallowed, but her throat was so dry she could barely manage. Where was Arwan when she needed him? The only explanation was too painful to consider.

She glared defiantly at Sarian.

He returned the gesture. "You prove to be more like your mother than I care to remember." He shoved her back, nearly throwing her to the ground.

More soil tapped over her shoulders. A thin layer of dirt now powdered the stone temple.

Sarian continued reading from the book. The ground below them writhed with roots. More of the tree's roots from above reached down, and more pushed up through the dusty earth. The temple trembled. Zanya grabbed on to a stone block and bent her knees so she wouldn't fall down the steps.

Thankfully, she still had control over her body.

Sarian didn't seem fazed by the churning ground and wild roots slashing at the air. Zanya's gaze flickered from him to the book while he dragged his finger along each line he read aloud.

This was the book from her dreams. It had the same curled corners, the same yellow tint, and the same textured pages.

Screams and shrieks replaced the underworlders' chants as roots coiled around their ankles and legs and dragged them under.

Gut-wrenching screams shook the air. Underworlders scattered in every direction, desperately seeking refuge from the hungry tree. Scarlet puddles sat on the dry surface. Soon, the ground looked like a sea of blood.

Sarian read line after line, page after page, and she could do nothing more than watch. Her stone was hexed with his underworld power, which was more powerful than anything she could control. She would have to be smart.

Zanya squared her jaw, examining Sarian. "Is this how you really want to win?"

He stopped reading and slowly turned his head toward her.

"I mean, this isn't even a fair fight. You really are a coward."

His upper lip twitched.

"Oh, so that's it. You're scared of me." She huffed. "Well, I should have guessed as much. My mother showed you up, so why wouldn't I? You couldn't take the same chance twice, so you took the coward's—"

He lunged toward her and clenched his hand around her throat. "Your mother, that *whore*, was no match for me. It's true she put up a reasonable fight, but I broke her." His grip tightened, cutting off her air. "And I will inevitably break you as well." He tilted his head to the side as she struggled to pull in a breath. The edges of her vision clouded with black. He released her throat just before she lost consciousness, and she gasped and coughed. "If you are suggesting you think you can defeat me in my own realm, I welcome you to try. Perhaps getting this over with early will be of more benefit." He turned back to the book.

She didn't have time to think, just react. With everything she had left, Zanya closed her eyes and searched her soul for the link connecting her to her stone. Though it was weak and struggling to hold on, the tether was there; like a single thread of spider web stretching from one branch to another, being battered by the wind. Zanya called to the stone. It was the only hope she had to recover even a small amount of power, even for a moment.

Her stone's distant whispers echoed back. The longing that exploded in Zanya's heart was like nothing she'd ever experienced. Not for a real home. Not for Jayden when he'd left. Not even for Tara, on the nights Zanya was forced to sleep in solitary after she woke from her nightmares with slashes clawed down her arm.

Something inside her snapped, and the bond to her stone began to grow. She clung to it, pulling harder until she could feel the link strengthen. The cool energy of her light spread through her chest, clashing with the sick heat of the cursed charm.

It was now or never. Energy flowed under her skin, through her limbs, and back to her chest. Her palms grew cold as she concentrated on collecting her powers and threw out her hands to strike him with an energy ball.

There was nothing.

Sarian grinned. "Did you honestly believe your abilities would simply return? That I would just give them back? Foolish girl." He shook his head. "Women are good for little more than to be subservient. I will never understand why the gods chose a female to guard the stone."

"Maybe because they knew what a complete ass you are, and there was no one better for the job." She lunged at the book and tore out several pages before he was able to react. The pages scattered around their feet.

He grabbed her wrists. "That, Guardian, was a step over the line." He pulled her so close their bodies touched. "You made the mistake of thinking I *need* you."

He knocked the wind out of her lungs with a punch to the gut. The taste of salt and metal coated her tongue, and warm liquid spread over her shirt. Zanya slowly lowered her gaze to see the handle of a knife protruding from her side.

Was it possible? Could somebody who was already dead, die?

Sarian shoved her back. A dull ache spread through her gut, and she fell to the ground, staring up at the ceiling of dirt and roots trapping in hell's sun. Cualli's emblem sat beside her. Zanya grabbed it and held it against her chest for comfort.

Everything had gone so wrong.

Sarian's expression changed. She pushed up on her forearms to see what was happening. The knife twisted under the effort, and she muffled a shriek by biting her lip. With a deep breath, she gripped the handle and yanked it out of her side in one swift jerk. It was impossible to trap in the scream. She let go of the blade, and it clattered to the ground. Her hand shook as she pressed her palm over the wound.

When Zanya was finally able to force herself to a sitting position, Sarian's posture had changed. He stared out at the ground, not reading, not moving. Zanya followed his gaze and spotted Contessa strolling through the genocide as if nothing were happening. Why would Sarian's ex-lover leave the comforts of her quant home in Moscow to come to the underworld? When Contessa was involved, the outcome was never good. Either she'd showed up just in time to watch Sarian finally get what he wanted, or she was up to something. The latter was Zanya's first bet.

Contessa didn't make any effort to pick up her gown or avoid stepping in puddles of scarlet as she strutted toward the temple. She twirled a strand of hair while passing the lifeless underworlders as they were dismembered and pulled beneath the earth.

The roots were now plump with blood, pulsing and writhing above the surface. As if they'd had their fill, they dodged Contessa's light footsteps.

"Hello, *lover*." Contessa's voice was like silk. She stopped at the altar's base. Her stance was wide, and she tapped her index finger against her bottom lip.

Deepening creases around Sarian's mouth gave away his disbelief.

"What? Not happy to see me?" Contessa looked at Zanya, whose muscles tensed. "Oh dear." She ticked her tongue. "I see you aren't doing very well." Instead of climbing the steps, she stood in place, her emerald eyes gleaming. "Allow me to make an educated guess." She tilted her head to the side. "Stabbed? Luckily for you it wasn't through the heart." She turned back to Sarian. "And *you*."

Sarian glanced around the quiet city. "This wasn't part of our agreement." Zanya might not have heard the quiver in his voice if she hadn't been so close.

"It may not have been part of your plan, but it was part of mine all along." She swayed her hips side to side, as if she were a playful child telling a story, delighted to be the center of attention. "You couldn't have honestly believed I would give up the lock of the guardian's hair so you could better control her stone. Why? Out of the kindness of my heart?" She paused. "Oh, wait. I don't have a heart any longer. *You pierced it.*"

"We agreed on a price, and you will get what you want as soon as I am finished with the book."

"Yes." Her smile vanished and her expression

turned to stone. "You can be sure I will get *everything* I want."

Sarian closed the Popol Vuh and scooped it under his arm. He shifted his weight. Zanya had never seen him look so nervous. "Stop playing games, Contessa." He scanned the bloodstained valley. "Where is he?"

"Who, pet?"

"The king. I assume you are here because you've informed him of my plans. Or are you here for another reason?" His shoulders relaxed, and he leaned on the altar with a smug grin. "A second chance at earning my good favor, perhaps?"

"As much as it would please you to have me groveling at your feet for an opportunity to claim the throne you once promised me, that's not at all why I'm here."

A shadow fell over Sarian—the first shadow Zanya had seen in this realm. It loomed over him and stretched across the altar, then down several of the stone steps.

Sarian stood up straight, his brows furrowed.

Contessa smiled widely. "I merely came to watch."

Zanya froze, her eyes wide and her breath stalled as Sarian slowly turned, finding himself face-to-face with a beast. Its muscular legs quivered under sleek black fur as if it had just learned to stand. Probably thirsty and weak like the others, it was most likely drawn there by the scent of blood.

Zanya pressed harder on her wound, but her hands were already coated in scarlet. Perhaps hers would be lost in the scent of the rest of the other blood.

The beast bared its teeth. The pads of its paws flattened against the stone when it took a step forward. Its breath blew a strand of Sarian's hair away from his face, now drained of color.

Zanya held her breath and hoped the creature didn't hear her pounding heart. Its dark eyes gleamed with specks of gold. Sleek, midnight-black fur covered its entire body. The only exception was a patch of gold on its chest.

The underworld animal snarled and lunged at Sarian before he had a chance to change and match the beast's size and strength. The animal's jaws clenched around Sarian's shoulder, and it thrashed its head side to side until the ground was dotted with a fresh coat of red.

Sarian's frantic efforts to morph into his beastly form only seemed to anger the creature. He managed to slice the animal's face with a sharp blow. It snarled and threw Sarian's mangled body against the altar, then towered over him. The beast's snout came within an inch of his face. Sarian dropped the book to the ground and reached out in a placating gesture, his hands now trembling as if he were a child. He opened his mouth to speak.

The beast didn't give him the chance. It snapped down and tore off Sarian's head. Blood sprayed over the steps as the animal discarded its trophy. Sarian's head bounced down the steps until it rolled to a stop at Contessa's feet.

Bile rose in Zanya's throat. She pressed her hands over her mouth and dug her back into the stone—as if curling into a ball would somehow make her invisible. She remembered doing the exact same thing in the orphanage while drifting off to sleep, hoping Sarian wouldn't be waiting for her in her dreams. It didn't work then, and she had no idea why she was doing it now. Maybe instinct. Maybe just wishful thinking.

Contessa stared down at the remains. She tilted her head to one side in morbid curiosity, and then she stepped over Sarian's head, as if it was merely a piece of garbage littering the ground.

CHAPTER NINE

"Rise up and stop cowering on the ground." Contessa paid no attention to Sarian's limp body lying beside the altar.

Zanya frantically searched for the beast.

"Child."

Contessa's cold tone brought Zanya's focus back to the woman—and the corpse. Sarian's hand twitched. Zanya clenched the wound on her gut. It would be *her* withering in the unforgiving sun if she didn't heal soon. The ache in her side grew into sharp spikes of agony.

Contessa stooped down, grabbed a handful of Zanya's hair, and lifted her head just enough to bring Zanya's ear to her lips. "Hear me, child. I will not repeat myself twice." Zanya swallowed and nodded the best she could. "You have done me a great justice today, and although it pains me to admit it…" Her lips puckered as if something bitter coated her tongue. "I am in your debt. Even the damned believe in honor."

Zanya would take what she could get, as long as

it meant going home. "I want to get the hell out of here." The blood from her wound had formed a pool beneath her, but she couldn't leave without taking back the one thing she'd come for in the first place. Not after everything that had happened. "But first I came here to get Jayden's soul back."

"That's right." Contessa let go of Zanya's hair, allowing her cheek to slap to the ground. "You still desire to retrieve your comrade's soul?"

Zanya struggled to sit up against the stone wall. "Yeah, but why do I get the feeling you know something I don't?"

"I know many things you do not."

Everything about Contessa's tone made Zanya uncomfortable. "Like?" She continued to probe, struggling to ignore the pain radiating through her muscles.

Contessa examined her face for a moment before speaking. "I shouldn't have expected you to understand." She sighed. "When you came to me for help after your comrade's passing, I found an opportunity I could not resist. I am not the only enemy Sarian has made over the years." She extended her hand to the quiet realm. "You see how little regard he has for the souls of the underworld. Many despise him, though none more than I." She dropped her hand back to her side, and her focus moved to the Sarian's corpse. She dug in his coat pocket and pulled out Zanya's stone. Zanya gasped and snatched it from Contessa's grasp, then hugged it to her chest.

Contessa stood, staring down at her. "I have no use for your little stone, child. When I approached him with your lock of hair, he was all too eager to agree to the trade. Your hair and a spell to finalize his control over the stone, in exchange for the Popol Vuh."

Zanya clenched her jaw. Of course Contessa would use Zanya's hair against her. But if Contessa lied to her once, then she could have lied about anything. "What about Jayden's spirit?"

Contessa cupped Zanya's chin delicately with her fingers. Zanya wanted to slap her hand away, but figured it better not to. "I knew who that foolish boy was as soon as I laid eyes on him, and I anticipated him following you here."

"Jayden didn't follow me. I followed him, in case you already forgot."

"I am not speaking of your fallen friend. I speak of the other—the dark one. I had no doubt he would exact revenge, which is no fault of mine, of course. The king can't possibly hold *me* responsible for the death of his general by—" She paused in consideration. "Well, the rest isn't important for now." She stood and pivoted away.

"Wait." Zanya reached out for her, and her breath caught in her throat. She swallowed, trying to block out the pain. "Are you talking about Arwan? The one with dark hair?" She hadn't seen him since they'd been submerged in the portal, and the reality of what may have happened to him nearly broke her. "He could be dead."

"You may have thanked me if that were the case." Contessa picked the book up off the ground and trotted down the hundreds of narrow steps.

The roots above them writhed as Contessa

continued down the temple toward the miles of blood-soaked ground. If Zanya stayed where she was, she'd die. Well, maybe not. But *not* dying here was worse than dying in the middleworld. She'd have to make nicey-nice with Contessa before she vanished—along with any chance of returning home.

Zanya ground her teeth and pushed to her feet, snatched up the loose pages from the book, and folded them in her pocket. She wobbled down the steps as fast as she could without losing her balance. It didn't help that every movement hurt like hell. "Wait." The temptress didn't stop walking. "Contessa, please. You didn't answer my question about Jayden. Where is he? Did you lie about Houn?"

The witch didn't reply.

"You said you were in my debt, remember?" If Arwan were in the underworld, he would have found her by now. If he was still in the caves, she had to find him. "I just want Jayden's soul, and I want to go home." Desperation cracked her voice.

Contessa paused on the final step of the temple. "Is that so?"

Panting, Zanya nodded. "Please." She swallowed. "Just help me get Jayden back and send me to the middleworld. I won't ask you for anything else."

Contessa turned to face her, one side of her mouth curling into a grin. "Very well. I will get his soul from Houn and have it returned to his body."

Zanya couldn't allow herself to feel any relief. She didn't trust Contessa. Unfortunately, she didn't have much of a choice.

Contessa gestured behind Zanya. "I believe you two have met."

Zanya turned to see the bearer of souls gliding over the first layer of the underworld, which was now eerily silent.

"He happens to owe me a favor. A few, in fact. And considering it's been some time since I've indulged, this is the perfect opportunity to call on such a favor." She locked her sights on Houn, and her bright green eyes grew black like onyx. The monster lurking just under her skin—the same glimpse of her ugly, damned soul Zanya had first seen on the streets of Moscow—flashed beneath her milky complexion.

Houn glided to Contessa's side and slowly removed the leather sack from his back. Contessa poised her hand over it. Houn pulled it open, and Contessa slowly reached inside.

Her eyes fluttered shut as her fair skin darkened with shadows. The pouch glowed, and screams filled the dead realm. Zanya clasped her hands over her ears and dropped to her knees, grinding her teeth under the assault.

The tree hadn't spared any souls. No one was left to scream. Zanya's gaze danced from the pouch to Contessa, who was somehow interacting with the trapped souls.

Zanya's lips parted and her stomach dropped.

No. Not interacting. Consuming. *Gorging.*

Zanya stood, still clasping her hands over her ears. Slowly, the screams faded. As each scream died, a distinct voice began to emerge.

A man's voice. A voice she recognized.

Zanya gasped. "Jayden!"

Contessa pulled her hand away from the empty carrier of souls and opened her eyes, now swirling with magic. "Stay back." Her voice was angelic, as if tiny bells were tinkling around them.

"What did you do to him?" Zanya shifted, balling her fists. "*What did you do?*"

"I intend to keep my word, though I'm afraid, child, your woes have just begun."

With a slight gesture of Contessa's hand, a root lunged from the earth above them and curled around Zanya's waist. Barbs stuck into her skin, and it jerked her into the air. The sudden movement made her stomach roll, and she screamed. On instinct, Zanya clenched her eyes shut just as her back slammed into the soil, knocking the air out of her lungs before she was sucked into the earth above.

***

Arwan

Cold shocked Arwan's body. He gasped in a scorching breath as he pried open his eyes. The dark cave did little to help him see, but from the humidity in the air and the sound of raindrops pattering on the ground outside, he knew he'd returned to the middleworld.

There was no rain where he was from.

With every movement his muscles weakened. A gust of wind ran over his naked body. It had been decades since the last time he changed, and he

85

hadn't been dressed when he returned to humanity back then, either.

Thankfully there were extra clothes in the pack he'd left behind. His body trembled as he slipped on a pair of sweats and a cotton T-shirt, and though his fingers were like ice, the warm jungle air had begun to thaw them out.

He'd fled the underworld after he'd torn Sarian apart, leaving Zanya behind. He had to find her. If anything happened to her, he'd never forgive himself.

His gut wrenched when he recalled the way she'd backed away from him in the caves. What she must have thought. The horrors that must have reeled through her mind. They would all be justified. He *was* a monster.

Arwan extended his hands and examined the lines tracing his palms. His life would never be the same. She had seen his true form. Worse, he'd killed Sarian right in front of her—as a beast. He still tasted the blood. Saliva pooled under his tongue, and he fisted his hands. He was no better than the world he came from or the monsters that lived in it.

Perhaps death would have been more merciful.

The echo of Zanya's moan made him jump. He peered out of the cave's entrance to see her lying on the ground outside. Arwan scrambled to his feet and stumbled toward her, using the cave's stone walls as support. He pushed hair out of his face and staggered out of the cave, then dropped to the ground beside her.

The heavy rain drenched him in seconds. The

soil had been dry for so long, it wouldn't absorb the water. The downpour sat on top of the ground, collecting pools and puddles in the places where it had nowhere to run.

Zanya lay on her stomach with her eyes closed and hair splayed over her face and neck. He gently brushed strands away from her cheek with the tips of his trembling fingers. "Zanya." Her name scraped out of his throat.

Her back rose and fell with shallow breaths. She was alive, and in the middleworld she would heal from her injuries. He grabbed her shoulder and rolled her over. Her fingers uncurled, and her stone slipped from her hand.

Zanya moaned and clenched her ribs. Her lips pressed tightly together while her fingers curled around her shirt, soaked in blood. He pulled it up to reveal a deep wound in her side, and watched, waiting for it to heal. But it only continued to bleed.

His turned his attention to the stone. It wasn't lit up or churning with colors. If he didn't know any better, he'd think it was just a regular river pebble. He grabbed the stone and a volt of energy threw him back to the ground.

Warm rain fell over him while he stared up at the sky. His inner beast rooted deeper inside of him like a blot of ink staining his soul. Arwan turned his head and stretched his fingers to touch Zanya's hand. This could be the last time he touched her.

A deep growl caught his attention, and he looked to see the speckled paws of a jaguar pad past him. Arwan tilted his head and met the animal's yellow eyes peering down at him.

"Foolish boy," spat an old woman's voice. The sound of hasty footsteps on wet ground grew louder until a woman with wrinkled skin and graying black hair loomed over him, blocking the big cat from his sight. With her hands perched on her hips, she seemed angry rather than concerned.

He furrowed his brows as his vision blurred. "*Tia* Drina?" He tried to focus, unsure if she was a hallucination from all he'd been through. Drina lived in Belize. They were nearly twelve hours away by bus from her village near Renato's home.

The woman held a stick in her hand and waved it in his face as she scowled. "I will build a fire, *t'en* beat you."

He exhaled, and his muscles relaxed against the cool, drenched earth. Without a doubt, it was Drina.

The crackling of the fire woke Arwan. The rain had stopped, leaving a humid, musky scent in the air. Tia Drina crouched on the soil beneath the jungle canopy, grinding herbs with a pestle and mortar. The frail woman's shoulders hunched as she toiled over the mixture, and a bead of sweat collected on her brow. She wiped it away with the back of her hand."

The warmth from the fire radiated across his skin. Zanya lay asleep on the other side of the flames. He observed her silhouette and listened to her steady breathing until he was satisfied she was all right. His senses seemed to be even more heightened now. He didn't have to strain to listen to the rhythmic *thud* of her heart.

He turned back to Drina. "How did you get here?" His voice was still raspy, though it was better than before. Most likely thanks to one of Drina's herbal treatments laced with magic.

"When Cualli calls, t'ere is no room to refuse." She huffed and pushed a lock of hair away from her face. "Even for an old woman."

"Cualli? She's here?"

Drina glanced at him, though it was more like a glare. "You are too eager. And foolish." She pounded the tool faster and with more power. "Nearly get yourself killed. And her." She gestured to Zanya with a nod. "You forget what is important and chase after revenge. Like a blind, scared animal."

Her words cut into him.

She paused and exhaled. "Did you get what you wanted?"

He had lost everything to gain so little. He'd always believed killing Sarian would bring back his humanity. Instead it had torn him further away.

He didn't remember choosing to change. The beast clawed out of him with such strength, he was stripped of any right to make a decision. He strained to remember his time as a beast, but the memories were fogged and unclear. One thing stood out: the deep, carnal need to tear through the man responsible for leading his mother to her death. His father might have killed her, but Sarian was the cause. As a beast, that desire had overpowered him.

Drina returned to pounding the herbs. "No matter. Is too late to t'ink on it. Important now is t'e guardian. She is hurt. It took strong magic—more t'an I was ready to make—but the link between her and her stone is alive. As is she. But it will still take time for her to heal." Panting, she stopped grinding the herbs, and her wrinkled hand trembled. "But she is ill. Not healing." Drina poured a steaming mixture over the herbs, then crushed it into a thick paste. Her rickety bones creaked as she stood.

Arwan nearly reached out to help her, but the old woman was too prideful for that. She would have swatted him away, or worse.

Drina hobbled to his side, scooped a clump of the mixture onto her fingers, and smeared it across his chest and over the gash on his cheek. It smelled horrible, but he didn't dare pull away. "Cuts will heal faster wit' salve." Drina turned, pressed the back of her hand against Zanya's forehead, and frowned.

Arwan grunted as he forced himself to his feet. He walked to Drina's side and crouched beside her. All of the color was drained from Zanya's cheeks. How could he have let this happen?

Drina's lips were still puckered, and the tension in her shoulders made it obvious she was unsettled.

"Will she be all right?"

Drina applied a new coat of salve over the wound in Zanya's side. "Yes, I t'ink so. But t'ere was dark magic used here. It weakened her powers. Somet'ing was used t'at belongs to her. Somet'ing personal."

Arwan dropped his head. He still blamed himself for not seeing it sooner. "Her hair. Contessa took it in Moscow when we went to her for help to find Sarian." He clenched his jaw. "I never should have let her give it to that witch, but it was what Contessa wanted in exchange."

"Yes. Hair would be very good for a spell." She twisted a cloth full of water over a terra-cotta pot and gently patted it over Zanya's forehead.

A heavy silence filled the air.

She dropped the cloth back into the bowl and continued to mix the salve unnecessarily. It was clear Drina was holding something back. She glanced up at him every chance she had, probably hoping he wouldn't notice.

He pretended not to. Drina was a rough woman. She had been alive far longer than her natural lifecycle would have allowed. If not for the blessings set over her by the village elders and the favor of the gods, she would have been gone and in the earth years ago. Still, all of her wisdom hadn't helped her in having a soft tongue.

So he would allow her to pound the herbs in silence.

The crackling of the fire mixed with the familiar jungle sounds soothed him. Arwan had spent so much time in the bush, it was like a second home. He drew in a deep breath, exhaled, and centered his mind while he examined Zanya's face, peaceful and content as she slept near the flames.

Life hadn't always been this complicated. There was a time when things were simple. A time he didn't know where he came from or what he really was. He hadn't always sensed the beast within him. It only began to claw its way out when he came of age, and the solstice first conjured it to life. So many changes had occurred at the same time. He filled out that year and became stronger. His mother hadn't been alive to scc how many changes had occurred at the same time. He became stronger and adopted martial arts as a hobby—to keep the effects of his dark side under control. The sport gave him something to focus on and something to do with his days other than pacing his room or running over the paths between villages.

A grin tugged at his lips.

As a boy, he was not above making mischief. Perhaps the fates had planned for him to join the other boys that day in throwing rocks at Drina's hut. She was, after all, a high priestess—a person the villagers both admired and feared.

Back then she had been much more nimble and quick on her feet. When she'd charged out of her hut, waving her fist in the air, the other boys ran. She locked eyes with Arwan, and her expression of anger melted away. He still recalled how her fist slowly relaxed and her arm dropped to her side. She recognized him, knew who he was, and loved him in spite of that.

"Cualli told me what happened." Drina's voice tore him out of his thoughts. "She called for me, knowing you would need someone." She set the stone bowl on the ground beside her. Her hands were stained dark brown from the mixture, much like the henna used to mark new Maya brides before they were given away. She traced the rim of the bowl with her wrinkled fingers. "Your love for t'e guardian has made you to do bold t'ings. Be brave. Face fears you have hidden away for many years."

He couldn't meet Drina's gaze out of his own humiliation.

"But you have loved selflessly."

She provided him little comfort. Nothing he could do would prove he was not a beast in his heart, where men built their destiny and chose who they would become.

Now he saw the knowledge in Renato's words. *You choose who you are, and the choice is yours alone.*

He finally met Drina's warm gaze. "She does not know, Arwan."

"What?"

"She woke while you were sleeping, and her first words were of you. She was worried. T'ought you were dead. Cried when she saw you."

He took Zanya's hand and pressed a kiss to her palm. Her skin was warm, and although she was asleep, her fingers curled and held his hand in return.

"Should I tell her?" He hoped for Drina's guidance. Instead she grabbed the bowl and returned to mixing the herbs.

To tell Zanya the truth would sever any chance of her seeing him the same way again. But not telling her could have the same consequences. She had already been hurt, and he swore he would not compromise her heart a second time.

CHAPTER TEN

Zanya

The whisper of soft voices woke Zanya from her sleep. She immediately groped for her stone in her pocket. Curling her fingers around its smooth surface, she exhaled, clinging to it with everything she had.

She smiled when the stone's tether tugged at her. It had missed her.

Plumes of smoke rose from the fire pit beside her. It must have been burning all night, but now the morning sun provided warmth and light. She sat up and looked at Arwan, who was speaking to an older woman just yards away.

They didn't notice she had woken up. Funny, Arwan was always observant. Now he looked so wrapped up in conversation that he'd forgotten about the world.

The woman beside him plucked leaves from a plant and replied to his whispers with a sober nod. It might be a good idea to let them know she'd woken up, but she didn't want to disturb them. The old woman had been so kind, and if Arwan trusted her, Zanya would do the same.

Besides, she had her own reasons to be thankful for the woman's kindness. She'd given Zanya water and stopped the bleeding from her wound with her herbal remedies. Zanya recalled drifting in and out of consciousness while the woman used several methods to bring her back to awareness. It all seemed like a dream now, though it had been very real.

The underworld was real. Contessa was real. The beast that had stolen Sarian's head—that was terrifyingly real.

And Jayden…

The anticipation of returning to Moscow was already too much to bear. Whether or not Contessa had returned Jayden's soul to the middleworld was still unclear. The only way to know for sure was to seek him.

Zanya cradled her stone to her chest and closed her eyes, drawing in deep, cleansing breaths. A sharp pain arched in her side, and made a mental note not to breathe in quite so deep next time.

As she focused on her powers, flashes of light beat like butterfly wings behind her eyelids. First there was darkness and static, followed by the sound of muffled breaths. Not her breaths, but someone else's. Jayden's maybe. But she couldn't see anything. Maybe his spirit was still trapped in Houn's possession.

Though if that were the case, she wouldn't be able to seek him. He had to be somewhere in the middleworld.

Suddenly, there was light. Zanya closed her eyes harder. A deep chill froze her to the bone. She shivered, holding the fuzzy image until she identified what was looming above him.

It was a big spotlight. She shivered again.

Someone groaned. "Fuck."

Zanya sucked in a breath at the sound of Jayden's voice—cursing, of course. She held the vision, experiencing his every sensation. This wasn't like the seeking she'd done before. This was more personal, as though she was experiencing everything with him.

Jayden rolled over and fell off the cold surface onto an even colder floor. The vision streaked in a haze of panic, and the breath was knocked out of her lungs. "What the hell…" Jayden rolled onto his back and cradled his ribs.

"Try to stay calm, Jayden." Renato was there. She recognized his voice immediately.

Zanya peered through Jayden's foggy vision. He blinked at the fuzzy image of Renato, who stood on the far side of the room.

Zanya's heart ached at the sight of his lean frame and dark hair.

When Jayden's focus finally centered, he scanned the contents of the room. Sleek counters with medical supplies organized on trays. A row of silver beds with hoses and drains in the floor. An industrial light fixed to the ceiling.

Was he in a…morgue?

"What. The. Fuck." Jayden shifted, still freezing cold.

"I understand you may be in shock." Renato kept his distance. "Perhaps it's better if you do not move. I am not entirely sure what changes have occurred, if any."

"Changes?" Zanya strained to keep a hold on Jayden. She couldn't lose him again, even for just a moment. Not when he was just waking from his ordeal and was clearly confused.

"Is this some kind of sick joke?" Jayden's voice drew her back to him, and her grip on the vision grew stronger. Jayden stared at a string tied around his toe with a tag dangling off the end. His muscles ached—as did hers. "What the hell's going on?"

"You are very lucky to be back." Renato shook his head, his eyes wide and fixed on him. "I had my doubts, but—" He extended his hand toward Jayden, as if offering proof. "You are very much alive."

"Then why was I just lying on a fucking steel bed?" Jayden scowled at his foot. "And why the hell is there a tag on my toe?" He tore it off and tossed it aside.

"Peter is on his way. He should be able to heal the rest of your wounds, but…" Renato continued to shake his head, as if he wanted to say something but didn't know how.

Jayden gathered the sheet in his hand and shifted his bare butt along the cold tile floor. He gripped the side of a steel examination bed and slowly pulled himself to his feet.

His legs wobbled and he groaned, his muscles raw like he'd been beaten with a bat.

Jayden smacked his lips. Thirst tore through

Zanya. Her throat tightened and every cell cried out for water.

She had never been so thirsty.

Her vision shifted as Jayden stumbled to a sink. He turned it on, tilted his head under the running water, and drank as fast as he could.

Zanya felt the cool water slide down her throat.

Water dripped over Jayden's lips and down his chin, and he drank until his stomach couldn't hold any more.

When he had his fill, he stood and wiped his mouth with the back of his hand, and turned off the faucet. Silence filled the room.

He leaned on the counter. "When will Peter be here?" When Renato didn't respond, Jayden ground his teeth. "Fine. I'll seek him myself."

Scalding pain sliced through Zanya's mind, throwing her back into her own surroundings.

She held her head as her vision continued to be assaulted by light. But this time it was sunlight. The light turned from a painful glare to warm rays, kissing her cheeks. Tree branches swayed above her in the distant breeze.

Jayden was back in the middle world, safe with Renato and Peter looking after him. Even if she didn't have the energy to seek him for a while, at least she didn't have to worry.

Zanya inhaled the fresh jungle air, which carried the scent of rain and warm earth. It was a welcome change from the bitter stench of the underworld.

"She lives." The old woman's voice was both soft and playful.

Zanya opened her eyes to the woman's wrinkled

face. She offered a smile. "Yep. I live."

The woman lifted Zanya's shirt just enough to the see the dried salve packed over the wound. She nodded and smiled softly. "Almost healed. You are very lucky to be alive."

Zanya swallowed as she recalled the instant rush of panic when Sarian had driven a knife into her gut. She'd had no way for her to fight back or run, not without her abilities or control over her stone. She'd been so helpless, and here in the middleworld, she had to deal with the physical repercussions.

The woman tugged the shirt back over her belly. "Stay here. Rest."

She stood and hobbled toward Arwan.

He was really here. Alive. Zanya bit her lip as he walked to her, and couldn't help but reach out to him. He took her hand and pulled her to her feet. She threw her arms around his neck and hugged him as tight as she could. He hugged her back, and it had never felt so good.

"I thought you were gone. I thought you didn't make it through the gate. I couldn't find you there, and with all of the blood and the—" She pulled away from him. He didn't know. "Sarian. He's dead. I saw it happen. Some kind of animal from the underworld must have smelled all the blood, and it just—" She was still a little unsure if it was really true.

Sarian had crept into her dreams her entire life, making every night a living hell and every day a reminder she'd eventually slip back into the horror of sleep. She had a difficult time wrapping her mind around the fact was gone. It was over, and he'd never hurt her again.

"It just…tore him apart."

The old woman stood with her back to them, her hunched figure lingering near bundles of wood and bushels of plants sorted into piles.

Arwan glanced over his shoulder. "That's Drina. I've known her for a long time. She's like my aunt."

"Really?" Zanya stole another glance at the woman. "Did you call her here?"

"No. Cualli did."

"Cualli? Is she here?"

"I don't know. Drina hasn't said much about it, and I haven't asked. She tends to have reasons why she doesn't elaborate on these things. I figured it's better to stay patient."

Patience was never her best quality.

"Hey." Arwan's voice brought her focus back to the warmth of his arms wrapped around her. Her lips parted as heat spread through her belly. Her cheeks flushed. *Damn this winter solstice thing.*

"Come on." He took her hand and led her toward the woman. "I'll introduce you. Then you'll have to take her advice and get some rest or both of us will be in trouble." He smirked and escorted her a few yards to where Drina plucked at bundles of herbs.

"Drina, this is Zanya, the guardian. Zanya, this is Tia Drina. She's a village elder from back home. One of the last."

The woman slowly straightened her posture, and the light in her eyes nearly took Zanya's breath away. She had an aura of magic about her that seemed to come directly from her soul. "I know you two have already met, but I thought it would be better to have a formal introduction."

Zanya cleared her throat. "I…" She paused, drawing a blank. "Thanks, for helping me—us." Damn it. Of course she'd make a stuttering idiot of herself.

Drina extended her hand. Cualli's pendant rested in her palm. "T'is belongs to you."

The wicker symbol was strung on a new chain made of leather string. She took it from the woman's hand and cradled the emblem against her chest. "Thank you. Thank you for fixing it."

"A gift from Cualli—you must be very special." She glanced at Arwan. "Very special indeed."

Zanya couldn't help but smile. She hadn't thought about it like that, but getting a gift from a goddess *was* pretty badass. She tied the emblem back around her neck. She'd thought it was lost forever when Sarian had torn it off her neck before Contessa—

Her features sobered when she recalled what the witch had done. "So, um." She crossed her arms over her chest. "Sorry to be a buzzkill, but we have a problem."

Drina glanced at Arwan with worried eyes.

"Contessa set us up. What happened in the underworld was her plan from the beginning. She wanted revenge on Sarian and showed up to make sure he got what was coming to him. But she promised she'd return Jayden to the middleworld, and she did."

"How do you know?" Arwan said.

Zanya bit her bottom lip. "I kind of sought him."

"You shouldn't be seeking right now. You need to rest."

"I know. I know. I just couldn't lie there wondering. I had to do something."

"For now let's stick to using the phone, okay?" Arwan walked to his pack and pulled out the satellite phone, then put it in her hand. "Deal?"

She nodded. "Deal. Speaking of, I'm sure Renato is worried about us. I should call him and let him know we're okay."

"Good idea. I'll pack our stuff."

She opened the contact list and scrolled down until the selector hovered over Renato's name. After a moment of consideration, she clicked on Tara's name below it.

Tara would be totally pissed at her, but Zanya owed it to her to call her first. It rang three times before Tara answered. "Hello?" Static clouded the line. "Hello?"

"Tara!" Zanya's heart swelled. Hearing her voice was like slipping on a pair of comfortable old jeans. "Tara, can you hear me?"

"Hello?"

She pressed the phone harder against her ear, as if that would help the static go away. "Tara, it's me."

There was nothing but static until her voice broke through. "Zanya?" Her tone was hesitant.

"Yeah, it's me. Is Jayden there? Is he okay?"

Zanya waited for her reply, but she could hardly hear Tara. She smacked the earpiece against her open palm. "Damn it. Stupid phone." The satellite icon indicated it was searching for a better signal.

She held it up in the air, but that didn't help, so she returned it to her ear. So much for satellite phones having a signal everywhere. "I don't know if you can hear me, but Jayden is back. Check if he's okay. Can you do that?"

Tara's voice was like mere whisper in the distance. "Zanya, I can barely hear you. Where are you?"

Ugh. Zanya raised her voice even louder to break through the white noise. "We did it. We're coming home, Tara. I'm coming home."

The phone bleeped and then went silent. A *signal lost* notice blinked on the screen. She exhaled and dropped her arm to her side, the phone clenched in her fist. They had to get moving—get back to Moscow and make sure Jayden was all right. That meant gathering their stuff, hiking out of the jungle, and grabbing another bus from the village back to civilization.

Luckily Arwan had gotten a head start and was just zipping up their stuffed packs. She walked to his side and handed him the phone. "We have to get back to Moscow."

He turned to Drina. "We'll bring you with us if you want. You're a long way from home."

"People do not belong in t'e sky. I will get home on my own, just as I got here."

It was rude to have to take off so quickly, especially after Drina had helped them so much, but Zanya didn't have a choice. There was no telling what kind of condition Jayden would be in. Even with Peter healing him.

A soft growl rumbled in front of her. It almost

sounded like a purr, but there were no house cats in the jungle. Just big ones, with teeth and claws.

Her stomach dropped, and she slowly lifted her head to see a jaguar pacing in front of her. Its tail flickered in the air, ears pinned back with its eyes locked on her.

The jaguar stalked low to the ground as if she were prey. Running wouldn't do any good. Screaming might just piss it off. She held her pack in front of her like a shield if it charged.

Arwan rested his hand on her shoulder, and the jaguar's muscles flexed under its speckled fur. He took several steps closer to the animal and then knelt on one knee.

Zanya's jaw dropped. "What are you doing?" she whispered harshly. "Are you nuts?" She secured her grip on her pack.

As if he had been brought in front of royalty, Arwan bowed his head in silence.

CHAPTER ELEVEN

Arwan

Arwan continued to kneel, as his people had done for generations before him when in front of one of the greatest Mayan deities.

The flapping of wings caught his ear, and he dared lift his gaze to see a white owl landing on a low-hanging tree branch. The bird examined him, though it was no ordinary bird.

The large cat circled them like a shark in murky waters. Arwan didn't want Zanya to be afraid. She had no idea this jaguar—the one she'd undoubtedly spotted before they arrived at the cave, was in fact Balam—the underworld jaguar who roamed the middleworld freely. Unlike the other underworld deities, Balam was not inherently evil.

The owl launched from the branch and spread its massive white wings, catching the jungle breeze, and exposing the bird's stark-white chest. Before it touched the ground, its wings morphed into a robe of shimmering feathers, and its face changed into the striking features of a woman.

Her feet rested gracefully on the ground, and she stood in front of them, silent and statuesque.

Cualli's robe of soft, down plumage draped over her milky skin, barely covering her breasts and thighs. Her long legs were shamelessly bare, as were her lean arms and the curves of her torso.

The goddess trailed her delicate fingers over Balam's back.

His ears twitched at every jungle sound. Balam huffed.

"Forgive Balam." Cualli's voice carried through the air like a song. Her skin shimmered like a sea of diamonds and flowers bloomed through the moss where she stood. With every step forward, more moss sprouted to cushion the bottoms of her bare feet, as if the earth wouldn't allow her skin to touch the gritty ground.

Cualli paused beside him, spilling her radiant energy over him. She was bound to sense the dark core of his being; there was nothing he could do mask it. Cualli's lips curved into a faint smile. "I see." She continued past Zanya to Drina, who hadn't moved or spoken. Cualli's now-full smile was as white as freshly fallen snow. The goddess rested her hand on Drina's shoulder. "Thank you for caring for them."

Drina bowed her head.

Cualli turned and tilted her head, examining Zanya. Waves of hair spilled over her chest and neck. "Why does the guardian not speak?"

"Uh…" Zanya's gaze darted between Drina and Arwan, but neither of them intervened.

Zanya was in fact the guardian, and this introduction to Cualli would be the first of many. At some point he would be forced to allow Zanya to make her own way. This was a good place to start.

Cualli held her hand out to Zanya, who hesitated at first, and then rested her hand in goddess'. "Nice to meet you." Zanya's voice trembled.

Arwan watched Balam's reaction. The cat flicked its ear and chuffed with approval.

He had never laid eyes on Cualli. Until this point, she was merely a name in the ancient folklore passed down through the generations. The story of her conception and deliverance to the middleworld was legendary, and one he'd shared with Zanya when they were in Belize. But to see her and Balam, still together after so many years, was like laying eyes on a relic.

"Come, outcast of outcasts. Come beside me." It took a moment for Arwan to realize Cualli was speaking to him. He did as instructed, and as he walked toward her, Balam followed by his side. The jaguar bared its teeth and let out a low growl, as if warning Arwan not to be a threat. When Arwan reached the goddess, Balam flicked his tail and stood between them, creating just enough distance to ensure her safety.

"Have faith, Balam." Cualli dragged her fingers down the cat's back. The jaguar arched his spine and purred, then lay at her feet, still keeping a close watch. "What I find here is a unique sight indeed." Cualli took Arwan's hand. Her bright energy sparked against his dark nature. "How do you keep your heart noble, outcast of outcasts?"

Arwan frowned. "Why do you keep calling me that?"

"That is what you are, is it not?"

He glanced at Zanya standing beside him. She seemed too entranced with Cualli to really consider her words. "I don't know."

"I do." Cualli smiled brightly, the warmth of her gaze washing over him. He admired her blonde hair, which glowed like the first light of dawn, and the way her robe never shifted out of place as she moved. It seemed as though it should have fallen from its precarious place on her shoulders.

She let Arwan's hand slip away, then reached out and traced the lines of her emblem hung around Zanya's neck. "I made it myself, from newly budded branches of a willow tree." Cualli's irises glittered like a sea of blue. Staring into her eyes was like peering into the universe—endless and beautiful. The longer he searched, the more secrets Cualli's gaze withheld. The entire history of mankind seemed to be pooled in one place, just out of his reach.

There was so much about his heritage Arwan didn't know, even after the years he'd spent with Renato. He had only himself to blame. He had spent so long denying his lineage. The wealth of his Mayan ancestry was uncultivated land. It was time to acknowledge it again. Perhaps even embrace it.

Cualli looked down at Balam, the subtle movement snapping Zanya out of her entrancement. The jaguar grunted, stood, and pinned back its ears with a low growl. Cualli let go of Arwan's hand and stepped away, sprouting more moss and flowers beneath her feet. Balam butted his head against Cualli's leg, and in return, she scratched between his ears.

"Balam does not like to be in his human form often. He is my protector and has watched over me from the time I was left on this earth. If you have need of him, Balam will be your protector as well."

The cat's jaws gaped in a deep yawn, and then blinked at Zanya, as if waiting for her response.

"Uh…" Zanya shifted her weight. "I don't want to take your guardian away from you. You may need him." The cat propped its head on the goddess's leg. "He seems to be pretty attached to you."

The curves of Cualli's rose-tinted lips curled into a smile. "I have been watching you. If you are in need, call on me." She rested her hand on Zanya's shoulder. "Your life, young one, is a path never traveled. It will be difficult but full of discovery and adventure." She glanced at Arwan. "Perhaps even love." Her focus shifted to the necklace one last time before she slipped her hand from Zanya's shoulder and turned to Arwan. "As our people say, '*Yu'um bootik.*'"

"May the gods go with you." They were words he hadn't whispered for years.

"Come, Balam. We have flowers to care for and crops to tend to. The humans need us." With her robe extended, Cualli morphed into her owl form and took flight.

The owl soared through a gap in the branches, and Balam followed her shadow into the jungle. The jaguar stopped and glanced back at Arwan.

With a deep growl, he turned and vanished into the foliage.

Drina hobbled to Arwan's, her pitiful stare boring into him. His entire body was rigid. He ran his fingers through his hair, and without another word, snatched his backpack off the ground.

After so many years of trying to pretend, he had no choice but to face the truth. He was, in fact, the outcast of outcasts. *That* he could never outrun.

"Let's go." He slung his pack over his shoulder. "We should get back to Renato."

Zanya took her pack, her other hand still clinging to Cualli's pendant. Arwan pressed a kiss on Drina's cheek.

The old woman gave him a tiny smile, then crinkled her nose and shooed him away. "Stop with your foolishness." She wiped her cheek with the back of her hand.

He grinned, though the sadness in his heart overwhelmed him.

CHAPTER TWELVE

Arwan led Zanya over the thin game path toward the village. Neither of them had said a word the entire hike. He was grateful for the silence. It had given him time to think. Zanya seemed to understand he needed that, even though she probably had a dozen questions burning on the tip of her tongue. He had some explaining to do, but the last thing he wanted was to hurt her. She deserved to know who he was. It was now or never.

Arwan slowed to a stop and heard her pulse quicken from where he stood. "I promised I would tell you everything. And I will. Right now, on our way back to the village. There's a lot to tell. Try to keep pace so we don't miss our bus."

She fell in pace beside him and followed him deeper into the jungle.

"I was born of a union between realms. The underworld and Riyata." Arwan's throat went dry. This was the first time he had acknowledged his bloodlines for as long as he could remember. The words put a bitter taste in his mouth. "I'm a hybrid.

A fuse of bloodlines none of the realms have ever seen."

"I thought the two realms were enemies?"

"They are, but my mother was seduced." His stomach clenched, and he swallowed a growing lump in his throat. "Or to be more accurate, raped. I was ten years old when Sarian delivered her to her death."

This wasn't the first time he'd spoke about Sarian's role in the loss of his mother, though he'd never been clear on who was actually responsible for taking her from this world. When he was ready, he'd tell her that part of the story.

"I wasn't there to save her." He swallowed. "When she left me in Belize, she didn't try to hide what was happening. She told me she was never coming back. At the time I didn't understand what she meant. I thought maybe she would change her mind. I was convinced she'd miss me enough—" The words caught in his throat.

He dared not look back at Zanya as he spoke. His shame was too heavily draped over his shoulders, weighing him down more with every word.

"Just before she sent me away, my mother said something I'll never forget. She said I was special, and someday, after many years of struggling and a lifetime of pain, I would understand how my existence would change the world, but until then, I needed to trust her and trust Renato. Take knowledge from his teaching. And most of all, when the time came, for me not to be afraid."

"Who told you what happened?" Her fingers were laced as she cradled her stone to her chest.

She must have needed comfort, but that was something he couldn't give her anymore.

He faced forward and pushed harder over the trail. "Drina. The middleword gods have been involved long before now. Or so Drina told me. She has been in touch with them since before I was born. She was the new priestess when my mother left. My mother's death saddened the gods enough to hand-deliver the message to her."

The gods were strange in their ways. They had been linked with Drina for centuries, yet today was the first time he'd laid eyes on Cualli and Balam. They'd waited so many years to show themselves. What had changed? Perhaps it was Sarian's death, or maybe something more than that. Perhaps it was Zanya.

"That's an honor, though, right? Your mom must have been more important than you realize."

He didn't acknowledge her words. Not because she was wrong, but he couldn't. Not without being brought to his knees. "We buried her near the sacred remains of an ancient ruin, far from Renato's home."

He'd have to go back once they returned to Belize, to pay his respects. Perhaps he would bring Zanya with him. It would be the first time anyone besides him, Drina, or Renato visited her grave.

"After my mother was gone, I spent my days with Drina and evenings with Renato, learning Maya legend and modern history. When I first sensed the darkness within me..." His voice softened and he slowed his pace. "I was relieved. Relieved my mother wasn't there to see me. See the monster I'd become."

"You can't be angry at yourself for who you are, Arwan."

She had no idea who he was. Not really.

"As a boy I vowed when the time came, I would kill Sarian and avenge my mother's death, even if that meant losing my life in the process." He touched the fading scar over his wrist. Even if it healed completely, he would never forget his blood sacrifice to gain entrance into the underworld. It would have killed him if Zanya weren't there to heal the wounds.

"Wait." She skipped a few steps ahead and caught up to him. "So you've kept all of this from me because you were afraid I wouldn't care about you anymore?"

He stopped and hung his head. "I know you may feel different about me now. I will always be damned. I have no hope for anything more than that. The darkness I'm made of is always ready and willing to take over. I don't know what it means for my future, but I'll be in the underworld after I die."

Zanya stopped walking, crossed her arms, and pushed out her chin. "What do you mean, 'take over'?" I've never seen you do anything to even insinuate you're…damned, or whatever you want to believe. You've always protected me and sided with Renato against the people who killed my mom. You're one of the good guys."

He stopped on the path and flexed his arms, unable to hide the tension winding his muscles. "Jayden. I could have killed him when he kissed you. I almost did. To this day I can't tell you exactly what happened. It was the first time in more years than I can remember that my dark side broke through. I just lost it. Everything fogged over and I saw red. I wanted to tear him off you and then tear him apart." He looked her in the eyes. "Is that the kind of man you want to be with, Zanya? The kind of guy who can snap at any moment and hurt people?" He worked his jaw, then looked away.

"Well, you didn't kill him, and, okay, so I was a little busy having a panic attack at the moment, but you have to remember that you let him go." She rested her hand on his chest, and his heart jumped under her touch. "You *let him go*." She pulled away, leaving his skin cold. "He was being a Grade A asshole. You *can* control it—this darkness you're talking about. Otherwise Jay would have been dead long before Sarian—" She blinked and shook her head. "I don't even know if he's okay, and here I am talking shit about him." She scoffed. "I'm some friend." She exhaled and slipped her backpack off, letting it fall to the ground.

Arwan softened his gaze. "I went with you because I know how much he means to you, and I couldn't live seeing you so heartbroken."

"I know." She exhaled and rolled her shoulders, craning her neck side to side. "And I appreciate that."

"And..." He ran his fingers through his hair, building the courage to say the words he had to say, even though every cell of his being protested against it. "I've been thinking. Perhaps I have been selfish. He may be different from the man I would have chosen for you."

"And who's that, exactly?" Zanya watched him intently.

She really was the most beautiful woman he'd ever seen. Long, dark hair and full lips. Wolf-gray eyes. Like some kind of dream made into reality as a reward for some noble conquest he'd never completed. Cualli may be a goddess, but even she paled in comparison to Zanya's bravery, humor, and beauty. For the rest of his days he would compare every woman to her, and for the rest of his days he'd live unsatisfied and lonely.

"I'd choose someone who would do anything to make you happy. Someone who would wake up and ask himself how he was going to make you smile. Someone who would listen to you. Find the things you love the most and surround you with them. Understand your heartache—no, take it away. And when he can't make it vanish, wish it were his own to bear." Arwan's eyebrows knitted together. "Someone who would walk beside you with a firm hold but a gentle touch. A man who was always there, but never drowned you in his own pride."

A tear streaked down Zanya's cheek.

Arwan reached out and wiped it away. His fingers lingered on her skin for a moment, and he pulled back. "But Jayden does care for you, and in some ways, he is better for you. Riyata are enlightened. He can give you things I can't. A long, happy life, both here and in the hereafter."

***

Zanya

Zanya narrowed her eyes and a fire sparked inside her. "Excuse me? Did you just try to tell me who I should choose to be with?"

"I'm just saying that in the future, you may wish you chose him instead."

"And who the hell are you to tell me something like that?" Her palms broke out in a cold sweat, and her blood rushed so fast she could hear it in her ears. It took everything she had to not spark an electricity ball in her hand and blast him into the bushes. Now that her stone was hers again, it wouldn't be hard.

"You are the one I want. And I'll be damned if you're going to sit here and tell me I made a mistake." She braced her hands on her hips. "Furthermore, I *am* pissed you didn't tell me about your *dark side*." She quoted the words in the air with her fingers. "Like you're freakin' Luke Skywalker or something. Who your parents are doesn't determine if you're a good person. If that were the case, half the world would be totally screwed. So don't you dare say I'm wrong to want to be with you, because if that's what you're saying, then…" Tears filled her eyes—more out of anger than sadness, but if she were honest with herself, it was a whole lot of both. "Then…well, damn it, you don't have a choice."

She threw her arms around him and kissed him.

Arwan worked his fingers through her hair. His breath was as hot as fire against her skin, and if it were up to her, she would submit to the heat and let it consume them both.

He ran his hands down her ass to the back of her thighs and lifted her off the ground. She wrapped her legs around his waist, pressing herself against his chest. He stepped forward and pinned her back against the smooth bark of a tree.

Electricity crawled over her skin and surrounded them both in a warm blanket of her energy.

He broke their kiss and pressed his forehead against hers. "This can't be possible." His words came out in a rasped whisper. "How can you still want me?" His grip on her waist tightened. "I won't ever be like you. I'm damned. I'm someone I don't want to be. Something—"

"Just stop. Please." There was no way she would believe the man cradling her against his body was evil. "I don't care how it changes you. The guy I know is the guy I want to be with, half-underworlder or not. *You're* the one I want."

He kissed her again. Her energy sparked and buzzed over their bodies. His lips curved into a grin. "You were right." He nibbled her bottom lip, and she let out a tiny moan.

He pressed his body against her, pinning her tighter against the tree. His firm muscles awoke her senses, making him all she saw, tasted, or touched in that moment. Being so close to him was an overload of sensations, and she wouldn't want it any other way.

"How can you keep torturing me like this?"

He chuckled. "The first time I saw your energy crawl over you like that, you said it tickled. You're right." He kissed the curve of her jaw. "It does."

His tongue parted her lips, and Zanya's heart skipped. He held her there as if she were as light as a feather.

The loud flapping of wings tore through the air. Zanya pushed against his chest and broke their kiss, then searched the treetops. A colorful parrot skipped along a thick branch. It grabbed hold of a fruit, and then took flight again.

"For a second there I thought it was…" Zanya's eyes grew wide. "Oh my God. Cualli."

"What about her?"

"She could be watching…like, right now." She slapped his shoulder lightly. "Put me down. Put me down." She squirmed until her feet touched the ground. "Cualli said she's been watching us, and we're still on her home turf."

"*Turf?*" He grinned.

"Oh shut up. You know what I mean." Her cheeks flushed with heat. "This is so humiliating."

He grabbed her hand and pulled her into him. "It's humiliating to be seen with me?"

Wow. His eyes were so amazing. Dark and searching…longing, and still somehow a little sad. "No." Heat spread through her body so fiercely, she could have combusted into flames. This whole solstice thing was torture. Cruel, inhuman torture. She cleared her throat. "Of course I'm not embarrassed to be seen with you. But do you feel comfortable knowing her and that jaguar, Balam, could be watching us? I mean, I don't."

Arwan pressed a kiss on her forehead. "Zanya, when I told you I'm patient, I meant it." He picked up his bag and slung it over his shoulder. "No rush."

He scooped up her pack and slipped it over his other shoulder, his muscles flexing under the weight. "Come on. The village is only about a mile away."

CHAPTER THIRTEEN

After hours of riding on a crowded bus that smelled like chickens and cabbage, Zanya's stomach rolled and pitched. The flight back to Moscow was smoother, but considering it was her second time on a plane in her entire life, the motion sickness lingered like a weight in her stomach.

Happy to have her feet on solid ground, Zanya walked beside Arwan through the airport. "What did Renato say?" She picked up the pace as they approached the pickup, drop-off area.

Arwan closed his phone and pushed it into his back pocket. "He's waiting outside."

Hopefully her uncle would have news about Jay.

The double doors slid open and cool air slammed into her. Winter had clearly set in. The foggy air sent a chill down the back of her legs.

A black SUV pulled up beside the curb. The passenger window rolled down, and Hawa hung out, resting on the doorframe. "Hey." She smiled, which was rare. "Gettin' in, or what?"

They climbed in the SUV. Before Zanya sat, she

threw her arms around Renato from behind and hugged him against his seat. Her cheek pressed against his, and she breathed in the earthy smell of tobacco infused in his hair.

He reached over his shoulder and rested his hand on her forearm before giving it a gentle squeeze. "I can't tell you how happy I am you've returned in one piece."

"Yeah, me too," Hawa said. "We're all *dying* with excitement. Now sit down so we can go."

Zanya sat back and took Arwan's hand as the car eased away from the curb and sped onto the highway. "So?" Zanya shifted in her seat, her gaze darting between Renato and Hawa. "How's Jayden? Is he all right?"

Renato watched her in the rearview mirror. "Yes. He's awake and at the hotel with Peter as we speak."

"Where are Marzena and Tara?"

"Tara's at the hotel," Hawa said. "Marzena took off back to Belize."

"There's quite a bit of work to be done on the house after Sarian's attack," Renato added. "I've arranged for workers to mend the cracks in the foundation, shattered windows, and also to clean so it's in livable condition. Someone must be there to manage them."

Hawa snorted. "I'd pay money to be there when all the workers realize they're taking orders from a kid."

Zanya melted into the seat and leaned her head back. Jayden was okay. She'd succeeded, and he came out of the ordeal alive.

"So." Hawa turned in her seat and faced Zanya. "Are you going to tell us about your great adventure or leave us hanging?"

"What do you want to know?" There was so much to tell. They'd been through hell and back over the last few days—literally.

"Everything." The curiosity in Hawa's eyes was endearing.

"I'll tell you what." Zanya covered her mouth through a yawn. "I'm tired. Neither of us has slept very much, so just give us a break on the way home and I'll tell you everything over a cup of coffee tomorrow morning. Deal?"

Well, almost everything. What Arwan had revealed about himself would stay between them.

Hawa parted her lips to say something but then pursed them shut. Her shoulders slumped forward. "Fine." She turned in her seat and opened a magazine.

"Oh, hey." Zanya leaned forward between the front seats. "How's your leg?"

Hawa made the okay sign with her fingers and flipped another page.

Zanya sat back in her seat, grinning. Typical Hawa. Zanya had missed her, tough exterior and all.

"Rest," Arwan said softly. "Maybe you can get some sleep while we drive."

Zanya closed her eyes and let her body relax. Her muscles ached, but at least the car was warm and nobody was trying to kill them. She'd almost forgotten what it was like just to breathe.

It would be hours before they reached the hotel in Moscow. Maybe she should check on Jayden when she got there. Even though she was confidant Renato, Peter, and Tara were taking care of him, it couldn't hurt to put her mind at rest.

She slid her hand into her pocket and glided her fingers over the smooth surface of her stone, calling on her inner powers. Tiny blasts of light flashed behind her lids as her seeking abilities reached out. The image wavered and burred, then slowly cleared.

Jayden laid back in his bed, tapping a pen against his knee. "I told you, I need more pills." A streak of pain zigzagged through Zanya's chest, stunting her breath. She curled her fingers into a fist and held the vision.

She was so cold—*Jayden* was so cold.

Peter searched a small duffle bag. "I don't have any more oxycodone. I took those from the hospital after we left the morgue. You finished the whole bottle in two days. They should have lasted two weeks."

Sweat collected on Jayden's brow, and he wiped it away with the back of his hand. He stilled the pen against his knee, then threw it across the room. It smacked the far wall and fell to the floor. "I need more fucking pain meds! What about that don't you understand?"

Zanya's arm trembled as a coil of pain strangled her muscles.

Jayden pulled his knee to his chest and leaned into it.

"I'll do what I can, but we need to do another healing session."

"Why? It hasn't done a damn thing."

"We can't just give up." Peter sat on the foot of

the bed, examining Jay with narrow eyes. "I can't explain it. Why aren't you healing?"

"Hell if I know." Jayden drew in a breath and pushed away the pain.

"Let's see how much progress you've made."

Jayden slowly and carefully rested his legs in front of him and pulled up his shirt.

Peter winced. "Not much progress."

Jayden slowly looked down at the swollen wounds, red and probably infected. The sutures held together tattered pieces of flesh from Sarian's attack.

"Maybe a little of the swelling has gone down, but other than that, it's going slow. Maybe it's because you were—"

"Don't say it."

Tara cracked open the door and slipped into the room. Jayden pulled his shirt down, hot bolts of pain rushing through his veins.

"How is he?" Red curls fell around Tara's face as she stood on the other side of the room, her arms crossed and her brows knitted together.

Peter glanced back at her. "Not great. But okay."

"What do you think it means?"

"I'm not sure."

"I'm right here." Jayden clenched his jaw. "But thanks for talking about me like I'm not."

Peter stood and met Tara in the center of the room. He whispered something to her. She nodded. "Okay, Jay. I'm going to get out of your hair so you can get some rest."

Jayden frowned. "Don't bother." He slowly forced himself off the bed, grinding his teeth with the effort.

Peter extended his hand. "Whoa. Slow down."

"Get away from me." Jayden smacked Peter's hand out of the way. "I'm fine."

"We don't know that." He pulled a small flashlight from his pocket and shined it in Jayden's eyes.

Zanya clenched her eyes shut even tighter. Her head spun, and her vision blurred.

"Are you having any other strange effects we should know about? Headaches? Fatigue?"

"Well, now that you mention it, there is this weird side effect I've noticed." He made a crisscross gesture over this chest. "I have a shitload of stitches that are causing a lot of pain. So yeah. Pain. Lots and lots of it." He grabbed the plastic bottle of meds and rattled the few pills left inside. "And I'm almost out of meds."

Peter frowned. "We've been over this. Anything else?"

Jayden shrugged. "Nope. Where's Zanya?"

"She's on her way with Renato. They'll be here soon."

Zanya blinked open her eyes, cutting off the vision. She glanced around the car at Renato, focusing on the road, Hawa still reading her magazine, and Arwan, asleep beside her.

She slowly blinked, rubbing her chest. Jayden's pain still lingered below her skin. He wasn't healing. Something was wrong, but she'd have to wait to find out what.

When they reach the hotel, Zanya popped open the back door. "What room is he in?"

"Zanya, I think it's better if you wait for me to examine him first." Renato shut off the engine. "He could be dangerous."

"Dangerous? I mean, an asshole, sure. But he's not dangerous."

Renato frowned. "Zanya—"

"*What room?*"

Renato exhaled. "One-twenty. First floor."

She jumped out of the SUV and barged through the hotel doors, past the clerk and down the hall. She turned the corner and stopped short, staring straight ahead.

Peter had his hands on Tara's shoulders, whispering to her in the hall. Zanya's chest tightened and she shifted her weight. "Tara?"

Curls bounced against Tara's shoulders when she turned toward Zanya. Her hazel eyes widened. "Zanya!" Tara ran toward her and plowed into her with a hug, nearly knocking Zanya to the Berber carpet. "You're okay." Tara squeezed her tighter, cutting off her breath.

Zanya patted her on the shoulder. "You're killing me."

Tara sucked in a breath and took a step back. "Sorry." She smiled, wiping away tears. "I'm just so happy to see you." She paused and her smile faded into a scowl. "And I'm so pissed at you!" She punched Zanya in the arm, leaving her with a low throb in her bicep. She deserved way worse. "What the hell is wrong with you, taking off like that? Are you crazy, or are you just stupid?"

"I'm sorry—"

"Sorry isn't going to cut it!" Tara crossed her

arms like a child throwing a temper tantrum. "You could have gotten yourself killed."

"I had to go back for him. I *had* to."

Tara's steel features softened, and she rolled her eyes. "You're still on my shit list."

"Fair enough."

"For, like, a long time."

Zanya cracked a smile. "Does that mean you forgive me?"

"No."

Zanya's smile widened. "It kind of does, doesn't it?"

Tara lifted her chin, examining her. "Not totally." She shrugged. "But a little."

Zanya chuckled. "A little is a start."

Renato, Hawa, and Arwan filed into the hall, and Tara glanced back at Peter, biting her lip. "Are you going to tell them before they see Jayden?"

Zanya shifted her weight. "Tell us what?"

One of the hotel room doors cracked open, and Jayden stepped out. He gripped on to the doorframe, leaning on the wall while he stepped forward.

Zanya parted her lips, staring at his hunched shoulders and pale skin, and the dark circles under his eyes. He looked even worse than when she'd sought him.

Zanya hurried to his side and hooked her hand around his waist to keep him on his feet. "What is going on? Why isn't he healing?"

"How do you know he's not healing?" Peter asked.

"I sought him on our way here."

Jayden snorted. "I guess you can never yell at me

again for seeking you."

"Oh shut up." She secured her grip around him. "Let's get you back to bed."

"No." He rested his hand against the floral wallpaper and steadied himself. "I'm fine."

Tara shook her head, backing away. "You're so far from being fine, Jay."

Peter moved to Renato's side and spoke to him in a low voice.

Renato stepped forward. "He isn't well. You should go to your room and get some rest, Zanya. You've had a long, hard journey."

"I'm fine."

"Zanya." Renato's tone deepened. "He may not be safe."

Jayden's eyes narrowed. "What the hell are you talking about? You're acting like I'd hurt her or something."

"Not intentionally."

Zanya scoffed. "That's crazy."

Peter stood in the threshold of Jayden's hotel room. "We could be bothering the other guests. Let's pick a room, for the sake of not having anyone see Jayden. They may panic."

"That's a good point," Zanya said. He did look like hell, even if she'd never say it aloud.

Jayden curled his lip. "Whatever." He limped back to his room.

Zanya rested her hand on Arwan's chest. "I need some time with him. Alone. He'll never talk if you're in the room."

Arwan's gaze darted to the open door and then back to her. He nodded. "Sure. No problem. I need to talk to Renato anyway." He held up the electronic key card. "Renato booked us our own rooms. I'm two doors down if you need anything."

"Thanks." Zanya walked through the doorway to see Jayden slouched against the wall. Peter followed her inside.

"Sorry to intrude, but I have to spend a few more minutes with Jayden," he said. "There's something I want to check."

Jayden groaned.

Zanya rolled her eyes. "Oh stop. Be a big boy and I'll give you a lollipop."

He pushed out his bottom lip. "Liar."

She chuckled.

Peter closed the door. "We need to talk." His tone had gone from suggestive to demanding.

"Yeah, no shit." Jayden lowered himself into a chair. "There's got to be something going on. Why don't you just come out with it?"

"I need to give you a physical."

"That sounds like a good idea," Zanya said. "Your healing hasn't been working."

"No, it hasn't." Peter removed a stethoscope from his little black bag.

"Go shopping for supplies?" Zanya asked.

"More like jacked them from the hospital, but we didn't have much choice. We had to get Jayden out of there before anyone spotted us." Peter hung the stethoscope around his neck. "By the way, I thought of a way to get you some more pain meds until you heal."

Jayden's head popped up to full attention. "Really?"

"There's this guy…but they're expensive—"

"Probably because it's not legal," Zanya grumbled.

"How did you know?"

"Because anytime someone says, 'there's this guy,' he's not talking about a pharmacist."

Peter removed a thermometer from the bag. "Well, it's either that or let him go without." He pushed the button on the thermometer until it beeped. "Here. Put this under your tongue."

Jayden snatched it from Peter's hand and shoved it in his mouth. The room fell silent as Peter placed the earpieces of the stethoscope in his ears and pressed the diaphragm over Jay's chest.

Peter's brow furrowed as he slid the piece from Jayden's right pectoral to his left, then just below his ribs.

Peter sat back and set the stethoscope on the table beside him, analyzing Jayden. "How do you feel?"

Jayden shrugged, the thermometer still in his mouth. Peter's foot bounced as if he were nervous. When the thermometer beeped, Peter brushed his fingertips together and then pulled it out of Jayden's mouth. He examined the results.

Zanya shifted and peered over Peter's shoulder. "What? Does he have a fever?"

Peter shook his head. "No fever. In fact…no temperature." He held up the thermometer with L* blinking on the digital screen, then turned back to Jay. "I don't know how to tell you this, but…you have no heartbeat."

CHAPTER FOURTEEN

Zanya snorted. "What do you mean no heartbeat? That's insane. He has to have a heartbeat."

"I can't explain it, but you can listen for yourself if you don't believe me."

Zanya blinked and her muscles locked. No heartbeat meant he wasn't alive, which meant he was…

"Dead?" Jayden's gaze darted between them. "Some healer you are. Can't even tell if someone's dead or alive. Your stupid little tool is just broken." Jay sat back in his bed. "Idiot."

"But…" The heat drained from her face. He looked like a corpse. And after everything Peter had tried, he still hadn't healed.

Jayden examined her. "Come on, Zanya."

Tears blurred her vision.

"Hey." He stood and wrapped his arms around her.

She hugged him back. "This is all my fault. I'm so sorry."

Jayden pulled away, staring at Peter. "This is just mean. Look what you're doing to her. Enough already."

Peter stood, chewing the inside of his cheek. "It doesn't totally make sense, does it?"

"See." Jayden wiped a tear from Zanya's cheek. "I'm fine."

"What about the pain?" Zanya looked to Peter for answers. "He's in pain, and he's hungry. How can he be—" She choked on the word.

"I think it's psychosomatic. See, his brain is telling him that logically, he should be in pain, so he is. I mean, he's spent his entire life knowing that if you're cut, it hurts. Or if you haven't eaten that day, you should be hungry." Peter reached for Jay's hand, but paused. "Can I check your pulse, just in case you're right about the stethoscope malfunction?"

Though it still didn't explain the low body temperature.

Jay hesitated at first, and then nodded. Peter rested his fingers over Jayden's wrist and waited and waited, then moved them to his neck. He lowered his hand and peered closely into Jayden's eyes.

Jay stepped back. "What?" He dragged his palms down his jeans.

Peter analyzed Jay's movements. "Are your palms sweating?"

Jayden nodded.

"I don't think you're actually sweating, because you're not hot."

"I can't fucking help it if I sweat."

"But you can't be sweating because your body tempe—"

"How do you know what I am, huh, healer?" Jayden stepped forward. "You think you know how I feel because I'm a vampire or some shit?"

Peter stretched his hands out in front of him, as if trying to calm Jay down. "No." His tone was lined with caution. "The more we try to understand what happened to you, the—"

"Stop. Talking." Jayden clenched his jaw and glared.

"Jay. He's just trying to help."

"I don't need his fucking help."

She took his hands and laced her fingers with his, and Jayden's focus broke from Peter. Zanya's throat ached as she worked to hold back tears. "But you're so cold. And you're not healing. It's taking twice the effort, and you're hardly making any progress." She swallowed. "It does make sense. It makes perfect sense." She had to stay strong for him, even if she wanted to come undone. "But it'll be okay. We'll figure this out. Meanwhile, I'll try to heal you. Maybe that'll make the difference."

His gaze darted to Peter. "That's what I said."

"Look," Peter said. "I've done the best I can under the circumstances, but maybe Zanya can do better." He walked toward the door. "I guess I'll go let Renato and Arwan know what's going on."

"Yeah." Jayden snorted. "Go to them with your zombie theory. I'm sure they'll buy into that real quick."

Zanya leaned close to Peter as he passed, making him pause. "Renato already thinks Jayden is some kind of threat," she said in a low voice. "After he hears about this, who knows what he'll want to do."

"I'll do my best to keep everyone calm." Peter walked out of the room.

Jayden grunted as he sat back on his bed and grabbed the remote. "So. What do you want to do? Watch a new-release marathon of pay-per-view or watch old horror flicks?"

Zanya arched an eyebrow. "Are you feeling up to it?"

"Well, coming back from the dead isn't exactly comfortable, especially when you're hamburger meat. But I could handle watching a few movies." He rested his hand over his chest and grimaced.

She couldn't just ignore everything Peter had said. She'd known Jayden for so long, it was obvious that was exactly what *he* was trying to do. "Let me see." She gestured to his chest.

"What? No. Forget about it." He patted the bed beside him. "Just relax and hang out with me. I missed you."

"I missed you too, Jay. But you need to let me see what we're dealing with. Peter's not the only one who can heal now, and—oh! Did anyone tell you? Sarian, he's—"

"Dead. Yeah. Peter told me before you came back." He took her hand and gently pulled her onto the bed beside him. "I know how much of a relief that must be for you, to know he can't hurt you anymore. All those years." He brushed his fingers over the top of her hand. "At least it's over now. You're fine, I'm fine, and we're gonna be—"

"Fine. Yeah. I know. But I still need to see

what's going on under there." She pointed to his shirt. "It won't be the first time I've seen you without a shirt on, so stop pretending to be shy. We both know you're not."

He braced himself on the bed and sat up as well as he could. "Apparently I'm not the only one anymore. I remember when you would blush every time you saw me without a shirt."

"Well." She tapped him twice on his leg, urging him to hurry up. "I've been through a lot and grown up a lot since then too. Don't make it out to be more than it is."

His eyebrows furrowed and the edges of his mouth turned down. "Right. I forgot. You're not into me like that anymore." His tight lips softened. "But you still came and got me, and that means something, whether you want to admit it or not."

Zanya sighed. "Believe whatever you want, Jay. You always do anyway."

He huffed, and then crossed his arms over his torso and grabbed the hem of his T-shirt. When he tried to peel it off, his arms trembled, and he couldn't lift it over his head.

"Wow." She gently pushed his hands back down to his sides. "You *are* in a lot of pain, aren't you?" Not that she didn't experience it herself while seeking him. He wasn't making it up. "I'm going to take this off for you. I'll be careful."

Surprisingly he didn't crack a wise comment and instead did as she asked. When she finally slipped the shirt over his head, she gasped. "You've barely healed at all."

Stitches wove his skin together as if he were

some kind of Raggedy Andy doll. They stretched from his collarbone and veined out in different directions across his chest. Stitches zigzagged across his chest, weaving his jagged flesh together.

"Okay. Scoot yourself down and lie completely flat." Zanya brushed her fingers together, gathering her courage. What she was about to do would be awkward but necessary. "Before I do this, let me just tell you that if you make any stupid comments, I'll kill you." Jayden's eyes widened when she stripped off her shirt and tossed it on the chair beside the bed.

He leaned up on his forearms. "What are you doing?"

"Just lie down, please." She took her stone from her pocket. She had a lot better of a chance to do this right if her stone was with her. She'd failed once at healing him, and she was determined not to do it again.

Zanya straddled him, and he rested his hand on her hip. She slapped it away and glared. "Be good." She closed her eyes and drew in a deep breath, channeling her energy. Tiny sparks fired over the surface of her hands.

She'd have to do better than that.

With more focus she sent energy up her arms and over the top half of her body.

Jayden shifted under her. "Since when do you decide to take off your shirt and hop into bed with me? Not that I'm complaining."

"Didn't we agree on no comments?" she said with her eyes still closed.

"I never agreed to that."

"Since you were torn apart and died because of me, okay? Now be quiet for a second. I need to concentrate." After a moment, the light in her chest burst to life. "This might hurt a little, but only from my weight." She planted her hands on either side of him and lowered her body over his. The stitches prickled her skin. Jayden let out a low groan.

He was as cold as ice. "I know it hurts. I'm sorry. Try not to move around too much." She laid her head on the curve of his shoulder and wrapped her arms under his. "Just breathe." She supported some of her own weight on her forearms. "The more of my skin that's touching yours, the better I'll be able to heal you."

He rested his hands on her lower back and trailed his fingers up to her shoulder blades.

Zanya lifted her head. "Are you okay? If it's too much, I can—"

"No." His voice was soft. "Stay. Please." The way his eyes begged her made her body flush.

Zanya swallowed. "Jayden."

"It's fine. I get it." His hands curved over her shoulders. "Just stay like this for a few more minutes. It's helping."

She hesitated but then rested her head back down on his shoulder. For the first time she realized just how much she missed him, and how afraid she was that he might have been gone forever.

Jayden's breaths steadied. "You know what happened to me wasn't your fault, right?" His voice was soft and raspy.

"Yes, it was. You were trying to protect me, and if it weren't for that, you would never have gone through any of this."

"And I never would have known how much you care about me. You came for me, Zanya. I love you for it."

Hearing him say that aloud made her chest tighten, but only because he meant it in a way she never could. Not like before.

Her fingertips tingled with numbness. Probably a sign to stop for the day. "I'm gonna get up now. Tell me if I'm hurting you." As she pushed herself off the bed, Jayden hooked his fingers around her arms and stopped her.

He pressed a kiss on her cheek. "Thanks, Zanya. I do feel a little better."

She moved and planted her feet on the floor. Her legs were wobbly and unstable as she slipped her shirt back on. "I'm sorry I can't do more now, but I have to rest. Healing seems to be harder than some of the other stuff." Her head spun, but it was a small sacrifice. Still, she needed rest. She hadn't slept in almost twenty-four hours and her body cried out for a fluffy robe, warm blankets, and a down pillow.

Jay was still sprawled out on the bed with his hands behind his head. She gave him a faint smile and stole a glance at the patch job on his chest. It seemed a tiny bit better, though not by much. "Well..." She shifted toward the door. "I'm going to go."

"Thanks for healing me. Again tomorrow?"

Zanya nodded. "But you know you should let Peter heal you too. He's just trying to help."

"I know. As long as I don't have to be around Renato. The guy doesn't like me, and he's crazy for thinking I'd hurt you."

"I know. I'm sorry about that." She walked toward the door. "He's just being protective."

"Yeah, maybe." Jayden sat up. "Hey. Will every healing session be like that?"

Zanya rolled her eyes. "Probably." It was obvious he was searching for something sarcastic to say. Maybe this time she'd beat him to the punch. "But you know if you let Peter heal you the way I did tonight…"

His eyes grew wide. "Oh hell no. There is no way in—"

Zanya chuckled. "Good night, Jay. Get some rest and I'll see you tomorrow."

He lay back down with a huff. "Fine."

Zanya opened the door, watching him pout like a child. "I missed you."

He smiled. A real smile. "I missed you, too."

Zanya walked into the hallway and exhaled. She rested her back against the patterned wallpaper and leaned her head back, closing her eyes.

It had been a long day, and nothing sounded more alluring than a hot shower and a pillow-top mattress.

Something crinkled in the back pocket of her jeans. When Zanya slid her fingers into the pocket, and her skin brushed against the rough texture of the paper, and she pulled out folded pages from the book. Pages she'd stolen from the underworld, just after Contessa had claimed the rest of the text.

Zanya groaned. A hot shower and a pillow-top mattress would have to wait. She had to bring the pages to Renato. Maybe he'd find something useful in the glyphs.

CHAPTER FIFTEEN

Arwan

Arwan stood on the far side of the room, leaning against the wall.

Tara sat on the bed beside Peter with her legs crossed, hugging a pillow to her chest.

Hawa was seated on the floor. With her back rested against the wall, she spun her ring in circles, listening to the conversation.

Arwan noted how pale Zanya was. The bags under her eyes had also gotten worse. Even the guardian needed rest.

"These are pages from the Popol Vuh?" Renato stood from the leather armchair and took the frail papers from Zanya's hand.

"Yeah, but I don't know what it says. What's it about?" Zanya yawned and rubbed her eyes.

"The Popol Vuh means *book of counsel*, or more literally, *book of the people*. It contains not only the original creation story of the Maya, but also information about genealogies that have been kept secret for thousands of years."

"So you can translate them, right?" Hawa asked.

Renato examined the papers, one after the other. "I recognize the numerical symbols in the corners, but I cannot read the glyphs. It's a formal dialect from the royal families of the original civilization."

"I tore out as many as I could. He was still reading when the roots of the tree pulled everyone under."

Renato looked up from behind the creased pages. "You witnessed that?"

Zanya nodded.

He returned his focus to the strange writing. "That must have been frightening."

Arwan tried not to cringe, recalling the change as it had torn through him and Zanya's terrified expression when she'd seen him in his alternate form.

"The ground was completely saturated with blood," Zanya said. "When Contessa showed up, it was like…" She crossed her arms, stretching her sleeves over her hands—just like she'd done when she first arrived at Renato's house. "Like she enjoyed watching it happen."

"So Contessa has the book now?" Peter asked.

Zanya nodded. "She took it after that underworld animal killed Sarian."

Arwan's stomach twisted. *That underworld animal.* Those words were all he could focus on.

"She waltzed right up the temple steps and took the book from the altar. She wasn't even scared."

"You couldn't stop her?" Peter said.

"I was a little busy bleeding to death. *Sorry.*"

She was tired and obviously irritable. He closed the distance between them and rested his hand on the small of her back. "You need to get some rest."

She responded by gesturing to the pages in Renato's hand. "Can these help us at all?"

"It's not often one has the opportunity to read even a small passage from the original Popol Vuh, but unfortunately, I'm not entirely sure if these particular scripts can do anything to help us find Contessa or the book."

"Drina." Arwan looked at Renato. "She was in Guatemala. She may be able to help."

"And Cualli said she would help if we needed her," Zanya added.

"Let's not bring the middleworld gods into this unless it is completely necessary." Renato tucked the papers into his jacket pocket. "We should head back to Belize as soon as possible. Marzena recently informed me the workers have finished fixing the damage to the house." His gaze moved on Arwan. "Also, if Contessa has the book, that means she is undoubtedly planning something. You need to return to training Peter. Zanya needs close-contact combat instruction as well and should learn how to better use her powers."

"Sounds like a plan," Zanya said, blinking slowly.

Hawa stood and smoothed down her shirt. "Well, if nobody minds, I'm going to check out some of the nightlife. Now that my leg is all healed up, I want to go dancing."

She opened the hotel room door and paused. "Anyone else want to come?"

Tara shook her head. "No. I think I've had my fill of clubs—forever."

Peter cracked a smile.

"All right. Well, I'm off." Hawa walked out and closed the door behind her.

Tara stood up as well. "I'm going to shower." She waved to Peter. "Come by my room if you want to watch a movie later."

Peter nodded. "I'll take you up on that."

When Tara left the room, Arwan turned to Zanya. "And you should get some sleep."

She glanced at Renato. "I have to talk to you first."

Renato stood up straighter. "All right. I'm listening."

"I just want to make sure everything's okay with you and Jay."

Renato's features sobered. "How so?"

"You know." She shrugged. "He says you're acting weird. Like you don't want him around anymore. I told him you were just stressed and—" She examined Renato's steely gaze. "It's not true...right?"

Renato curled his fingers around the lapel of his coat. "Jayden is an unknown. Do you believe we can continue to trust him?"

"Wow." Her flat tone made Arwan shift his weight. "You know, I stuck up for you. I told him you were just being protective and to cut you some slack. But he was right. You really don't want him here anymore."

This conversation wouldn't end well for anyone. Arwan stepped closer to them both. "Maybe we should all get some rest before talking about this."

Renato nodded. "I think that's a—"

"Admit it." Zanya braced her hands on her hips.

"Very well," Renato said. "He may be dangerous, and I believe it is for the best if he keeps his distance. At least until we can identify what the cause of his…illness is."

"You can keep all the distance you want, but don't expect me to stay away. He's one of us. You should know that better than anyone." Her eyes narrowed. "You were the one who hired him to find me in the first place."

They all knew what she really meant. When she and Jayden grew close, Renato ordered him to stay, aware that when he left, it would break her heart.

Renato's chest sank with a deep exhale, and he looked away.

Silence filled the room.

Zanya glanced at him and Peter. "I don't want to talk about this again." She walked into the hall, leaving Arwan alone with Peter and Renato.

Arwan exhaled, considering his mentor's undeniable concern. "What do you think this situation with Jayden means? Is he an underworlder now?"

"I have no idea." Peter shrugged. "It is what it is, whether she wants to face it or not."

Renato reached in the inner pocket of his jacket and pulled out his pipe. "I will get in touch with Marzena. She may know more about this than I."

Arwan turned to Renato. "I want to examine him myself."

"Why?" Peter asked.

"I may be able to sense something you can't." Like the inherent darkness of an underworlder. It lingered deep in every being from that realm, and every underworlder could sense it.

"Whatever you want to do," Peter said. "Zanya already tried to heal him. Now is as good of a time as any."

Arwan narrowed his eyes. "She's was with him alone?"

Peter nodded.

Under the circumstances, Arwan sided with Renato. Leaving them alone was risky. Even if she was the guardian.

Arwan walked across the room and flung open the door. He stalked down the hallway and pounded on Jayden's door, then listened to the line of mumbled curses from the other side.

Jayden cracked open the door and peered out. "What do you want?"

"Can I come in?"

"Thanks, but no thanks."

The seeker tried to shove the door closed. Arwan planted his hand on it and pushed it open, forcing him to stumble back. "Let me be clear. I'm coming in."

Jayden leaned on the wall, his chest rising and falling as he struggled to stand up straight. "No. I'm not busy. Come on in." Sarcasm drenched his tone.

Arwan shut the door and locked it.

Jayden's gaze flickered to the steel bolt. "What are you doing?"

The seeker appeared much too weak to struggle. "I just want to see something. Hold still."

When Arwan stepped forward, Jayden staggered back a few steps. Arwan caught him by his shoulders and stared into the seeker's eyes.

"If you're here to ask me on a date, you should have just said so." Jayden's arms quivered and his heartbeat accelerated.

He was in pain.

"Stop talking." Arwan hadn't intentionally tuned in to his dark side in longer than he could remember. If he wasn't able to control it, he may morph right in the hotel room.

Arwan drew in a deep breath. His inner beast clashed and sparked against his will to keep it caged. He searched Jayden for any hint of underworld energy but found none. He needed to look deeper.

"I'm going to need you to bleed."

Jayden glared. "*Now* you want a piece of me?"

"I don't want to hurt you. But I have to." Arwan removed a small dagger from a sheath in his belt he always carried.

Jayden pulled back, his face contorting under the effort.

"Hold still." Arwan grabbed Jayden's wrist and steadied the blade over his forearm. "I just need—"

A punch to his cheekbone cut him off. "Fuck you!" Jayden shouted and doubled over holding his chest.

Arwan clenched his jaw as the darkness clawed its way out. This time he didn't work as hard to hold it back.

He gripped Jayden's neck and slammed him against the wall, applying just enough pressure to keep him in place. "I'm not here to kill you, *seeker*. But if you won't hold still, I just might."

He let go of Jayden's neck and nicked Jayden's arm with the blade.

Jayden flinched.

His blood didn't flow.

Arwan waited, but there was nothing. "You're not bleeding."

Jayden jerked his arm out of Arwan's grasp and stared at the cut. "I'm not bleeding…"

Arwan grabbed his arm and brought it to his nose. He inhaled, searching for the underworld smell.

A bitter stench shot up his nose and burned his throat.

"What the hell are you doing?" Jayden pulled his arm back, and this time Arwan let him have his way.

The stink of the dark realm ran deep through Jayden's veins—or what was left of them.

Zanya would be crushed to find out both of the men she cared for were tainted by the underworld.

Arwan cleared his throat and stepped back. "Nothing. I'm not doing anything."

Jayden's glare intensified. "Nothing my ass. I know about you."

Maybe Zanya had told the seeker about him. In that case, everything he had known since he was a boy was about to change, because the seeker would not stay quiet. Peter, Tara, Hawa, and Marzena still weren't aware of his origins, and he intended to keep it that way. He stepped forward. "What do you know, exactly?"

"I haven't forgotten what you did at Renato's house. How you lifted me off the ground. Renato couldn't even pull you off me. And your eyes." Jayden held his gaze. "You're not normal. You're not human."

Arwan scoffed. "And you are?"

"More so than you, even as fucked up as I am." Jayden stood up straight and pushed out his chest. His shoulders quivered, and his lips pursed into a tight line. "I'm better for her than you are, and you know it."

Arwan clenched his fists. He'd told himself the same thing dozens of times, but hearing the seeker say it to his face made his blood seethe. "She wouldn't have reached the underworld if I hadn't gone with her." Arwan stepped back. "Remember that, seeker." He turned and opened the hotel room door, then paused in the threshold. "It doesn't matter who or what you are now. Zanya cares for you. But if you do anything to hurt her, I'll kill you with my bare hands."

Arwan walked into the hall, past Renato's door that still hung open. Renato stepped out and waited for him to speak. Arwan looked his mentor in the eyes and gently shook his head. "I can't sense anything on him." The lie tasted better on his tongue than the bitter truth. He took the key card out of his pocket. "I guess we'll just have to wait and see."

Renato exhaled and his shoulders relaxed. "That's certainly good news."

"What's good news?" Peter asked from inside the room.

Renato glanced over his shoulder. "Oh." He patted Arwan on the shoulder, as if telling him to go rest. "There seems to be some improvement with Jayden." Renato joined Peter into the room before shutting the door, leaving Arwan standing in the hall.

Arwan dropped his head. He'd never lied to his mentor, but Renato would get rid of the seeker the first chance he could if he was even remotely a threat.

Arwan ran his fingers through his hair. If anything did happen, he would be solely responsible.

***

Zanya

Zanya sifted through the clothes on her hotel room floor, all of which were dirty. She picked up a tank top and pressed it to her nose, then frowned at the stale scent. She hadn't done any laundry since they'd left Renato's house.

A few solid knocks on the door made Zanya jump. She walked to the peephole and spied through it to see a hazel eye with red lashes staring back at her. Zanya grinned and opened the door.

Tara smiled, cradling a basket of laundry in her arms. "Wanna keep me company?"

"Wow. You read my mind." Zanya tossed her tank top into Tara's basket and gathered the rest of her clothes. "There's a laundromat here?"

"Yep. First floor. And I have a pocket full of

Russian coins, in case you need some."

"You're a lifesaver." She snatched a pair of jeans off the floor and bunched the rest of her clothes in her arms. "I'm surprised you didn't go out with Hawa. Dancing sounds way more exciting than doing laundry." Zanya walked back to Tara and propped the door open with her foot.

"Not really my scene."

Zanya grabbed her keycard and stepped into the hall. Tara let the door fall closed. "All you ever talked about in the orphanage was getting out and doing stuff like that."

"Yeah." Tara swallowed as she walked beside Zanya toward the elevator. "I guess I've had my fill." She pressed the Down button outside of the elevator doors.

"I find that hard to believe." Zanya chuckled.

The doors pinged open, and they both filed inside. Tara jabbed the button for the first floor, and glanced at Zanya. "Yeah, well…"

The hesitation in her friend's voice made Zanya still. The elevator pinged, and the doors slid shut, sealing them inside. "Well, what?"

"Stuff…might have happened while you were gone."

Zanya's brows shot up. "*Stuff*?"

"Yep." Her lips popped at the end of the word. "Stuff."

Zanya's stomach rose in her throat, only partially because the elevator's downward drop. "Are you going to elaborate?"

Tara examined the elevator walls. "Not in here."

"Why not?"

"Because if you freak out, you could kill us both."

"What would I have to freak out about, *exactly*?"

Tara pursed her lips, looking around the small space as if Zanya hadn't said a word.

"Seriously?" When Tara didn't respond, Zanya grit her teeth and watched as the digital display above the elevator door counted down from the tenth floor. When the doors pinged open, they exited the elevator and followed the signs pointing to the laundromat. "Okay, so…" Zanya continued.

"I kind of met a guy."

Zanya stopped midstride. "Excuse me?" She was sure Tara and Peter were soul mates. How could this happen?

Tara rolled her eyes "Not *that* kind of *met*. Just a guy."

Zanya clung tighter to her wad of clothes. "What about him?"

"His name was Malachi." Tara pushed open a door. The low hum of machines and the scent of fabric softener drifted into the hall. "Come on. I'll tell you about it while we're sorting our clothes."

Zanya walked silently through the door into the room of stacked washers and dryers. Tara placed her basket on top of a folding area. "Colors first?" She plucked out a few garments and tossed them in the washing machine beside her.

"I guess." Zanya dumped her clothes next to Tara's. Zanya watched as Tara sorted her laundry as though they weren't in the middle of a conversation. "Are you trying to torture me?"

Tara slid a line of quarters into the coin deposit.

"Promise you won't freak out."

Zanya held her breath and nodded.

"Okay." Tara turned and leaned her back against the folding counter. "I met a guy named Malachi who took me to a dance club. I kind of got in some trouble." She examined Zanya. "And after Marzena used my memories to find Sarian, I remembered what happened when Sarian took me."

Zanya balled her fists. "What?"

Tara held her finger in the air. "You said you wouldn't freak out."

Zanya slowly uncurled her fingers and took a deep breath. "I'm not."

"I was lost. You weren't here, and Peter couldn't make the memories go away. Then I met Malachi and found out that some people can be good and evil at the same time." Tara smiled. "I helped a group of girls who needed saving. I was pretty proud of myself, actually."

Zanya arched an eyebrow. "Helped, how?"

"Rescuing them. I was able to be the person I wish I'd had when I needed help the most." Tara bit her lip, smiling through the words. "It was good. I'm good."

"But you remember."

Tara's smile softened. "Yeah. But the nightmares are gone, so I just try not to think about it. That seems to work most of the time."

"And when it doesn't?"

Tara shrugged. "I have Peter. I have you." She bumped Zanya with her hip. "I'm okay."

It was all her fault. If Zanya could have found Sarian first or if she had been there instead of going with Arwan to the underworld, maybe she could have stopped Tara's pain. "Was remembering worth it?"

Tara paused and then nodded. "I know who I am now, and I believe in myself. That makes it all worth it."

CHAPTER SIXTEEN

While Renato checked out of the hotel, Zanya settled into an oversized chair in the lobby and sipped the dark roast coffee she'd snagged from the continental breakfast.

"Feeling better?" Arwan took a seat across from her with a crooked grin.

"Much. Thanks."

He glanced at the clock mounted to the far wall. "We're running late."

"I'm sure Jayden will be down soon." She glanced at the black SUV parked out front. "Everyone else is in the car?"

Arwan nodded.

"Maybe I should check on Contessa. Who knows what she's doing with the book."

"Are you sure this is a good place to do that? There are a lot of people around. What if something goes wrong?"

"I could do it on the plane, but that'd cause a massive scene." Especially if it were anything close to what had happened when Sarian broke the obedience spell on her stone, it'd be newsworthy.

"How about the car."

"Yeah, while we're going seventy-five miles an hour on the highway." She chuckled. "It'll be fine. Now be quiet so I can concentrate."

He didn't protest anymore, though he had a point. If something went wrong while she sought Contessa, everyone in the lobby would see it. She would have to have faith in her ability, and her stone.

Zanya closed her eyes and concentrated on Contessa's long red hair, bright green eyes, and angelic voice. Fog and light flickered behind her eyelids, and a mental window opened to Contessa standing in her living room. The witch mumbled to herself as she read the pages of the Popol Vuh tacked to her walls. She must have disassembled the book and tacked each page to the plaster, lining her home with the ancient texts. Contessa paced, her normally smooth waves now wild and untamed, matching the feral gleam in her eyes.

The witch doubled over and grabbed the corner of the wall while gripping her gut. After a moment, she dragged herself into the far bedroom of her quaint home.

Zanya struggled to follow her through the house. Contessa's black magic was stronger than Sarian's. Maybe her strength was the reason he wanted Contessa dead in the first place.

Zanya settled deeper into her chair, reached into her pocket, and curled her fingers around her stone. It gave her the extra pulse of energy necessary to peer through the fog of Contessa's black magic.

When the vision cleared, her breath stalled and her muscles coiled.

Maybe nearly a dozen bodies, all of them men, were splayed out lifelessly over the floor. Some were half-dressed, but all of them displayed the same wide eyes and gaping mouths—terror frozen across their faces.

Contessa sorted through the corpses, growing more and more agitated when she didn't find a single one of them still alive. She turned back toward her door, seething, her hands balled into fists. She stormed into her bathroom and turned on the shower. Steam rose into the air and fogged the room with a soft cloud.

"Not enough. Not enough." She frantically arranged beauty products on the vanity.

The air sparked with dark magic, and pain shot through Zanya's temples. She gripped the armrests of her chair while focusing on the image. There could be something worth finding if she held the link long enough.

Contessa stepped in front of a full-length mirror fastened to the wall and analyzed her reflection. With a shrug, her robe slipped off her body and floated to the tile floor.

Her skin, once milky and flawless, was now covered in blue-and-purple bruises.

Contessa's eyes narrowed as she ran her fingers through the length of her hair, smoothing it down to resemble her usual glossy waves. When she pulled her hand away, a mass of red strands were caught between her fingers. She stared down at the clump and clenched her hand into a fist. Her gaze slowly rose back to her own reflection, and a shriek tore out of her lungs. The mirror shattered, spitting glass at her feet.

Zanya jerked out of the vision, coming back to the hotel lobby with a sharp pain shooting through her temples. "Ouch."

Arwan watched her without saying a word. He was obviously concerned, though there was nothing he could do to help. Head-splitting migraines were just one of the many perks of being the guardian.

"Contessa is definitely up to something." She rubbed her eyes. "She's been gorging on souls and it still isn't enough. She looks weak."

"She's using all of her energy."

"After the bag full of souls she sucked up in the underworld, that can't be good."

"Renato strode across the marble floor, his black shoes gleaming under the bright lights. "We're all checked out. As soon as Jayden comes down, we'll leave." He checked his pocket watch. "We cannot wait long."

Zanya checked her watch and frowned. "Yeah, we're cutting it close." Her phone buzzed. She grabbed it out of her bag and read the text from Jayden.

Jayden: Room service kicked me out.

She stood from her chair with a smirk. "Speak of the devil. He's on his way."

They all walked to the SUV. Arwan opened the door for her, and she climbed, settling beside Hawa, who looked half-asleep with a cup of Starbucks coffee cradled in her hands. Arwan sat beside Zanya and shut the door.

Renato sat behind the steering wheel and turned in his seat. "Should we be expecting one more?"

"Yeah. He said—"

The passenger door opened on the other side.

Hawa squinted at the sun. "Hey!"

Jayden stared at Zanya for a moment, then glanced at the others. "Sorry. I'll get in the back." He looked at Tara, who was sitting in one of the two remaining seats. "Unless..." He eyed the spot beside her.

Tara's cheeks flushed, and she patted the empty space. "Come sit next to me."

Jayden flashed a subtle smile and squeezed between Zanya and Hawa to the back of the SUV. Once he settled down, Tara punched him in the arm. "How ya feeling?"

He rubbed his bicep. "Better, until now." He grinned.

Zanya turned to face the front and let out a long breath. Thank God. Things would have been awkward the entire way back to Belize if Tara were still freaked out. But, whether Jayden liked it or not, when they returned home, they would have to figure out exactly what had happened to him.

Salty air poured through the open car window, tickling Zanya's nose. She smiled softly at the sight of the sandy coast as they drove past it toward Renato's home. The humidity stirred memories of her arrival at his estate and the fascination of first strolling down the winding beach.

Everyone had been civil on the way home. She

was thankful for that. No drilling Jayden with questions. No prying stares. No smartass comments or bitter attitudes. Everyone seemed to just want to relax and decompress.

Renato steered the SUV onto the bumpy road that led to the house, and Zanya sat up straight when the estate came into view. She couldn't help but smile.

"Welcome home," Renato said as he slowed the car to a stop. Zanya was the first to step out.

Renato wasn't kidding when he said Marzena was overseeing renovations. The roof, which used to be aged terra-cotta, was now made of copper that glistened under the tropical sun. The cracks that ran along the stone exterior had been filled and blended until they were no longer visible, and the stained-glass windows had all been replaced.

Marzena stepped out of the front door, anticipation flooding her childlike features. Her hair was in a tight bun, and her emerald eyes were glued to the driver's side of the car.

Renato stepped out of the vehicle, cueing Marzena's smile—something Zanya had never seen before.

While Arwan and Peter unloaded the bags, Zanya walked with her uncle to greet the timeless dreamwalker. As they approached, Marzena was focused on Renato, probably communicating with him using her telepathic abilities.

Renato paused in front of her. "It's good to see you too, my old friend."

Marzena's gaze traveled to the car behind them, and her smile vanished.

Zanya turned to see Jayden walking toward them. Renato had surely told Marzena about Jayden's condition. Hopefully she wouldn't object to Jay staying at the house. After all, Marzena may have looked young, but Zanya was all too familiar with her power. The seemingly innocent girl was capable of doing some serious damage.

"Hey, Marzena." Zanya smiled. "It's good to be home."

"It is good to have you home, where you belong," Marzena's voice echoed in Zanya's thoughts. Zanya winced. It had been a while since the dreamwalker had spoken to her using her mind. Maybe one day she'd use her voice, if she even had one. It wasn't apparent if Marzena could actually speak.

Zanya scaled her gaze over the house. "Great job with the upgrades. Looks amazing."

Arwan and Peter scooted past them with luggage. Tara wasn't far behind, leaving Hawa to drag herself out of the car.

Zanya waited for Jay to go inside. Instead, he lingered behind her, making the awkward air even thicker than it already was. Zanya grabbed his arm and tugged him past Marzena, holding her gaze. "We've all had a really long day. I'm going to get Jay settled in and get some rest before dinner." Zanya offered a smile before pulling him up the stairs and into her bedroom. Once she was safely out of their earshot, she shut the door and rested her back against it. "What's wrong with you? Why didn't you just go to your wing?"

"Because. I saw the way that dreamwalker was

staring at me—like children of the freakin' corn. Creepy."

"Oh stop. She just doesn't understand. Not yet. Give her some time to get used to the idea."

"What idea?"

"Of…you know."

"A dead guy living in her house?"

She scrutinized his body. He was walking better, without a limp like before. "Have you healed at all?"

He shook his head.

"Well, are you still in pain? You don't seem to be." She stepped toward him.

He backed away.

She narrowed her eyes. "What's wrong?"

He shrugged. "I'm just…I don't know."

"You can talk to me, Jay."

"Yeah. I know." He rubbed the back of his neck with one hand. "Do you think it's true, what they said about me?"

She let out a long sigh. "I really don't know. All of us are a little—"

"Freaked out?"

"I was going to say confused, but thanks for putting words in my mouth."

He dropped his shoulders. "Sorry."

"Can I take a look?" She gestured to his chest.

"No."

"What do you mean, 'no'?" She reached toward him. "I just want to see—"

He stepped back. "Stay away from me, Zanya. I mean it. I don't want to hurt you." He hung his head. "I don't know what I'm capable of anymore."

"What are you talking about?"

"Never mind."

"To hell with that. I dragged your ass back from the underworld and then vouched for you to Renato. So if there's something I should know, you need to tell me."

He exhaled. "I…" He swallowed. "Look." He slowly dragged his sleeve up his arm, exposing long, deep gashes.

Zanya gasped. "What did you do?"

"Don't worry. It doesn't hurt." He yanked his sleeve back down. "Nothing hurts. Not anymore. I'm a monster, Zanya. I'm not even alive." His jaw flexed. "I had to find out for myself."

"*You* did that?" She pressed her fingers over her mouth.

"It only hurt at first, but when I stopped thinking about it…" He shook his head. "It just didn't anymore. Do you think I'll…?" He avoided eye contact for a moment, and then gathered the courage to meet her gaze. "Do you think I'll start to…?" He rubbed his eyes. "Damn it. Do you think I'll start to rot or something?"

Zanya's lips parted. "Oh, that wouldn't be good."

"Yeah, no shit."

"Um…I…" Jayden had always been so confident, usually to the point of arrogance. Now he was like a child who needed to be shielded from the world. He was searching for some kind of comfort, and all she could do was sputter like a moron. "Look." She took his hand. His fingers were like ice, and she resisted the urge to pull away. "I know you're scared, but everything's going to be okay. I'll keep healing you. Every day if I have to."

His features softened. "Thanks, Zanya."

"Of course." She yawned. "You want to crash out in my room tonight? You can sleep on the weird, curvy couch thing over there." She pointed toward the white chaise on the far side of her room.

He grinned. "As tempting as that is, I think I'll sleep in my bed. Besides, I'm sure Arnie and the healer will wonder where I am if I'm not in the west wing where they can keep an eye on me."

He had a point. Everyone was on edge. "All right. Then I'll see you tomorrow?"

"Yep." He opened the door and moved into the hall. "So, that healing session you mentioned. Tomorrow morning?" His grin widened.

She rolled her eyes. "Yeah, yeah. Milk it, because it's only going to last so long."

"Oh, I plan to."

"Good-bye, Jay."

When she tried to shut the door, he stopped it and stuck his head back in her room. "Hey. One more thing." He reached out and touched her cheek. "Thanks for coming for me."

She smirked. "You owe me. You know that, right?"

He withdrew his hand, winked, and shut the door, leaving her alone in her room. Thank God, because she needed to get some rest. Tomorrow would be a big day—the day they started on their to-do list.

One. Go to Drina's house and ask her to examine the pages from the Popol Vuh.

Two. Find out how and why Jayden had become the walking dead.

Three. Train.

CHAPTER SEVENTEEN

The next morning, Zanya stretched in the sun beaming through her bedroom window, buried beneath down blankets. She sat up and twisted her hair into a bun. They'd spent so much time traveling and sleeping in strange places, it was good to wake up somewhere that was simply hers. She stood and slipped on her robe before heading downstairs.

Everything about the house was familiar. Nostalgia filled her as she wove through the halls and down the winding staircase.

The French doors creaked open in the kitchen. Maybe it was Tara. If Zanya were lucky, she was late enough to have missed Peter's horrible daily pancake breakfast.

When she turned into the kitchen, the doors leading to the veranda hung open. "Hello?" She walked toward them and poked her head outside. Gulls screamed in the sky and the waves crashed on the coast. "Tara?"

The hairs on the back of her neck stood up.

She sensed someone behind her. Someone who

shouldn't be there. Electricity sparked over her skin when the light in her chest jumped to life.

"I see you're still learning to control your abilities." The woman's voice was familiar.

Zanya's breath stalled. She swallowed and then slowly turned. The heat drained from her cheeks at the sight of the woman with brown hair and wolf-gray eyes standing in the kitchen. She stood like a warrior, her stance gaped and chin tilted up. Her dark hair was pulled back, showcasing sharp cheekbones and long lashes. Her fitted shirt and pants were ordinary enough, except the armored shields on her forearms, thighs, and shins. Were the shields made of…rubber?

Zanya dropped her hand from the doorknob. This couldn't be happening. Her mother was dead—killed by Sarian years ago.

A rush of sick heat tore through her gut. There was another possibility—the *only* other possibility.

Contessa.

Zanya curled her fingers into a fist, charging an electrical pulse in her palm. "You must think I'm really stupid." She'd shock the temptress bitch until she couldn't breathe.

The woman raised her hands. "I know this is a shock to you."

"Not as much as it'll be to you." She spun and swung a heavy right hook.

The woman leapt to the side and pulled a baton from her belt. "You need to calm down."

Zanya snarled and shot an electric orb straight at the impostor's chest. The woman used a shield mounted to her forearm to deflect the attack.

"Zanya, stop it. I don't want to hurt you."

"You shouldn't have come here, Contessa." Zanya gathered tension in her muscles to strike with deadly force. She still hadn't mastered the strength Renato held, but she was sure she could pound the witch into the ground if she tried.

The woman ground her teeth and gripped her weapon tighter. "I'm not Contessa, and I'm not here to hurt you. Believe me."

"Go to hell!" Zanya swung hard, barely missing the witch when she ducked out of the way.

The woman struck Zanya in the stomach with her baton. The blow knocked the air from her lungs and doubled her over. Zanya gasped and coughed, forcing herself to draw in a breath as she looked up.

"Damn it!" The woman lowered her weapon, staring down at Zanya with a sharp gaze. "I didn't want to do that."

Renato skidded into the kitchen and stopped in the doorway, gawking at them with wide eyes. "Ellie?"

The woman stepped in front of Zanya in a defensive posture.

"No!" Zanya wheezed, reaching for Renato. "It's not her."

The woman spun around and glared down at Zanya. "Search my mind if you don't believe it's me." She extended her hand. "Use your abilities, and it'll prove I'm not that black-hearted whore."

The room fell silent as Zanya slowly stood up straight. She searched the woman's face. "Fine." If she were lying, Zanya would shock her hard enough to stop her heart.

Zanya grasped the woman's forearm and opened her mind, peering into the woman's eyes. So far, she had only used her mental abilities to seek like Jayden and communicate like Marzena. With her stone tucked away upstairs, she would have to pull this off on her own.

It took focus, but Zanya found the power deep within. She pushed through the mental barrier into the woman's subconscious.

The memory of her mother's gentle smile washed over her. Her calm, confident gaze. Her gentle touch. Her mother's spirit shone bright from behind the woman's now-cold, calculating stare.

Zanya gasped and yanked her hand back.

"There." Her mother nodded and slid the baton back into its holder. "Now you can stop trying to kill me." She stepped around Zanya and shut the French doors, then pulled the curtains closed.

"Wait." Zanya swallowed, anxiety bubbling in her chest. "How is this—?"

"Are we safe here?" She turned to Renato, who seemed even more stunned than Zanya. "Where are the others?"

Her mother seemed so different—her features sleek and sharp, and her hair pulled back in a high ponytail. It was really her, but Zanya hardly recognized this woman compared to the mother she had once met.

Eleuia's brow turned down. "Why isn't anyone answering me?" She rested her hands on Zanya's shoulders. "Are you okay? Are you hurt?"

"Hurt? No." Her mind reeled. "Mom...how are you here?"

Her mother paused. "It's a long story, but right now we have to secure the house."

Zanya threw her arms around her mother and hugged her as tight as she could. "I thought I'd never see you again." Her voice quivered as she held back tears.

Her mom hugged her back, though only briefly. "We have to move. We're in danger."

Zanya pulled away. "Why?"

Renato scooped her off the floor with a hug. "My God, it's a miracle."

"I'm afraid not," Eleuia said as Renato set her back down. "We need to get Zanya to a safe place."

"How are you here? What's going on?" Zanya said, desperate for an explanation.

"Do you have the stone?" her mother asked.

"It's in my bedroom."

Eleuia's jaw flexed. "You should carry it with you at all times. We have to get it, then get out of here as quickly as we can." She grabbed Zanya's wrist.

Zanya glanced over her shoulder at Renato as her mother dragged her toward the stairs. "She doesn't know," Zanya said, glancing over her shoulder at Renato. She dug her heels into the ground and stopped her mother from pulling her any farther. "Mom, Sarian is dead."

Her mother froze. "Dead?"

Zanya nodded. "He was killed right in front of me."

Her face paled. "This is worse than I thought."

Zanya's eyebrows arched. "I don't understand. I thought you'd be—"

Arwan walked into the foyer.

Her mother pulled a blade from a scabbard tucked in her boot and extended the knife. "*You.*"

Zanya moved between them. "What are you doing? He's not—"

"Get out of the way, Zanya!" Her mother jerked her back and lunged at Arwan with the blade. "I'll kill you!"

Arwan's eyes widened, and he leaped to the side. Renato grasped at Eleuia. "Ellie, no!"

She sliced at Arwan, her eyes lit with fury. "You bastard!" She lunged at him again. He grabbed her wrist and wrenched it back, locking her arm behind her. The knife clattered to the floor. Ellie spun and kicked him in the chest, and Arwan slammed into the railing. He grabbed on to the wood and pulled himself upright as Renato snatched the knife from the floor. "Ellie, stop this!"

She reached to her belt for a black handle. It was a gun—one Zanya hadn't noticed until now.

Her lips parted. She really meant to kill him.

Her mother pulled the pistol and took aim. Zanya threw out a shield, knocking Eleuia to the floor and Arwan even harder against the far wall. The gun skidded across the hardwood to Zanya's feet, and she picked it up. The weight of the cold metal made her heart race even faster.

"Let me take that." Renato slowly removed the pistol from her hand.

Arwan righted himself, his gaze flickering between Zanya and her mother.

The chaos was just too much. She'd just woken up. She hadn't even had her first cup of coffee, for

God's sake. "Someone better tell me what the hell is going on!" Zanya should have been able to enjoy the fact that her mother was back from the dead. Instead, Eleuia had come back as a cold woman with a chip on her shoulder.

Eleuia slowly picked herself off the floor, and the sharpness in her gaze deepened Zanya's guilt. "I'm sorry, Mom, but you almost killed him."

"I'd be doing you a favor." Eleuia grabbed the knife from Renato's hand and shoved it back into its sheath. She extended her hand, waiting for her gun.

Renato ejected the clip and cocked it, releasing the single bullet from the chamber. He slowly set the piece in her hand.

She snatched it, glaring. "Mind telling me why the hell that *thing* is in our house, near my daughter? You were supposed to protect her from his kind."

"Ellie, he isn't who you believe him to be."

"Oh really?" She let out a haughty laugh. "So he's not the heir to the underworld? He's not a monster?" Her eyes narrowed. "I know, Renato. I know much more than you're giving me credit for."

Zanya's gut rolled and pitched. Her gaze rested on Arwan as her stomach clenched. She swallowed down the saliva pooled under her tongue. "What is she talking about?"

He analyzed her apprehensive stance, and nodded. "It's true. I am." A tremor ran up his arm. "I am all of those things. And worse."

"See." Eleuia stepped beside Zanya. "He's not even trying to deny it." She looked toward Renato. "And you knew all along. This is how you protect her?"

Renato analyzed Eleuia with a sober stare. "You are out of line, Ellie. He may be the rightful heir, but he is not like them. He never has been. You have no idea—"

"Heir to what, exactly?" Zanya's gaze darted between them.

Renato shook his head. "It's not how it sounds."

"Yes." Arwan clenched and unclenched his fist. "Yes it is. Zanya has the right to know who I am." He met her gaze. "I should tell her myself. I should have told her a long time ago." When he stepped forward, Zanya's breath caught in her throat. "She deserves that much."

"Arwan…" Her heart ached as she hoped this was all a huge mistake.

"I wanted to tell you, to be honest with you from the start." His chest rose as he drew in a breath. "I'm so sorry, Zanya. I am who they say I am. Heir to the throne of the underworld, son of the king. I hate it—hate myself for it—but I can't keep running away."

"It's too late for confessions, you mongrel half-breed." Eleuia's arms were thin and lean, but the armor made her look fierce. "You have never belonged here, and I'll be damned to the world you came from if I escaped Sarian's capture just to watch you pollute my only daughter." She pulled a second pistol from a hidden holster in her belt.

"Mom." Zanya extended her hands. "You can't be serious."

"Try to stop me again, Zanya, and I'll put a hole in his heart." She glared at Arwan. "Apparently I'm the only one left with any sense. This boy—this creature—is only going to destroy you. He's dark. Riyata and underworlders have been enemies since time began, and for good reason."

"He's not like that." She inched forward. Maybe she could snatch the gun from her mother's grip before it was too late.

Eleuia took aim.

"No!" Renato jumped into the path of the bullet just before the gunshot rang through the house. The bullet struck him in the shoulder but didn't stop him from tackling her mother to the floor.

"Let go of me!" Eleuia screamed, struggling to twist out of Renato's grasp as blood tricked down his arm. "You let him in here! You let that thing in our house!"

"So help me, Ellie. If you do not calm down, I will be forced to do something I would otherwise never do."

Zanya turned back to Arwan, but he was gone. The French door in the kitchen hung open, the breeze tossing the curtains side to side.

CHAPTER EIGHTEEN

Zanya sat near Renato's desk, listening to her mom and Renato bicker in the back of the study. It had been almost impossible to sleep the night before while knowing her mother was in the house and Arwan still hadn't returned. She had so many questions, but she'd have to wait until they stopped arguing to get a word in edgewise.

"How could you let this happen?" Eleuia whispered harshly.

"Now wait a moment." Renato lifted his hand, but Eleuia slapped it away.

"I'm the guardian for centuries, and as soon as I leave, there is an underworld half-breed living in my house?"

She'd had just about enough of this "underworld half-breed" crap. If they weren't going to offer her the answers she needed, she'd have to take them.

Zanya stood and stalked toward them. Of course they were so focused on each other, they didn't even notice her approach. If only she could go back to the first time she'd met her mother—back when

Arwan had bent time and risked his life to save Tara and retrieve the stone. Her mother should have been thanking him.

Zanya paused beside the bickering pair and waiting for her opportunity to speak. She eyed Renato's shoulder. The wound seemed to be healing quickly, thanks to Peter's handiwork. The fact it was only a flesh wound helped. Still, her mother didn't seem at all apologetic for the accident.

Her uncle pinched the bridge of his nose. "If you would stop being so stubborn and just listen to what I have to say—"

"Hey, guys…" Neither of them looked at her.

"Right, so you can keep telling me how he's really a good guy?"

"Mom…"

Eleuia scoffed and continued her argument. "Do you even realize that boy has more power than Sarian, or anyone from his realm? And he is inherently programmed to use his power for evil. Nothing, and I mean *nothing* can change that."

Zanya balled her fists. *"Excuse me."*

"That is not up to you to judge, Ellie. There are some circumstances that call for a more thorough explanation."

"Yeah, how about that? Let's start with how you could let him in my house to begin with!"

Zanya ground her teeth. "Hey!" The two froze and stared at her. Zanya exhaled. "Can you guys shut up for two seconds?" She swallowed the lump in her throat. "First—" she looked at her mother, "—you seriously need to lay off. Whatever you think Arwan is, *he's not.* He's fought with us this entire time, and if it weren't for him, I never would have bonded with the stone. How can you forget how much he's helped us?"

Eleuia's eyes narrowed. "You're right." Her tone had softened. "I wish I could have recognized him sooner. I was so stupid." Her mother turned and paced in front of the fireplace. "A timebender. I knew it wasn't possible. Only deities or crossbreeds have the ability to do that."

"*Stop calling him that.*" Zanya crossed her arms as her mother paced like a madwoman. "And stop treating him like a criminal for something he can't control."

"It's the harsh truth, Zanya." Eleuia stopped pacing and squared her stance. "Sometimes life deals you shit and you can either wallow in it or make the best of your situation and keep going."

Zanya's shoulders dropped. She examined her mother's sharp features. "What happened to you? You were so different when I first met you. You were strong and elegant. You were…my mom." She tilted her head. "Now you're like someone else. Someone I don't even recognize."

Her mother cast down her gaze. "I'm sorry. I'm not the same woman you met. I wish I could do it all over again. I never wanted to lose you, but that's what life dealt me." She glanced at Renato, this time with a bit of humility. "And I chose to survive."

"Survive what?" Zanya asked. "What happened? You still haven't told us how you escaped Sarian. How? When?"

Eleuia slowly lowered herself into a chair. Zanya

remembered watching her mom in the same exact spot when they had gone back in time. Back when her mother wore a pregnant belly, and soft waves cascaded over her shoulders. Now she was half the woman, in more ways than one.

Zanya and her uncle cautiously sat in the chairs beside her. Renato still hadn't lost his intense focus. She didn't like to see him so conflicted, but something had happened. Something that had changed the ripples of life.

"After you came to the house…" Eleuia settled deeper in her chair. "After you bonded with the stone, my fate was sealed. I was stripped of my powers. The only gift a guardian retains after they give the stone to the next in line is their longevity. But the future had to play out the way it had the first time. So I had you and then sent you away with your father."

Zanya sat up straight in her chair, hope swirling in her chest.

"No." Eleuia lifted her hand. "He isn't here. It just wasn't meant to be."

Zanya slumped back. It would have been too good to be true.

"Sarian found me and expected to find the stone," her mother continued. "Except this time it was gone. I was powerless, and he was angry over all of the wasted years he'd spent chasing me." She rested her hand on her chest. "But he found other ways to keep himself entertained." She let out a shaky breath. "And he kept me alive for years."

Nausea slithered in Zanya's gut. She had seen that same expression on Tara's face every time she spoke about her abuse. Now her mother's features were riddled with shame, and Zanya couldn't do a damn thing to make it better. "He was supposed to kill you. What happened?"

"Sarian and I spent a lot of time together, Zanya. After being his prisoner that long, he began to open up to me. He bragged about his plans. That's when I found out about that *boy* and how Sarian was going to take down the king of the underworld and kill the prince. He wanted the king's realm but couldn't have it as long as an heir was around."

"Mom." Zanya leaned forward in her chair. "Are you saying Arwan is a demigod like Sarian was?"

"Something like that. To be honest, we aren't really sure, exactly."

"The prince?" Zanya sat back. All this time and he hadn't told her. He'd had every chance in the world, and he'd still hidden who he truly was.

"What do you mean, *we* aren't sure?" Renato said.

"I'm not the only Riyata left. There are others, like us, who have been helping me survive all this time. I couldn't do it alone. Not without my abilities. Not without the stone."

He rubbed his chin. "Are they willing to fight?"

She nodded. "For the right cause."

"Fight who?" Zanya said. "Sarian's gone."

"Which is what I was afraid of." Eleuia traced her fingers over a scar on her wrist. "I've seen what would happen if Sarian died. I've seen a lot of things I shouldn't have. Things only gods and underworlders are meant to see." Sweat collected on her brow. "Now that Sarian's gone, the doors are open to someone much worse, more powerful, with absolutely no moral boundaries."

"Contessa," Zanya whispered.

Eleuia examined her carefully. "How did you know?"

"Um…" Zanya exchanged glances with Renato. "We sort of asked her for help a while back."

"What?" her mother snarled through clenched teeth and peered at Renato. "You brought my daughter to see that demon?" She slammed her fist against the table beside her, rattling the tiny crystals that hung from the lampshade. "What the hell were you thinking?"

"It was my idea," Zanya said. "So stop freaking out on him. It's not Renato's fault. He hasn't done anything but worry about me and protect us this entire time you were—" She bit back the rest of her sentence.

"I know I haven't been here. But I am now, and that's all you can ask of me."

"That—and some humility."

Her mother's lips parted. "Excuse me?"

"Arwan may be a lot of things, but he's not evil." She'd deal with his half-truth confession later. For now, she had to convince her mother to let him back in the house without trying to kill him. "As far as I'm concerned, he's one of us."

Eleuia sat up straight, her hands draped over the armrests of the leather chair. "This is my house, and I will say who is welcome and who is not."

Zanya pushed to her feet. "Fine, but I'm the guardian now. You may regret that, but you can't take it back. As long as the stone and I are bonded, I have to do what's right for us." She squared her shoulders. "It's time for me to step up and be the leader I'm supposed to be. Not just for me, but for everyone." She turned and walked toward the door. There clearly wouldn't be any smiles, hugs, or nights spent reminiscing and telling stories about their lives. Things would be different. Colder. More distant.

When she reached the threshold, her mother spoke. "I hope you're not in love with him."

Zanya paused at the door.

"You can never be with him. He's an underworlder and you're Riyata. You're not compatible, and you never will be. There is nowhere in any realm where you both belong."

"Ellie," Renato scolded.

"No. She needs to hear this."

Zanya listened with her back still turned, her chest rising and falling with every short breath.

"Even if you do love him, you need to let him go. He'll only bring heartache and destruction to you. To us all."

CHAPTER NINETEEN

Zanya descended the spiral staircase in the main wing. It was early, and the hike to Drina's would be a long one. They needed to find out more about the salvaged pages of the book. Thankfully, Renato was an early riser and had already begun his day in his study.

She paused in the entrance, expecting to see her mother as well. Instead, Renato sat at his desk in the otherwise vacant room.

She'd sort of hoped her mom would be there so they could talk about the night before. What her mother had been through was unfortunate, but Zanya's life hadn't been peaches and cream, either.

Renato studied her as she approached his desk. With his brow raised, he leaned back in his chair. "May I ask the occasion?"

Zanya squirmed under his gaze. The amount of skin her gear showed wasn't at all in her comfort zone. "No occasion." She adjusted the braided shoulder strap, showing off her torso in the corset-like training shirt with leather chest shields.

He laced his fingers and rested his hands on his desk. "You look exactly like your mother in her old training gear."

"It was in my closet." At the bottom of her closet, actually. In a box…that was locked. She'd broken the lock to get in…after smashing it with her stone. "I didn't think she'd mind."

"It is good to see the gear in use. Are you training today?"

"First I have to find Drina and ask her to look at the pages of the book. We need to know exactly what they say. At least I know *she'll* tell me everything."

Renato tilted his head and narrowed his eyes. "Is there something on your mind?"

"I just can't help but wonder why nobody told me the truth about what's really going on here."

"We have been truthful with you, Zanya. As truthful as we could be."

"Oh, don't give me that crap. You knew about Arwan and you didn't tell me. *That* is *not* being truthful." She turned and walked toward the door.

"You shouldn't try to find Drina's home."

"Why not?"

"Because you don't know where she lives, and you may get lost in the jungle."

"My stone will guide me." She paused in the threshold and glanced over her shoulder. "Or did you forget that now *I'm* the guardian?"

Renato stood and straightened his jacket. "I understand you are angry, but I *am* trying to reason with Ellie. She has been through more than you can imagine, and you can't blame her for having some trouble adjusting."

She turned to face him. "That's fine. She can take all the time she needs to adjust, but I have to do what I am meant to do—what you *dragged* me here for."

His shoulders dropped, as did his gaze.

She bit her lip. Being pissed at Renato sucked. He didn't deserve her shitty attitude, but she was sick and tired of being sick and tired, and her anger was all she had to grasp on to. Still, they would have to work together if they wanted to make any progress. She drew in a deep breath and swallowed the urge to deliver another dose of resentment. "Contessa is up to something, and we need to find out what."

"Agreed. But please take someone with you, just so I know you are safe."

"Safe?" How could he continue to treat her like a child? After almost being killed by some cave demon, a bloody battle against Sarian's incubi, traveling through time, winning back the stone at Jayden's expense, and then venturing to the depths of the underworld where she was almost eaten by the tree of Yaxche, apparently she still hadn't proven herself.

Zanya stepped toward him and cued the light in her chest. The tips of her fingertips burned while she formed an energy ball in her hand. She pushed harder, sending electrical currents over her skin and causing the current to roll and spark in her palm. Her breathing steadied and she widened her stance, focused on conjuring winds. "I'm pretty sure I can take care of myself," she shouted over the low roar of the building cyclone. The air current picked up, snatching up papers and tearing a few photos off the walls. Renato squinted through the windstorm. His tie danced over his chest, and his usually manicured hair was tousled in the spinning current.

She dimmed her light and let the winds die out. Loose papers glided silently to the floor.

Renato ran his fingers through his hair and straightened his tie. "Was that entirely necessary?"

"Apparently it was. You don't think I can tap into my powers. I had to show you otherwise." She lowered her hands and took a normal stance. "And with this solstice thing around the corner, my abilities have gotten stronger."

"Ah." He straightened his button-down vest. "Your mother and I were just speaking about our travel plans."

"Where are you going?"

"We. Where are *we* going?" He rounded his desk, stepping over broken glass from one of the small paintings. A tinge of guilt streaked through her. "The solstice is an important event to our kind, and your mother hasn't been able to attend a ceremony since before she left. She's rather looking forward to it."

"Where is she, anyway?"

"She is staying in a room in my wing." He averted his gaze. "I believe staying in the room she and your father once shared was too painful for her to even consider."

"Oh." She relaxed her shoulders and leaned on the wall. "How is she? I mean, is she okay?"

"She is coping." His deep brown eyes carried

unwavering wisdom and confidence. "But I cannot begin to imagine how difficult this has been for you. I know you are hurting, and not just over your mother." Renato walked toward her and stopped several feet away. He pushed out his chest and rested his hand over his heart. "I'm sorry I've failed you, Zanya. I never intended to keep secrets from you, but some secrets were not mine to disclose." His tone carried more pain than she was prepared for and more hurt than he deserved.

She wouldn't lie and say she wasn't still angry. But it wasn't all his fault. They were Arwan's secrets, after all, and he was the one who should have told her the truth.

"The solstice ceremony will be on the twenty-first of December—the shortest day of the year."

"December twenty-first? Isn't that the day everyone was freaking out over the world ending?"

"Back in the year 2012, yes. But it was an unfounded concern. Our ancestors did not predict the end of the world. It was merely the end of the thirteenth baktun."

If she'd kept up with her reading like she was supposed to, she'd know what that was. "Okay, I'll bite. What's a baktun?"

He pinched the bridge of his nose and sighed. "A baktun is a cycle of time equaling nearly four hundred years. And unlike the belief of many, the end of the thirteenth baktun was a time for hope and change. But it is also a time for bonding and reuniting with long-lost friends. It is a family gathering of sorts, with the purpose of creating new spirit bonds."

"You keep saying *bonding*, and I'll be honest, it's kind of freaking me out."

Renato walked to a bookshelf and slid a book out of the long row. "Bonding is the unity of two souls, much more powerful than any vow of a traditional marriage." He opened the book and searched through the pages while walking toward her. "It is a commitment solidified by the lights of Aurora. A solidification that cannot be revoked." He extended the book. "It is a sacred event for all Riyata."

Zanya took the book and skimmed over the text about the ceremony. "So…" She glanced up at him. "Why are we going? I mean, nobody here is bonding." Her thoughts flashed to Arwan, who hadn't been back to the house since her mother returned. She missed him, and worse, she was worried about him. Maybe later she would try seeking him, even though she promised herself she would give him the space he was clearly looking for.

"Because it is a tradition for our people, begun by the earliest of the Maya. It marks the shortest day and the longest night of the year. Every day to follow will be one step closer to spring, and therefore new life. It is not strictly for bonding. It is a holiday. A celebration of life."

"Oh." She closed the book and held it up. "Can I take this back to my room?"

Renato nodded. "As long as you return it with the others you took last night."

"Uh, yeah. Sorry about that."

"And before you leave, kindly clean up this mess." He nudged a piece of paper on the floor with the polished toe of his shoe.

Zanya looked around the study and dropped her shoulders. "Right."

"Perhaps this is your first training lesson." He sat behind his desk. "Do not use your abilities unless you can clean up after them."

***

The jungle had always stirred a sense of curiosity in Zanya. She marveled at the trees, so tall and vast, reaching toward the sun like living skyscrapers. But unlike the times she'd hiked with Arwan, today the forest was nearly silent, and a layer of thick fog blanketed the ground.

Zanya chose each foothold with care. She stepped over a fallen tree, slicked with moss. A humid breeze wove through the foliage and swept her hair off her shoulders. The cool air soothed her flushed cheeks.

A fork in the path presented itself. One sloped toward the coast and what looked like a village. She peered at the pitched roofs of tiny huts, all clustered together near the tree line.

The other path wound up the side of a steep incline and over a peak.

When she'd first arrived at Renato's house, Arwan gave her a tour of the estate. He'd mentioned nearby villages he often visited. She pivoted toward the descending path. Maybe that was where she'd find him.

She'd tried to call him, but each attempt was forwarded straight to his voice mail. Peter had told her Arwan had left his phone in the west wing. Apparently he hadn't taken anything with him, which was worrisome.

Her stone vibrated in her pocket, and she traced her fingers over its smooth surface. Its whispers directed her to the inclined path. She bit her lip. It was important to find Drina, but her stomach had been in knots since Arwan had left, and she wanted to be sure he was all right.

The stone sent a more forceful current through her this time. She swallowed and secured her hold around it. "I hear you. You don't need to yell." She exhaled and started up the inclined path. The farther she hiked, the steeper the trail became. Before long, she was forced to cling to trees and rocks for leverage.

The end of the trail was straight ahead. Her stone acted like a compass, delivering a low, steady stream of energy as long as she was headed the right way. She reached the top and clung to a branch while she surveyed the land. Her stone fell silent. "Am I close?" All that surrounded her was more thick jungle. Not a hut or home in sight. She pulled her stone out of her pocket. "Hey you," she said in a sweet tone. "Did you fall asleep or something?"

Before Sarian had taken her stone, she didn't have time to get to know it very well. It was, after all, somehow a living thing, churning with magic and power, its very existence woven into her soul. Now they were working together, as they should be. Or so she'd thought.

She sighed when it replied with silence. "All right. I guess you would rather I find my own way from here?" Her stone sent out a tiny burst of light. "I figured as much."

After she tucked the stone back in her pocket, she considered the surrounding paths. "Okay. Looks like that's where I need to go." She turned toward a thin, well-worn trail that snaked around the side of the hill.

She rounded a turn and paused in front of a jungle clearing straight ahead. Each step led her closer to the butterfly field Arwan had once brought her to.

The field housed thin bushes with tiny purple blooms, shaded by the mature trees that formed a canopy overhead—exactly the way it had been the first time she'd seen it. This time of day the flowers were closed, waiting for the warmth of the sun and the cold morning dew to slide off their leaves.

Zanya stood on the edge of the clearing, admiring the collection of bushes that had once served as refuge to thousands of butterflies.

She let out a deep sigh. The bare spot in the center of the clearing was still there. She swallowed and looked away.

The birds in the trees exploded in chatter and chirps while the branches of the canopy shook with screaming apes and small jungle creatures. Zanya searched the thick foliage surrounding her.

The loud snap of branches tore through the air. Zanya spun and searched for any movement. A deep growl surrounded her. The hairs on her arms stood up, and she crouched in a defensive stance.

A black figure flashed past, concealed by thick leaves and vines.

Her stone sent a shock through her. Zanya had never experienced such a charge in her life, as though her abilities had been given a shot of adrenaline. She could practically hear her powers winding tighter inside her. The light in her chest burst to life, churning with blue, white, and silver. The air was sucked out of her lungs, and she gasped, gripping a nearby tree to keep from falling to her knees.

The figure darted past her again, closer this time. Her stone wouldn't have reacted this way if it were an ordinary animal. No. Zanya sensed a dark presence deep in her bones.

Hot air brushed against the back of her neck. A growl slid over her skin.

Zanya let go of the tree and stood up straight. She brushed her fingers together, grinding her foot into the soil for some balance.

Another hot breath sent chills down the back of her legs.

With a clenched jaw, she spun into a side kick.

Her attack landed. A shock rippled through the air. Something dark and heavy flew back and slammed into an immense oak. The impact splintered bark and wood in every direction.

The creature with black fur scrambled to its paws and shook leaves and soil from its body. The beast bared its teeth, growling.

Zanya's eyes widened.

Its fur was wet and tousled. The scruff on its neck stood on end with its ears pinned back.

This beast was no stranger. The underworld demon was the same creature that had killed Sarian.

It must have followed her to the middleworld, or more likely, was set free by Contessa.

The beast's paws shifted in the cool earth. Zanya cocked her head and stretched her hands out to her sides. It was time to use her offensive abilities—powers she had never used before.

She gathered power deep in her gut. Electricity sparked over her skin, and strands of hair lifted off her shoulders with the electrical charge.

Lightning flashed through the air, followed by a clap of thunder through the otherwise weary morning. A bolt struck a nearby tree, splitting it in half. The shredded trunk tilted toward the beast.

It leapt out of the way, then wound between the trees, its tail whipping side to side. Its black eyes, dotted with flecks of gold, stayed locked on her.

The fear and hesitation she expected never came. Her stone's power coursed through her veins, supercharging her abilities.

This is what she was meant to do. Who she was destined to be.

Only one of them would leave this battle alive.

CHAPTER TWENTY

Arwan

This wasn't supposed to happen. She wasn't supposed to see him this way. Not in this form. Not under these circumstances.

Arwan's fur twitched as he wove through the trees, tension coiling in his muscles. He was foolish to have come here, to the spot he and Zanya first connected. He should have stayed far from home—from her.

An electric ball sparked in Zanya's hand. She wound her arm back and launched it directly at his head. He ducked, and the assault struck a tree behind him, blowing a hole right through it.

He let out a low growl.

Clearly her mother had told her who he was— what he was—and she hated him because of it. He should have told her the truth from the beginning, even if it meant losing her.

Another blast struck the earth beside his paws. Currents flowed through the soil, vibrating the ground beneath him.

He snarled, and she pursed her lips and squared her stance. She wouldn't leave him alone. Not after she'd seen what he did to Sarian—what he was capable of doing to anyone.

His only two options were to flee or fight. Fighting would result in tragedy. He'd rather die than hurt her, though he wasn't ready to die today.

He pinned back his ears and dashed into the jungle. Tree branches and leaves slashed at his snout as he sprinted forward. He would keep running until he reached the river. Once he crossed the water, the terrain would become too steep for her to follow.

A bolt of lightning struck the ground in front of him. He dug his claws into the loose soil, sliding to a stop just before he plummeted into the crater. Another bolt struck the earth behind him. Trapped, he turned to face her.

Zanya emerged from the trees, her hair whipping around her face, and her wolf-gray eyes illuminated with power.

Conjured winds tore through the jungle, blowing the trees with the power of a hurricane. He squinted and clenched his jaws, digging into the soil with his paws. He had to find cover or be thrown into the storm.

Her face tilted toward the sky, and scattered clouds gathered into a dense cyclone. The vortex reached for him. Trees cracked and bent under the velocity of the winds. Lightning flashed around them, so bright his vision blurred after every strike. Leaves and thorny branches whipped by.

She would destroy the entire jungle at this rate.

Zanya extended her hands and threw an energy ball, which struck him in the shoulder, and he flew back and slammed into a rock face. He huffed and scrambled to his feet, still fighting against the roar of the storm.

A tree uprooted from the forest floor and tumbled toward him. Before he could move, it plowed him into a rock and pinned him down. He snapped and clawed at the solid wood.

The wind died down, and Zanya stalked toward him.

She gave him no choice.

He called on all of his strength and pushed away the tree. He righted himself, his tail whipping side to side.

Her eyes were cold as steel, and her scowl only deepened the sharp stab through his chest.

"I know who sent you," Zanya said as she built energy in her palm. "And when you see her in hell, you can tell her I was the one who sent you there."

She threw a burst of power, and this one struck him in the chest. Electric shock racked his muscles. His vision went black, and the hum of the current rang in his ears.

He pulled in a breath. When the fog lifted from his sight, Zanya stood over him with a dagger clenched in one hand. She lifted it over her head, electricity crawling around her arms in preparation to deliver a fatal blow.

He huffed and clawed at the earth, but there was no point. If all he had left was to hide in the jungle all of his life, in the body of this beast, death was surely more merciful.

He rested his head on the ground and closed his eyes, soaking in the rays of sun. The light warmed his body.

He opened his eyes and stared up at her, then let out a soft whimper. Her hand shook with the blade still poised overhead. Sweat collected on her brow.

He wanted to tell her it was all right.

He slowly turned onto his side and lifted one paw into the air, exposing his chest. The quicker it was over with, the sooner he could forget about all of this.

Zanya plunged the knife into his chest. Hot, scalding pain shot through him as the blade drove deeper. He gagged and coiled into a ball, all the while fighting the instinctual urge to claw at the handle of the knife.

***

Zanya

Zanya stared down at the beast lying on the ground, blood pooling under its enormous body. There was no need to throw a force field up like she had anticipated. The animal didn't even fight back. She stepped away as its chest rose and fell with longer pauses in between each breath.

The adrenaline that coursed through her veins had begun to fade, but she was still on edge. She had never killed anything before, and some part of her, deep down, ached with remorse. But it had to be done, and she was the only person capable of fighting such a beast. It was her role—one she'd have to get used to.

Zanya glanced up at the thick clouds dispersing overhead. She had called them there. This was the first time she'd used her abilities to manipulate the weather, and now her limbs felt heavy from the raw fatigue that followed.

Thankfully the fight with the creature was over, because she couldn't have kept the cyclone going much longer. She slumped against a tree, her breath in rhythm with the creature's as it began to slip into unawareness.

The sun cast warm light on the wolf-like animal. Its long tail lay lifeless over the ground, and its paws were padded more like a cat's than a dog's.

"Stupid boy."

Zanya spun and threw an energy ball at the source of the voice. It crashed into Drina, but the attack simply washed over her, and she continued to stalk forward.

Zanya gasped and drew her hands back to her chest. She could have killed the old woman. Another lesson she needed to implement: don't be so quick on the draw.

"Don't come over here. It's not dead yet."

The old woman hobbled closer. If the creature lashed out in one last effort to kill, Zanya might not be able to protect them both.

"I told you, didn't I?" Drina shouted, shaking her finger at the beast. "I told you, you silly, foolish boy, but you don't listen. Stubborn!"

Zanya glanced back at the fading creature. Was Drina talking to it?

"You t'ink like a dumb animal." Drina stalked past Zanya and approached the creature. She crouched beside it and extended her wrinkled hand, blotting its blood-soaked fur with her fingertips. A deep sigh escaped her chest. She slowly stood. "You will die if you stay like t'is."

The beast let out a low rumble and pawed at the ground.

Drina shook her head, digging into a leather sack slung over her shoulder. "Change, and I will treat you."

Its massive form and mud-caked fur shrank into the figure of a man.

But not just any man.

Arwan.

Zanya's eyes widened, and she stumbled, grasping at branches to keep from falling to the ground. Her back slammed into a tree and the air was knocked out of her lungs.

Drina removed a scarf from her bag and draped it over Arwan's naked form. He lay on the fallen leaves, his eyes closed and the color drained from his face.

Zanya's limbs were heavy, and her head was spinning so fast, everything around her turned into a blur of green. She closed her eyes and swallowed, struggling to get her shit together. The panic attack had already wrapped around her lungs and heart. She fell to her knees, gripping her chest.

How could this be happening? How could he…? Zanya peered through the dark fog clouding the edges of her vision. Drina yanked the blade from Arwan's chest, and a desperate cry tore through the air before Arwan's body fell limp.

"No," Zanya whispered. "He can't be—"

Her eyes fluttered shut and she collapsed, her cheek pressed against the cool earth.

CHAPTER TWENTY-ONE

Arwan

Quiet mumbles woke Arwan from his sleep. Before opening his eyes, he drew in a deep breath and touched his face.

No fur.

The scent of herbs and tea infused the air. He pried open his eyes and turned his head. The muscles in his shoulders and neck throbbed with every movement, and the wound in his chest burned with protest.

Drina was hunched in the corner of her small home, grinding herbs in a large basin. The light in the hut was low. He was thankful for that. His vision after changing back to his human form was always slightly impaired. It was something he would have to adapt to again—a side effect he'd completely forgotten about.

Drina scowled. "Foolish." She continued to grind the herbs.

Arwan didn't remember walking back to her hut,

and there was no way she could have carried him. He shifted under a blanket covering him from the waist down. He held the quilt in place and pushed to a sitting position, groaning under the effort.

Drina stood and hobbled toward him with more salve. The bitter, pungent scent invaded his nose and throat. He turned his head as Drina brought it closer. His senses were still heightened.

"Salve will help you heal," she mumbled, scooping a clump into her hand.

"I don't want it." He suppressed the urge to gag.

"I don' ask if you wanted it." She smeared the goo across the wound.

Arwan sucked in a breath and clenched his jaw as the salve hardened over the injury.

"Does it hurt?"

All he could do was nod.

"Good!" She slapped another layer over it and sat back as he grumbled and lay down again. The old woman huffed. "You are lucky. She nearly killed you."

"That was the idea," he mumbled. Sweat collected on his brow. He squeezed the blanket with all of his strength to take his mind off the searing heat from the new layer of herbs. "I don't want to be this…" He swallowed against a dry throat. "This thing."

"You are who you are. Not me or her or anyone can change t'at." He heard her moving through the house but was too tired to open his eyes. "How did I get here?"

A low bubbling noise caught his attention, paired with the gamey, salty aroma of freshly cooked rabbit. He licked his lips.

"Balam. You almost died. I could not drag your lifeless body alone."

Her comment carried more annoyance than he expected, but probably not as much as he deserved. She was right. He owed her more gratitude than what he was showing her—even if she had prevented him from passing into his next stage of life.

The scent of the food suffused the air, and his stomach growled.

Drina lifted a bowl of stew under his nose. "Be careful. It is hot."

The rich aroma gave him the strength to sit up enough to eat. He took the terra-cotta bowl and brought it to his lips. He blew on the stew before taking in a mouthful.

Drina slapped his leg haphazardly. "Slow, boy. Eat slow."

He paused, and then swallowed down more of the savory broth. He had never been so hungry in his entire life.

"What did you hope to gain from showing yourself to her?" Drina scooped some stew out for herself and settled on the floor beside him. She cupped the bowl in her hands and rested it in her lap, waiting for him to respond.

Arwan wiped broth off his chin with the back of his hand. "She wasn't supposed to see me."

"And the jungle? The trees are stripped of t'eir leaves. May not recover."

Arwan frowned. "I couldn't stop her. She was too powerful." The hatred in her eyes had torn into him. His stomach rolled in protest of eating anything else. "Where is she? Is she all right?"

Drina gestured outside. "She is here, waiting for me outside. Needs help. Confused. Angry."

Arwan sat up straight—too quickly. His wound throbbed.

Drina huffed. "You have no sense. No sense at all." She shuffled to her feet. "The guardian needs food. Guidance." She glanced at the door to her hut, covered with a single piece of fabric. "You must stay here and rest."

Drina dished up another bowl of stew and carried it outside. Fresh, crisp sunlight assaulted his eyes. He shielded his face until the flap of fabric fell limp over the door once again, shrouding the room in shadow.

This was his chance to talk to her. To explain. It may backfire, but he had to at least try. That, or spend the rest of his life wishing he would have.

His clothes had been torn to shreds when he shifted to his other form. There was nothing else but the quilt to cover him, so he gathered it around his waist and limped toward the arched door.

Warm winds pushed aside the flap of fabric and caressed his skin. He drew in a deep breath and stepped outside.

Zanya sat on a log beside Drina, who was examining large, crumpled papers. That must have been why she was still here. Surely she hadn't stayed for him.

Zanya was dressed in training gear, something he hadn't noticed in his other form. She raised her gaze. They locked eyes for a mere moment, and the air between them immediately thickened with tension. She looked away and shifted her weight.

He balled his fists as the darkness inside of him clawed and scratched in his core. He bore down, suppressing it until the urge to change subsided.

With the solstice quickly approaching, and him changing for the first few times in decades, the power of his dark side was stronger than ever. He drew in more deep breaths until the beast within fell silent.

He could control it. And he would. Somehow.

He would not let him and Zanya end like this.

Not because he was afraid.

***

Zanya

Zanya struggled to focus on Drina, but the raging heat in her veins drowned out the woman's voice. She swallowed down the lump in her throat, hoping with everything she had Arwan would leave her alone.

He limped toward them, struggling to hold a tattered quilt around his waist. A thick patch of salve was piled over the knife wound on his chest. His tanned skin glistened under the midafternoon sun, and his muscles twisted and bulged with each advance.

She looked at Drina, whose wrinkles deepened with a puckered frown.

Arwan stopped feet away. "Zanya."

His silky voice tore away what little patience she

had. She stood, her stomach tightening more with every second she looked into his dark eyes. "You stay away from me. Far, *far* away." The light in her chest burst to life for all the wrong reasons, but she wouldn't give any effort to suppress it. Not for his sake. Not anymore.

"I know you're angry."

"*That* is an understatement." She glared. "You're a damn liar."

He winced at her words. "I'm sorry."

"Just leave me alone." She stepped back. "I don't have anything to say to you."

"I understand if you don't want to see me right now—"

"*Right now?*" The pain and heartache exploded from inside her, and she threw an electrical ball straight at his chest.

He ducked, effectively dodging the attack. When he rose, he stared at her with wide eyes—and no blanket wrapped around his waist.

Her body flushed with blistering heat. Zanya gasped and spun around. "Can you *please* put something on?" For God's sake, the pull of the solstice didn't give her any mercy. Her heart pounded, and her body ached with raw hunger for his touch.

"I don't have any clothes."

"Well, that's not really my problem." She crossed her arms, tapping her foot. "Can I turn around now?"

There was a short pause before he spoke again. "Yes."

When she did, Arwan was tightening a knot in

the blanket, which was now secured around his waist. His legs trembled, and he rested against a tree for support. "I didn't want any of this to happen."

"You lied to me. I could have dealt with the whole half-underworlder thing. I may have even learned to be okay with you being the crown-freaking-prince of darkness. But…" She examined him. He looked so different from his beast form. "What the hell are you?"

He pushed back strands of hair that had fallen in front of his face, offering nothing but silence.

"It's fine. Don't bother explaining. All those things you said, all the bullshit you fed me about how you would never hurt me…did you forget all that?"

He squared his jaw. "I haven't forgotten."

"Then you sure as hell didn't mean it. Not a damn word." The last statement came out in a breathless whisper.

"I meant it, Zanya." He stepped toward her, his gaze intense. "I never wanted to hurt you. All I have ever wanted was to keep you safe."

"And who the hell is supposed to keep me safe from *you*?" She bit her lip, her throat aching. "I don't know you, Arwan." She shook her head. "And it's pretty damn obvious I never did."

Arwan staggered back. The shattered look in his eyes cut her even deeper, but she held strong. How could she allow herself to be so vulnerable? Her heart had already been broken once by a guy who wasn't who he'd said he was. Falling for Jayden was a stupid mistake. A mistake she'd *never* make again.

"Look." She swallowed. "I'm not going to tell you to stay away from Renato's house. That's not my place. Just—" She sat beside Drina on the fallen log. "Just stay away from me."

"T'at…" Drina tipped her chin up and looked at him. "T'at cannot happen." The old woman stood and turned to Zanya. What seemed to be raw, untainted panic flooded her wrinkled features. "You must. You *must* be toget'er. You must, or…" She held the pages out to Zanya. "Or the middleworld is destined to burn."

CHAPTER TWENTY-TWO

Zanya stormed out of the jungle toward Renato's house. "Un-freaking-believable." She glanced over her shoulder at Arwan following close behind.

When Zanya approached the kitchen entrance near the veranda, she spotted Jayden sitting outside. He slowly stood, his gaze darting between her and Arwan.

"Zanya, please." Arwan was struggling to catch up. If he didn't fall back, she'd make sure he struggled a whole lot more. "Wait a second."

"Wait for what? To be told there's yet another aspect of my life I have zero control over?" She stormed up the path to the house and pushed through the door into the kitchen.

Jayden followed her into the entryway, then paused, staring at Arwan as he finally stumbled inside. Jayden smirked. "Dude. What did you do?" He eyed Arwan. "And what the hell are you wearing? You look like a seriously jacked-up Tarzan."

Arwan pointed at him with a vicious glare. "Shut

up."

Jay snorted. "I haven't seen Zanya this pissed off since…well, since I got here." He groped in his pocket. "Oh my God, dude. Just stay right there. I have to take a picture. Don't move."

Arwan's glare intensified. "You're not helping."

Zanya groaned and continued upstairs. Tara peeked her head out of her bedroom. "What the heck is going on? I could hear you shouting all the way from up here."

Zanya's mind was too scattered to explain. She retreated into her room, slammed the door behind her, and locked it, swallowing down the urge to scream.

Tara's muffled voice pushed under the door from the hall. "Is everything all right?"

"Some kind of lovers' spat, if I had to guess," Jayden said from the hall.

"Stop being such an asshole. Can't you see she's totally freaking out? We should try to talk to her."

Zanya paced the room, unable to block out their voices while she desperately tried to sort her thoughts.

"Uh…you want me to go in there?"

"You're her friend too," Tara whispered harshly.

"Last time I put myself in her line of fire, she almost knocked me on my ass. Not doing that again."

"Jayden, stop being a pansy and knock on the door."

"No way."

Tara scoffed. "Pansy. Move out of the way."

There was a knock on the door.

Zanya stopped and fisted her hands. "What!"

"I told you to give her some time to cool off," Jayden said from the hall. "She's like Wonder Woman on her…you know."

Zanya rubbed small circles over her temples. "I can hear you."

"Idiot!" There was a smack.

"Ouch!"

"That's what you get. Now shut up." There was another moment of silence before Tara's voice continued steady and strong. "Hey, honey. We're here. Everything okay?"

"No, everything is definitely not okay." Zanya flung open the door and paused when her focus landed on Jayden. "Just perfect." She turned and stormed back into her room.

"Do I have to go in there?" Jayden asked.

Tara grabbed his arm and dragged him through the doorway, then closed the door behind them.

Zanya crossed her arms as her breaths quick and sharp. "What are you doing here?"

Jay pointed at Tara.

Zanya pursed her lips. "Great. Now if we bring Arwan up here, we can have both of the guys who screwed me over in the same room, like a little reunion. Wouldn't that be fun?"

Jayden cringed and stepped back. "I vote *no*."

Zanya glared. "You would!"

"Hey, don't get mad at me because of some other guy's—"

Zanya pointed at him. He snapped his jaw shut midsentence, staring at her finger as if it were a magic wand.

She conjured a spark of electricity to her fingertip. The surge rolled over her hand and up her arm. "You are just as much to blame as he is." She narrowed her eyes further. "It must be a male DNA deformation that makes you all liars."

Jayden's eyebrows shot up. "I haven't lied to you since…" He fell silent. "Never mind."

Zanya scoffed and paced along the wall, burying her fingers in her hair. "Do you have any idea what just happened?"

Tara stepped toward her. "Sweetie, you have to calm down. You're starting to freak me out."

"If you're freaked out now, just wait until you hear this." Zanya resumed packing while she counted the points on her fingers.

"A, I just fought the same animal who killed Sarian in the underworld. B, turns out the beast was Arwan, and apparently he's some kind of werewolf-underworlder-thing. C, the pages of the book do have some *useful information*." She quoted the last two words in the air with her fingers.

"And D…" She stopped dead in her tracks and locked eyes with Tara, whose breath hitched. The heat drained from Zanya's cheeks and she sucked in a few panicked breaths. "Shit, not again." She gripped her chest and grabbed on to the bedframe for support.

"Oh boy." Tara rushed to her side and guided her to the bed. "I thought you were done having panic attacks.

"Me too," Zanya wheezed.

Jayden crouched in front of her. "Breathe. Just breathe." He rested his hand on hers. "What's D?"

She clenched her eyes shut, shaking her head. A hot tear rolled down her cheek. "I'm destined to be with him. *Fated.* Created to bond." When she opened her eyes, both Jay and Tara were staring at her with parted lips. "The book said I have to be with the one man on earth, touched by darkness, who walks among man. Half-evil, half-light."

"That could be…" Tara glanced at Jayden. "A lot of people."

Jayden walked to her side. "You're not destined to be with anyone. Not even me. Don't believe that bullshit."

Zanya swallowed and took a few deep breaths to compose herself. "The book is talking about him. He's the only one it could be."

Tara ran her hand down her own arm, still staring at Jay. "That's not entirely true."

The door burst open, and Zanya's mother barged into her room. "What the hell is going on in here?" Her eyes softened when she saw Zanya. When she walked to Zanya's side, Jayden moved out of the way.

Her mother quickly examined everyone in the room. "What's happened?"

Zanya stared up at her—the one person she wanted to confide in and the one person she couldn't. "I can't do this right now. Not with you."

Her mother looked at Tara, who froze like a deer in headlights. Eleuia turned to Jayden, who shifted his weight.

"Wonderful. It's the dead kid." Eleuia exhaled. "Are *you* going to tell me what happened?"

Jayden shook his head. "I'm not sure." He

glanced at her clenched fists. "Ma'am."

Eleuia rolled her eyes and turned back to Zanya. "Honey…" She slowly sat on the bed. "I know I've been a little…harsh since I came back. I just want to protect you. So much has changed since we last saw each other. You couldn't have known about the boy." When Zanya didn't answer, her mother's shoulders dropped.

Eleuia stood, surveying the room. She traced her fingers along the engravings of vines and leaves on the wooden bedpost. "I haven't been in this room since…" She pulled her hand back to her chest. "Since I last saw your father." She stood a moment longer before walking toward the door. "I'll be in Renato's wing if you need me. I won't keep bothering you." She paused and turned at Tara and Jayden. "You seem to have some good friends. Maybe you don't need a mom anymore."

CHAPTER TWENTY-THREE

Arwan

Arwan flung open his bedroom door in the west wing. He grabbed a pair of shorts and a T-shirt from his drawer and laid the pages of the book on his bed, staring down at the taunting symbols. He narrowed his eyes. His attention shifted to the drawings of his mother that hung on his wall. Her face was so familiar, yet it seemed he didn't know the woman nearly as well as he thought.

The stink of Drina's healing salve broke his concentration.

First he would shower, then he would figure out what do to next. The pages presented more questions than answers, and he refused to believe what the book insinuated about his mother.

She had been a windbender—a Riyata forced into compliance by the underworld king. She had been a victim, sucked into the darker realm. That was what he knew and what he would continue to believe, no matter what the book said.

He walked into the bathroom and turned on the hot water, eager to rinse off the herbal treatment and loosen his muscles. He untied the tattered quilt from his waist and tossed it into the laundry basket before stepping under the running water. He braced his hands on the tile wall and let hot water run over his head and down his back.

Drina's desperation left him unsettled. He had never seen the priestess so shaken. If he was destined to bond with Zanya, there was more to his past than what he'd been told.

He and Zanya were destined bonds, born into the world to find each other and unite for a common purpose.

It all made sense now.

He didn't understand the immediate attraction when they first met. It slammed into him like an asteroid. Whatever it was, it was more than just a crush. Something deeper linked them, and now he had a small understanding why.

Still, not everything made total sense. The passage in the book—the one fleeting line that hinted to his lineage—was not enough to convince him that his mother was anything but a victim.

He finished his shower and slipped on clean clothes.

He'd have to travel light.

Some cash, his cell phone, and a small duffle bag packed with a couple changes of clothes would hold him over for a few days. That was all he would need to get to Moscow and back.

He had to see Contessa.

According to Zanya's last vision, the witch still

had the book. If it contained the rest of his mother's story, what would that mean for his future?

He descended the stairs and walked through the west wing, leaving through the back door before he checked his watch. If he made it to the airport in an hour, he could catch the six o'clock flight out of Belize.

That meant he'd have to take the sports car.

He walked into the covered garage and grabbed the key fob to the Infiniti Coupe.

He paused at the sound of a thudding heartbeat, and turned. Eleuia was leaning against the passenger door of the car, her arms crossed.

"What do you want?" he said.

She glanced at his bag. "Going somewhere?"

"Depends. Do you have your gun?"

Eleuia snorted. "This whole mess you've dragged my daughter into hasn't ended well for you. I had a feeling you wouldn't stick around."

"Great. Anything else?" He had to leave, and Eleuia was clearly just trying to agitate him.

"You know, Zanya is up in her room right now crying her eyes out."

He bit the inside of his cheek. What did she expect him to do? Apologize? He didn't owe her anything. He pushed the Unlock button on the keychain. The headlights blinked and the horn let out a short beep. "Please get away from the car." He opened the trunk and threw in his bag, then slammed it closed.

Eleuia rested her forearms on the hood, peering at him as he walked to the driver's side. "So how did you do it, exactly? You just waltzed right into my house and charmed my brother into thinking you're some kind of changed man? That you turned over a new leaf? That you're not an abomination?"

Arwan worked his jaw while he opened the door. He watched her over the roof, considering whether there was any use in talking to her at all. "You don't know anything about me, and whether you like me or not, I'm part of your daughter's life." He had to believe that.

Eleuia pushed off the car. "Not anymore."

Talking to her was a waste of time—time he should be using to drive as fast as he could to the airport so he didn't miss his flight. "I have to go." He sat and slammed the door, then pushed the Start button. The car roared to life. It had been a while since he'd driven, but the hum of the engine was a welcomed familiar. He rested his hand on the stick shift.

Eleuia tapped on the passenger window.

Arwan dropped his head. He shouldn't bother rolling it down.

"Half-breed," she said in a singsong tone.

As much as he hated it, Eleuia was still Zanya's mother, and out of respect to *her*, he'd listen to what she had to say—though he had a feeling he'd regret it.

He pushed a button and the window slid down. He stared straight ahead, wringing the leather steering wheel.

"You know you'll never be able to make her happy, don't you?"

Arwan swallowed, his body heat rising. He drew in a deep breath and suppressed the call of the beast.

"It's sick, really." She slowly backed away from the car. "You played with her heart all this time, knowing damn well anyone with underworld blood can't bond with a Riyata. You set her up, *half-breed*, and she'll never forgive you for it."

He pushed the stick into first gear and slammed his foot on the gas. The wheels spun, and the tires screeched against the asphalt.

***

Zanya

When Zanya walked into the study, everyone was huddled around Renato's desk. Arwan was the only one missing. She couldn't help but feel relieved. He was the last person she wanted to see at the moment. Maybe ever again.

Zanya approached the chattering group and leaned on Tara, peeking over her shoulder. "What's going on?"

"Renato found something about Jayden's *condition*."

"Really?" She stretched on her tippy-toes and spied a book splayed open on Renato's desk.

Someone tapped her shoulder. Zanya glanced back at Eleuia, who now stood behind her. Zanya gave her a haphazard smile. "Hey."

"I bet you're pretty happy about all this." She gestured to the book.

"That depends on what Renato found."

"Well, it looks like your zombie friend is going to be okay."

Zanya suppressed the urge to roll her eyes. "That's great, but he's having a hard enough time dealing with what happened without you cracking walking-dead jokes every two seconds."

"Fair enough." She lifted her hands in a gesture of surrender.

Renato scanned the group. "I have very good news. It seems there *has* been one other case like Jayden recorded by the scribes." Renato extended the book. Zanya took it and examined the pages. "His name was Canek, which means 'black serpent.' He was a prince set to inherit the throne of Chichen Itza."

"Where's that?" Zanya asked.

"It's in central Mexico," Eleuia replied. "It's an old Yucatan civilization."

"That's correct." Renato flipped to another page, scanning the entries. "The scribe's journal says the same day Canek was crowned king, he met a princess named Sac-Nicte. They fell in love, but she was betrothed to the much younger prince of Uxmal. On the day of the princess's wedding, Canek arrived and stole his beloved back from the undeserving king. But when she tried to flee with Canek, he was killed by one of the prince's guards.

"The princess was heartbroken, and in mourning, she gave all of her riches to a high priestess in exchange for a powerful blood offering as a payment to Houn to return Canek's soul. Once his soul was returned, the princess ran away with Canek, abandoning their city.

"The scribe wrote that Canek was never the same after his soul touched the underworld. His heart ceased to beat and his body did not need rest. Fearful his beloved would be afraid of him, Canek told the princess it was her love that kept him alive."

Tara sighed and leaned against Peter. "That's so sweet."

"A sweet lie," Zanya mumbled.

"Sometimes a small lie is more humane than the truth," Renato said. "If you know the truth will hurt the one you love."

Zanya huffed. "I'd rather have the cold truth than be lead to believe I know a complete stranger."

"I have to agree with Zanya on this one." Hawa shrugged. "The truth is always better."

"So I'm gonna be okay?" Jayden asked. "Or does that matter to anyone?"

"According to the scribe's journal, the prince retained his immortality in a seemingly healthy state. So, yes, it appears you will be fine."

Hawa grabbed her clutch purse from the corner of Renato's desk. The rhinestones glittered against the light pouring in from the stained-glass windows. "Good. Now we can all go. I have a date tonight." She twirled in her scarlet dress and then strutted toward the door.

"I'm afraid you will have to cancel your plans," Renato said.

Hawa froze and slowly turned. "Excuse me?"

He looked at Zanya. "We have training to do."

***

Arwan

It took almost more than a day to reach Moscow. The airport was crowded and decorated with wreaths and brightly colored lights. Arwan had nearly forgotten that most people in the city celebrated Christmas this time of year.

He stepped out of the building into the night air. Rain soaked the roads beyond the covered area, and the bitter cold sent a chill deep into his bones. He flagged a cab and climbed in the backseat, thankful to be off the plane and in a car. The inside of the bright yellow taxi smelled like pine. The driver turned in his seat and flashed a smile. "Happy Holiday."

Arwan nodded out of respect, though he didn't necessarily agree. The solstice was usually the only time of the year he felt whole. This year he was empty and alone.

"Traveling to see family?" The cabby pulled away from the curb.

Arwan dug in his bag and pulled out some cash. "No." He extended a fifty-dollar bill.

The driver glanced at it in the rearview mirror and took it without turning around.

"Take me to Red Square."

"Sure thing." The driver was quiet the rest of the drive. The streets of Moscow were pitch-black, except for the reflection of the streetlamps on the rain-covered roads.

He pulled to the curb and stopped the meter. "Red Square, sir. This is the side entrance." He pointed toward a narrow street. "Not many people use it, though nothing'll be crowded this time of night."

"Thanks." He grabbed his bag and opened the door. "Any idea where I can find the food market?" That was where the witch had lured Peter into her home. Once he found his way there, he would be able to find Contessa.

"It's a bit of a walk," he said, pointing across the square. "Once you get to those buildings, you have to go all the way back to the market area. But nobody'll be open. They went home hours ago."

"Thanks." He stepped out of the cab and shut the door. The car pulled away, casting red light over the ground when it braked at the stop sign.

Arwan flipped up the collar of his jacket and secured his bag around his shoulder. He followed the cabby's instructions until he reached an alleyway, tucked in the back of the quiet city.

Last time he was here, tourists swarmed the streets. Fresh produce was stacked, carts lined up along the back roads. Now the residents slept, sheltered in their homes from the bitter cold.

Small landmarks led him closer to the witch's home. A yellow-and-green fire hydrant. A small cafe with odd-shaped chairs. A bronze statue of a stately man in a trench coat. It wasn't much farther.

The patter of his shoes striking puddles with each step was a soothing rhythm compared to his chaotic thoughts. He had no way of telling if this would end well, but if he wanted to be truthful with himself, he had nothing to lose even if it went very, very badly.

He and Zanya may be fated, but he would not try

to force her to care for him again. She would have to do that on her own or not at all. And the chances of that happening seemed less and less likely as the days passed, especially with her mother around.

He turned a corner into a shadowed alley, where. townhouses lined each side of the familiar cobblestone street. He crept down the path and paused at a black door with a silver serpent as a knocker. He squared his shoulders and faced the quant home, where a single candlelight flickered in the second-story window.

Just beyond that door were the witch, the book, and more importantly, the truth.

CHAPTER TWENTY-FOUR

Zanya

Zanya readied herself on the mat in the dojo, dressed in her mom's old training gear. She crouched while Peter circled her.

Renato, Hawa, Tara, and her mother stood on the sidelines, watching and coaching her as needed. Jayden and Tara sat on the sidelines.

Zanya had never trained in hand-to-hand combat, but Renato had insisted she learn how to defend herself in case she ran into another situation where her abilities didn't work.

"Be sure to stay balanced and light on your feet," Renato instructed. Zanya leaned forward on the balls of her feet, pivoting with Peter.

Peter charged toward her with an aluminum training knife clenched in his hand. Her stomach jumped and she threw up an electric shield. Peter smacked into it and flew across the mat.

Tara stood from her chair and gasped. Peter skidded to a stop and peered up at Zanya. "No powers." He groaned as he stood. "That's the whole point of this."

She lowered her hands, and her shield instantly dropped. "I am *so* sorry. I got scared, and it just happened."

Peter smoothed out his clothing and then snatched the training weapon off the floor and held it in front of him. "We'll go again."

Zanya nodded and crouched into a fighting stance. "Okay. Ready."

Peter charged.

Zanya leaped to the side and glanced at Renato for instruction. "What now? What if I can't move out of the way?"

"Then the next course of action should be to subdue your opponent using nonlethal force. We do not kill unless it is our last option."

Before Zanya could respond, Peter charged at her again, this time wielding the knife in his opposite hand.

Her stomach clenched, and she threw a kick that landed right between his legs.

Peter's face flushed, and he doubled over on the mat.

Eleuia laughed. "That's some pretty effective nonlethal force."

Peter rolled on the floor, cupping his groin with his hands. Zanya crouched beside him, hovering her hands over his body. "Oh my God, Peter. I'm so sorry."

Tara rushed over and knelt beside him. She shot Zanya a glare. "Are you trying to kill him?"

Zanya stood and looked at Renato. "I suck at

this. Can we stop?"

"Absolutely not. But perhaps it is time for Peter to take a break."

Tara gripped Peter's arm and helped him to his feet, and then guided him to the closest chair.

Zanya hung her head. "I can't believe I did that."

"All right," Hawa said. She stripped off her jacket and dropped it to the floor, grinning while she approached Zanya on the mat. "My turn."

"Are you sure you want to do this?" Zanya asked. "I think I hurt Peter pretty bad." She bit her lip as Tara activated an ice pack.

"Stop procrastinating."

Zanya sighed. "All right. What next?"

"Sprinting isn't just about moving fast," Hawa said. "It's about seeing everything around you in as much detail as possible while moving too fast to be attacked. You will pick out details others can't, and then use your knowledge against your opponent."

"I didn't see details when I was running through Moscow."

"No offense, but that's because you suck at sprinting." Hawa stretched her legs as she elaborated. "You were moving fast, but not fast enough. Once you hit that sweet spot, you'll see a whole new side of your ability." She waved Zanya forward. "Come on. Charge me as fast as you can. No holding back."

"Okay." She crouched like a sprinter on her mark. "Ready?"

Hawa stood casually with her arms crossed. "Just go."

Zanya burst toward Hawa with all of her

strength. It seemed like a split second before she had to screech to a stop so she didn't crash face-first into the mirror lining the back wall.

Hawa stood behind her on the other end of the mat. "You didn't even see me move, did you?"

Zanya shook her head.

Hawa examined the room. "There's not enough space in here. We need to move outside."

"But it's raining," Renato said. "Are you sure it is a good idea?"

Hawa shrugged. "A little rain never hurt anyone. Besides, it'll give her some practice in less than ideal conditions. It won't always be sunny and dry when she needs to sprint like I do."

"I think we're going to stay behind," Tara said, still nursing Peter.

Peter gave a thumbs-up. "I'm good," he grunted.

Zanya sighed. "I feel so bad."

"He's a healer," Renato said. "He will be back to new in no time."

She was thankful for that, but it didn't make her feel any better.

Zanya followed Renato, her mother, Hawa, and Jayden out the back door to the beach. The skies were a deep gray, and the sand was wet and hard with rain.

"Okay." Hawa threw her hair in a ponytail and dug her feet into the sand. "Just try to keep up. I'll start slow."

Zanya mimicked her cousin's stance. "Ready."

Hawa nodded. "Let's hit it." Before Zanya could respond, Hawa was gone.

Zanya sprinted forward.

The sea and cliffs on either side of her blurred into indiscernible smears, though the small roadblocks were still clearly visible.

A piece of driftwood washed up on the beach.

A large rock sat in the sand.

The rain smacked her in the face as she pushed harder to find Hawa. The plump drops of water turned into tiny razors biting at her skin. She finally caught up with her cousin and fell in pace beside her. The ends of Hawa's hair feathered out into what looked like strokes of watercolor in midnight black.

"Nice to see you finally caught up," Hawa said. Her voice sounded so far away. "Let's pick up the pace. You good?"

Zanya nodded.

Hawa pushed ahead. Zanya squinted against the rain and wind, prompting her body to move faster, stronger, more aerodynamically.

The air rippled, and suddenly everything around her slowed down. The raindrops fell, exploding against the packed sand when they made impact. The waves seemed to pause. Each blade of grass, bent over from the force of the cold breeze, creaked with stress. She heard everything, saw everything so clearly. It didn't seem real.

Hawa smiled. "There you go."

Her cousin seemed like a completely different person as an expression of joy and playfulness washed over her. Hawa wasn't just a professional at sprinting, she truly loved it. Now it was obvious why.

"Is that all you got?" Zanya shouted. There was

no telling how far they'd run, but from her best guess, it was at least five miles. "Last one home cooks breakfast tomorrow."

Hawa nodded. "Just so you know, I like my eggs over medium." She pushed forward, flying ahead at an impossible speed.

Zanya hooked a U-turn just seconds before she spotted everyone gathered on the beach ahead. She skidded to a halt, plowing her feet deep in the sand. They covered their faces with their hands as grains showered over them.

Zanya smiled, panting. "Oops."

Hawa stood with one hand propped on her hip. She strutted back to the house. "And biscuits," she said over her shoulder. "With apple butter."

Zanya dusted the sand off her clothes and looked at Renato, whose prideful gaze mirrored her mother's expression.

"I did good?"

Eleuia stepped forward. "You did great."

Zanya's muscles were suddenly weighed down with exhaustion. She swallowed as waves of dizziness threw her off-balance. "Whoa."

Her mother reached out and steadied her. "Take it easy. The vertigo after sprinting that fast can put you on your ass."

Zanya used her mom as an anchor until the tornado in her head stilled. "Yeah, no kidding. Will that happen every time?"

"No. You'll get used to it. It'll just take some practice." Her mother slowly let go of her arm. "Are you okay?"

"Yeah. Thanks." Zanya smiled softly and let go

of her.

Jayden strutted toward her with a crooked grin. "Pretty impressive. You got moves."

Zanya smiled. "Thanks. It was actually pretty cool."

Eleuia's gaze ping-ponged between them and settled on Zanya. "Well, it looks like you need some rest. Maybe your friend here can get you something to eat and keep you company."

"I think I can make it to the kitchen on my own." The vertigo had passed, and now she was just sleepy.

"Yeah." Her mother shrugged. "I just thought you could use some company. Plus he's cute. It couldn't hurt, right?"

Zanya's lips parted. "He's my *friend*."

"But you guys used to date, right?"

"Wha—" She shifted her weight. "How do you know that?"

Eleuia glanced at Renato.

Zanya exhaled and rested her hands on her hips, glaring at her uncle.

"Don't be mad. I dragged it out of him." Eleuia tugged playfully on Zanya's hair. "Besides, the dead kid is well-intended, and at least *he* isn't evil." She analyzed Jayden. "Dead, and still an improvement on your last pick."

Jayden stood silent until her mother left. With his brow raised, he leaned in close to Zanya. "Did your mom just drop a hint about us?"

"*So* not her place."

The door to the house opened, and Zanya glanced back at Tara, who stood in the doorway.

"Done?"

Zanya looked back at Jay. "Do you mind? Even though we live in the same house—in the same wing—somehow I haven't seen Tara for what feels like forever."

His smile faded and he lowered his head. "Oh. No, it's cool."

A streak of guilt ran through her. Besides her and Tara, Jay didn't have anyone to hang out with. "You want to come?"

His head popped up. "Really?"

With everything he'd been through, it wouldn't be right to leave him. "Yeah, really."

He threw his arm over her shoulder, and they started the walk back to the house. It was nice to have Jay back, even if he was a total asshat half the time, and even if he was kinda dead.

"I miss the hell out of you, Zanya. I mean, when you're not around."

"When am I not around?"

He paused and then pressed a kiss on the top of her head. "Never mind. Don't listen to me."

"Jay." She took his ice-cold hand. "I don't care what anyone else thinks about you. I'll always be around. You can't get rid of me."

He walked ahead in silence. Before long, a chuckle pushed out of his chest. "Damn it, Zanya. You have to stop doing this to me."

"Doing what?"

"Saying stuff that makes me think you're not still in love with jungle boy."

Her breath hitched, and the ache in her heart flared. "You can't love someone you never knew."

"But you liked the side of him you did know."

Her heartache dulled, overrun by resentment. She'd been so stupid. After everything they'd been through, he'd screwed her over anyway. "When it comes down to it, we're not over because of who he is. I'm done because he crossed a line. He did the one thing I told him was a deal breaker. Lying by omission is just as bad as lying to my face."

"So you don't believe in the whole *destined to be together* thing anymore?"

She shrugged. "I don't know what to believe, but I do know how I feel. Right now that's all I can depend on."

They walked silently for a while before he spoke again. "Hey, what about the healing sessions?"

Zanya's eyes widened. "Oh my God. I'm so sorry. I forgot all about it since you haven't been in pain."

"It's cool. But I would eventually like for my chest to not look like a piece of gnawed-on trash dragged out by the neighborhood alley cat."

Zanya crinkled her nose. "That's gross, Jay."

"Yeah, no kidding. So, tonight? My room?"

She nodded. "Sure."

They approached Tara, who waited with her foot propping the door open.

Jay held the door open for her. "I think I'll let you two chill without me in the way."

Zanya paused. "But I thought you wanted to come?"

When Tara disappeared into the house, Jay grinned. "Nah. I just wanted to know you wanted me to come."

CHAPTER TWENTY-FIVE

Arwan

Arwan knocked on the door of Contessa's home. It creaked open, allowing warm light to pour out. The scent of savory food wafted from inside.

He stepped back. Everything about the witch put him on edge. She wasn't just powerful but cunning, and the feats of magic she was capable of would keep him cautious. He took off his bag and leaned it against the side of her house.

"Contessa." He dared not enter her home without seeing the temptress—knowing where she was and keeping a constant eye on her.

The voice of a woman echoed from inside.

Arwan arched his brows. The woman's voice was not Contessa's. He would recognize her snaky tone. The voice he heard was soft and silky, full of joy and familiarity.

He pushed the door open to a room lit with the warmth of candlelight flickering in every corner. His mind was pulled back to the home he and his mother had shared when he was a young boy—to the ten nights before solstice, when they spent the evenings filling their home with scented candles, lighting them each by hand to signify the arrival of spring and new life. It wasn't a common practice but something they had begun as a family tradition. He missed it dearly.

He stepped through the threshold, entering a dreamlike atmosphere. A soft haze blanketed the scene in front of him.

A young boy with black hair played with a wooden train on the living room floor. Arwan stared down at the foggy image of himself, all those years ago.

It could not be real, no matter how much he wished it were. Still, he ignored his instincts, all of which were telling him to get out while he could. He hadn't seen his old house since before his mother had passed. It was the only place he'd ever really felt safe.

When he reached out to touch the boy, a woman glided into the room. Her thick, black hair was pulled back in a French braid, and her heart-shaped face beamed with serenity and light. Big, brown eyes gazed down at the boy as she passed.

Arwan's throat ached while he stared after the woman—his mother. He cautiously followed her into the kitchen, where he found her humming as she arranged bundles of herbs in vases. She pressed her nose into a bushel of what looked like mint, and her lips spread into a soft smile.

She raised her gaze, showering him in angelic light beaming from behind her eyes.

He extended his hand, and her image wavered like a mirage. She examined his gesture, then offered her outstretched hand in return.

Her soft laugh carried through the air, becoming louder until it filled the space. The dreamy atmosphere shook with dark energy. Arwan pulled back his hand, and the scene around him melted into puddles of muddled color. His mother's features twisted and contorted into something unworldly. The mask fell away to reveal Contessa, leaning against the counter in a bloodstained satin slip.

A noxious stink filled the air and invaded his nose. The windows were all closed, trapping the odor inside the gloomy room.

Contessa tried to stand straight while gripping her stomach, both amusement and pain woven into her features. Taking slow, backward steps, he examined pages from the book tacked on her walls, many of them now marked with blood.

He'd come here to get something, and he wouldn't leave without it.

"You poor, pathetic boy." She cackled, limping toward him. Her legs were dotted in deep-colored bruises, and her arms crawled with purple veins stretching up her neck. Arwan didn't know much about Contessa, but the witch was obviously clinging to life. She sucked in a gasp and hunched, gripping her ribs. The power radiating from her pressed against his skin. She turned her head to expose a bald scalp on one side.

Arwan squared his shoulders, his eyes locked with the witch's. He had to be calm and strategic. Hopefully, if his plan didn't go well, she would be too weak to fight, and he would escape with his life.

Her eyes narrowed, and she forced herself to stand up straight. Contessa dragged her gaze over the walls of her home, examining the pages on display. "You've come for something in my possession."

She tore a page off the wall and waved it in the air, watching his reaction with a calmness that made his stomach pitch. "I believe this is why you came. To uncover the mystery surrounding your tainted lineage."

Bile churned in his gut from the stench of rot and death.

"As you can tell…" She gasped short, labored breaths. "I am not at my best." Her focus was trained on the pages he held. "Though you could assist me with that, considering I have something of great value to you."

He shouldn't engage her in negotiation, as no encounter with the black temptress would end in his favor. But the truth was, while he stared into her eyes, shimmering with underworld magic, he was not all that different from her. They both shared a common spawning, and if anyone could sway the woman, it was him.

He drew in a deep breath and refocused himself. "What does the page say?"

Her lip curled into a snarl. "If you're willing to give me a fair trade, you'll soon find out." Her face twitched. "Speak quickly, boy."

He studied her failing body. "You've been exhausting yourself. Why?"

She slowly craned her neck and tilted her head,

leering at him with a predatory gaze. "I need more. More than what these weak, insufficient humans can provide. More to complete what I must do." Her sudden fascination with him made the hair on the back of his neck stand on edge. "We can assist each other. You can return my power, and I can provide you with freedom—a way to win back your guardian's affections and rid yourself of the burden you carry." She pursed her lips, gazing into his face. "Such a heavy cross you bear."

The air sparked with black magic. He tried not to notice the dark energy caressing his skin, awakening the dormant creature deep within.

Arwan clenched his fists.

"Ahh." The moan passing through Contessa's lips enticed his darker half, already awakened by the pull of the solstice. "I see you," she said in a singsong tone. "The real you, deep down, fighting to get out." She inched toward him, the page still clenched in her hand. "I can give you peace. All I want in exchange is something you wish to rid yourself of. I can take away your pain." She stretched out her hand and rested her index finger against his chest. "I will tear the darkness out of you." His skin burned from her touch. "And she can love you again."

A war raged beneath the calm surface of his gaze. Their energies clashed and danced. Without some kind of escape, the worst would happen.

Contessa examined the page in her hand. "It speaks of your beloved mother, the martyr."

The way she said the last two words sent a blaze of heat coursing through his veins. He watched the life in her eyes dim as she struggled to keep her finger pressed against his chest. Her arm trembled under the stress.

"What do you mean, 'martyr'?"

"Oh, my poor boy." Her touch scorched his skin, and a crawling ache wound around his lungs. "Your mother was not killed because she bore you. She met her end at her own hand."

The ache clenched like an iron claw, forcing the air out of his lungs. "What? Are you saying my mother committed suicide?"

"This single page will make it clear."

A low growl escaped his throat as his inner darkness bled into his mind, polluting him with thoughts of underworld savagery.

Contessa curled her fingertips into his muscle. "And as for the rest…" Her lips parted, her eyes shining with desire. "I cannot take it without your consent. You are heir to the throne, after all, and your father is still king. You must say it. Say you will give me your power of your own free will."

"You can do that? You can…make me normal?"

"Better than normal, boy. *Immortal*. You can spend the rest of your life with the one you love. Everything you want, I can give to you. All you need to do is to say yes."

Chapter Twenty-Six

Zanya

Zanya sat on the floor of Tara's bedroom, her legs stretched out in front of her.

The brightly decorated room was adorned with Moroccan curtains, woven throw rugs, and satin pillows, all shimmering with silken threads. The curtains on the large bay window were pulled aside, allowing moonlight to spill over the floor, where they lounged on oversized pillows.

They kept the conversation light and casual. Her muscles were still achy from training, and she still hadn't shaken off the waves of dizzy spells from sprinting for the first time. Zanya sighed and rubbed a knot in her shoulder. "I need a massage."

"I thought you were supposed to magically heal from everything, like Peter."

"You'd think so, but using my abilities pretty much strips my energy to nothing."

Tara bit her lip. "Other than that, how are you holding up?"

Zanya shrugged. "Okay, I guess. It's a lot to take in, but I've gotten kinda used to that."

Tara nodded, her red curls bobbing with the gesture. "It's cool you're back, and your mom, too. She seems…" She pursed her lips. "Mmm, different."

Zanya sighed. "Yeah. Too different. I'm trying to get used to it, not that I ever really knew her in the first place."

"You spent a lot of years wishing you did."

Zanya pulled her legs to her chest. "I dreamed about her so much when I was a kid, always wondering what she'd be like. Then when I met her, that image of her was all I had. And now…"

"She's a stranger." Tara's eyebrows drew together. "It's okay if you're disappointed."

Zanya played absentmindedly with a string from the pillow she sat on. "I don't know. It's just weird. My mom is alive. I really shouldn't be complaining." She paused, watching her friend chew on her bottom lip. "What?"

"Nothing…"

Zanya narrowed her eyes.

"I was just thinking about you and Arwan…but I wasn't sure if I should ask."

Zanya blinked, and then lowered her gaze. "I guess I don't know what to say. He seriously betrayed my trust. I'll never be able to look at him the same way again."

"You don't think he deserves a second chance? I mean, I can kind of understand why he didn't tell you."

Zanya jerked her head up. "What?"

Tara shrugged. "Think about it from his point of view. He totally digs you, and it's a fair assumption you wouldn't want to be with him once you found out who he is." She twisted a curl around her finger. "I don't go airing my past out to every person I meet." She ran her hand down her arm. "Not exactly proud of it, you know?"

"You were a little kid when that happened, and it's not even close to the same thing. You can't seriously be sticking up for him."

Tara shrugged. "It's just that I can relate."

"*Unbelievable.*"

"Hey, don't get your panties in a bunch. I'm just trying to be honest. You guys *are* destined to be together, right? Why not at least let him explain?"

"This is ridiculous. What would you possibly have to gain by—" Zanya's shoulders slumped forward. "Oh, of course. I should have seen it sooner."

Tara scratched her arm—a telltale itch that nipped at her skin whenever she was nervous.

"Peter put you up to this, didn't he?" When Tara didn't respond, Zanya lazily pushed to her feet. "Tell Peter I appreciate the sentiment, but I'll deal with my own love life." She tugged on one of Tara's curls to let her know she wasn't completely furious, then checked the clock on the wall. "I have to go. I promised Jay I'd heal him tonight."

"'K," Tara said softly. "But…"

Zanya paused at the door. "But what?"

"Pete's a healer, and he said he can sense it."

"It?"

Tara's green eyes shimmered under the silky

moonlight. "Your broken heart."

***

The warm hardwood floor creaked under her feet as Zanya walked into the west wing, scouting for any sign of Peter or Jay. The bachelor pad was empty and dark, except an idle light from the TV, and a nightlight plugged in halfway up the stairs. "Jay, you here?"

"Up here."

She followed his voice to the top floor and down the hall, where his door hung open. Jay sat on the bed, a guitar cradled in his arms.

She smiled. "Hey, I forgot you started playing that thing. Any better than you were the first time I heard you?"

"I think so. Listen to this." He pressed the tips of his fingers over a few strings on the neck of the guitar. With a pick pinched between his fingers, he strummed an entire song from start to finish without fumbling once.

Zanya smiled. "That was awesome. How did you learn how to play so well?"

He held his hands in the air as if declaring his honesty. "I swear, it's like this kinda-dead thing is helping my memory. I read that book—" he pointed to a how-to guide on the floor, "—and after I did it once, I had it down. It just flows."

She didn't want to be a buzzkill, but any side effects should be noted. "Anything else the *kinda-dead* thing has done to you?"

"Like what?"

She shrugged. "I don't know. Stuff I should know about?"

"Oh." He pointed over his shoulder with this thumb. "Like the wings that are growing from my back?"

She sucked in a breath.

"I'm joking. Calm down."

"That's wasn't funny."

"I have to disagree." He chuckled. "Oh, but there is one other thing. Well, two, actually."

"Okay." She walked to his bed and sat beside him. "What is it?"

"I've been experimenting the last few days, and I've realized I don't actually need to sleep. I wondered if I was the same as the guy in that story, and after I stayed up for a few nights, I wasn't tired. But I get really hungry when I don't sleep.

Zanya's eyes widened. "How hungry, exactly?" If he had developed a hankering for human flesh, they had a problem.

"I ate, like, four sandwiches last night. And a pie."

"A *whole* pie?"

"Hey. I told you I was hungry."

"What about, oh, I don't know…" She glanced at him. "Raw meat?"

Jay crinkled his nose. "Gross."

The knot in her stomach fell loose. "Okay. Not so bad. That's it?"

He shrugged. "So far." He flashed a grin. "I guess you're here for my session, Doctor." He stripped off his shirt.

Thankfully, for whatever reason, the solstice

issue she had around Arwan didn't carry over to her time with Jay.

He pushed scattered strands of hair out of his eyes and lay down on the mattress. Zanya stripped off her shirt. "I won't be able to do this for very long since I've been training all day, but I figure a little is better than nothing." She lowered herself on top of him.

He wrapped his arms around her waist. She resisted the urge to smack away his ice-cold hands. "I'm ready to go if you are. Let's get this party started."

She jerked her head back. "What?"

He raised an eyebrow. "My healing."

Her cheeks flushed with heat. "Right."

His chest jumped with a chuckle.

She aligned their bodies and rested her cheek on the curve of his shoulder. Goose bumps prickled her skin. "God, Jay. You're freezing." She shivered.

"Sorry. Not really something I can control."

"Is it uncomfortable being so cold all the time?"

"At first, but I don't feel it anymore."

She drew in a deep breath, channeling her energy to the surface of her skin. Before long, the healing heat move from her body into his.

Jayden exhaled and laid his head back. His expression turned solemn. She lifted her head and looked down at him. More blond hair was sloppily draped over his forehead, and his crystal-blue eyes were focused on the ceiling. His Adam's apple bobbed when he swallowed.

"You okay?" He nodded. "I would ask if you're in pain, but—" She blinked when the back of his fingers brushed against her cheek. "Jay…"

He ran his thumb over her lips.

"You know…" His voice was soft in the dimly lit room. "I know I've done a lot of shit that makes me a Grade A asshole, but out of it all, I've only regretted one thing." His gaze intensified.

Suddenly she was hyperaware that she wasn't wearing a shirt. She swallowed against a dry throat. "Jay, I don't know if we should be talking about this right now."

"I just want to ask you for a favor. One favor and I'll never ask you to do anything for me again."

She smirked. "Can I get that in writing?"

"Yes."

The complete lack of sarcasm in his tone made her grin vanish. "What is it?"

He quietly contemplated his words. The fact he was thinking—actually thinking before he spoke—set their conversation on a whole new level. A level that made her stomach drop.

He cupped her face and ran his thumb over her cheek. "The one thing I regret is never kissing you good-bye."

Red flags and screeching sirens went off in her mind. "Oh, Jay. No. You can't—"

"Please." The broken expression behind his eyes tore at her. "Just once, without worrying about anything or anyone. Like it used to be. Just this one time. For me." His eyes softened with the arch of his brows. "I should have kissed you good-bye, and it kills me to know I didn't. I should have told you before I left the orphanage, Zanya. And I'm sorry. I never should have left at all."

Her throat ached, her heart racing.

His gaze flickered to her mouth. He lifted his head off the pillow and brought his lips closer to hers. Static and confusion scrambled her thoughts.

All she'd ever wanted was a normal life, with a normal boyfriend who drove a normal car. She wanted to do what regular high school graduates did. Apply to college. Worry about their grades. Live in a crammed dorm room, and stay up late for a party instead of studying for finals.

Now it was clear her life would never be normal. She would never have those things, and she would eventually have to embrace the fact that her future would always be unknown. No stability. No plan. No quaint wedding followed by a house with a picket fence and two kids. She would always live on the edge, and by accepting the responsibility of protecting the stone, she had also accepted her fate.

Jayden's lips brushed against hers. His breath was cold. Everything was so cold.

She rested her hand on his forearm and let her fingers trace his tattoos.

He combed his fingers through her hair and squeezed her tighter.

This was a place she'd never thought she would be again—cradled in Jayden's arms. Getting here had been a roller coaster of ups and downs, and now she may as well have been free-falling.

The ache in her chest flared when her thoughts snapped back to Arwan.

She broke their kiss and scrambled off the bed.

"Zanya." Jayden sat up and watched her slip her shirt back on.

"That shouldn't have happened." Jay didn't respond. She straightened her clothes and walked to the door.

When she paused and looked over her shoulder, his eyes pleaded with her to stay.

"I think it's better if Peter does your healing from now on." She did her best to ignore the softness of his gaze that always drew her to him. He looked at everyone the same way—like cold steel—except when he looked at her. He *saw* her, and *that* was what had caught her heart.

Zanya opened the door and stepped into the hall. "We can't be together like this. Not the way you want to." The cool of his lips lingered over hers. "That can never happen again."

CHAPTER TWENTY-SEVEN

Arwan

Arwan burst out of Contessa's front door into the dreary street. Sweat collected on his brow, his body shaking.

He stumbled forward and grabbed his bag from the ground. It weighed a hundred pounds under his fatigued and battered muscles. He would be lucky to make it to a hotel for the night.

He staggered through the streets like a drunkard, grinding his teeth to push down the urge to vomit. A neon flashing sign reading **'vacancy'** was his salvation.

He slumped against the hotel door and grabbed the handle. He nearly fell onto the office floor when he pushed inside.

The clerk working the night shift slowly stood from his chair. Arwan leaned on the check-in desk, struggling to keep standing. He dug some money out of his pocket and spilled it onto the counter in a crumbled pile.

The clerk stared at him. "Dude. You okay? You look like shit."

An American. Thank God. Arwan pushed the cash closer to the clerk. "I need a room." His voice was raw and coarse. He hardly recognized it.

"Um, okay." The clerk counted the cash and then offered a key dangling from a heavy blue marker that read *room eight*. "Bottom floor."

Arwan's head pounded, and his vision blurred when he reached for the key.

The clerk pulled it out of his reach. "No trouble, right? My boss would kill me if someone died of an overdose on my shift."

Arwan's legs quivered and nearly buckled. He clung on to the cold, dirty counter and shook his head. "No trouble."

The clerk slowly lowered the key into Arwan's hand.

It took every ounce of strength to drag his bag to his room. Arwan fumbled the key into the lock and managed to push the door open. He flipped on the yellow-tinted light to reveal a narrow bed made with a faded brown blanket, a round poker table with a fold-up chair, and a floor lamp in the corner.

He slipped inside and shut the door, then pulled the curtains aside and scanned the empty street for any signs he'd been followed. He would have preferred a hotel farther from Contessa's home, but this was the best he could do under the circumstances.

He snapped the curtains shut and collapsed onto the bed. Springs groaned under his weight, and the scratchy blanket prickled his sweat-slicked skin.

Tomorrow he would find a flight back to Belize. Renato's house. His home.

He closed his eyes, and his mind wandered to an image of Zanya's face.

Her touch.

Her smell.

The force of the solstice kept his heart true to her. Everything he had done was so they could be together.

Hopefully what Contessa had done to him would not have any long-term effects, though only time would tell.

***

Nearly three days later, Arwan landed in Belize. The airports were packed with holiday commuters traveling to see family. This time he was just part of the wandering crowd as he wove between people toward the exit.

Though the fatigue was still settled deep in his bones, his condition was better than it had been the day before. Each morning seemed to bring improvement, and the fact he had not succumbed to any other effects from Contessa's magic left him optimistic.

He caught a trolley to the long-term parking and unlocked the Coupe, then sat in the driver's seat. The engine purred when he turned on the car.

He pulled out of the parking lot, onto the highway. The drive gave him time to think—to wonder what the page of the book would say. Could Contessa have been right when she said his mother had taken her own life?

He gripped the steering wheel tighter, making the color drain from his knuckles. If that were the case, his entire life had been a lie. He'd spent most of his life hating the underworld king, who he'd believed was responsible for her death. All along he should have been angry with her, or maybe himself for becoming the creature she wanted to escape from.

Perhaps *he* had been to blame all along.

Nearly two hours later Arwan pulled into the covered garage at Renato's home. His first priority was to find his mentor and explain where he had been for the last five days. Other than Zanya's mother, nobody was aware he'd gone far enough away to need a car.

The house was empty as he wandered through the wings. Even Renato's study was quiet. He slipped down the hall toward the main wing.

Distant, echoing voices caught his attention. He approached the door to the dojo and quietly pushed it open. Everyone was gathered around the blue training mat. Zanya and Peter were in the center, and her mother, Renato, and Hawa stood on the sidelines.

Arwan softly cleared his throat. Renato glanced over his shoulder and studied Arwan for a moment before slipping away.

Everyone else was too caught up in Zanya's training to notice Renato's absence. His mentor met him in the hall. "Where have you been?" His tone was deep, calm, and yet somehow intense.

Arwan held out the page bearing the Maya

hieroglyphs in fading ink.

Renato let out a deep sigh. "That was what I was afraid of." He pinched the bridge of his nose in silence and then snatched the paper from Arwan's grasp. "You traveled there without me—without anyone knowing, to get *this*?" He shoved the paper against Arwan's chest. "You could have been killed."

Arwan lowered his head. "I know. I almost was." He held the page against his chest with his flattened palm. "She's up to something, Renato. Something terrible. She was deteriorating."

"Did she hurt you?"

"Yes…no." He still wasn't entirely sure. "I managed to escape her house with my life, barely. Her darkness made me sick for days. She touched me. I think that was what caused it."

"But did she cast on you?"

"No. She wasn't able to. She was too weak. But she offered to give me something. Something I had no idea was even possible."

Renato's eyes narrowed. "No gift from that witch is worth accepting. Not when she is so deeply invested in working against our cause."

"Renato." Arwan shifted closer to him. "She told me she could make me normal. Riyata, without the darker half. That she could tear it out of my soul."

His mentor's lips parted and his eyes widened with alarm. "Dear gods in the heavens, please tell me you did not allow her to do this."

Arwan swallowed and took a step back. "Not knowing what she might do with it, I couldn't."

Renato let out a long exhale and patted Arwan on

the shoulder. "Very good, young man. Well done."

"But I still needed this page." Arwan reexamined the symbols. "She said this page contains a piece of my past. Something about my mother."

Zanya's mother approached the open doorway, her focus locked on Arwan. "What the hell are you doing back here?"

"Ellie, please," Renato said sternly. "As far as I remember, this is my home as well, and I welcome him here as long as he needs to stay."

"Fine. But if he's going to stay here, he has to earn his keep." She gestured to the dojo. "Zanya needs training and she's kicking Peter's ass."

Arwan turned to Renato. "This isn't the best time—"

"I wasn't asking." Eleuia stepped aside. "Go ahead. Renato tells me you're quite the martial artist."

Arwan held the paper out to his mentor. "Keep this safe. I'll bring it to Drina for translating as soon as I'm done."

Renato cautiously accepted the page. "Zanya has become quite powerful. Are you sure you want to train her right now? I believe she is rather upset with you."

"Snap-snap," Eleuia interrupted. "We don't have all day. Move it."

Arwan glanced at Zanya's mother, then back to Renato. "It seems I don't have much of a choice."

CHAPTER TWENTY-EIGHT

Zanya

Zanya shifted her weight on the mat as Arwan walked toward the center of the room, Renato and her mom bickering behind him.

"Oh thank God." Peter cradled his ribs. "Where have you been?"

Hawa stood silent while Tara glanced nervously at Zanya. She had every right to be worried. If Arwan stepped one foot on the mat, Zanya would conjure a lightning storm and finish what she'd started.

"Well?" Eleuia said to Arwan. "What are you waiting for? Show her your moves."

Arwan's jaw visibly flexed. He slid off his shoes.

Was he seriously going to try to train her? Zanya exhaled, annoyance stripping away any patience she had left. She had been in the dojo all day. With few breaks and little sleep the night before, she wasn't in the brightest of moods as it was.

Arwan moved to the center of the mat, avoiding

eye contact.

"What are you training on?" When nobody answered, he looked at Zanya.

She turned to Renato. "Is this really necessary? Peter and I were doing fine."

"What?" Peter was still clenching his ribs when he glanced between Zanya and Renato. "But it's good to train with more than one person. That way you can test yourself with different levels of skill." He locked his eyes on Renato. "Right? Tell her I'm right," he whispered harshly.

"Of course he's right," Eleuia said. "Give the poor healer a break. He's done enough work for one day."

Peter mumbled, limping off the mat.

Coward.

"Fine." Zanya threw her hair into a messy bun. "Basic defensive blocks. Upper, middle, lower, and X-block. Got it?"

Arwan nodded. "Ready?"

Her mother laughed and then pressed her fingers over her lips, her eyes bright with amusement.

"Whenever you are," Zanya said.

Arwan threw a basic forward punch. She countered with a side block, and Arwan flew back. Her arm sparked with electricity.

He shook out his hand. "I thought you weren't using your powers."

She grinned. "Oops."

He settled into a fighting stance. "Again." He charged, throwing a downward strike with a hammer fist.

She used an X-block to counter, and the force of

her energy pitched him across the room. He tumbled to a stop at the edge of the mat and slowly picked himself up. He shook his head as if his vision were impaired and rubbed his eyes.

She threw her hands in the air. "You know what? This is a waste of time. I can clearly take care of myself."

"But it's funny as hell." Hawa chuckled, standing beside Eleuia. Now both of them were snickering.

"You may be able to defend yourself with your abilities, but without them, you panic." Renato's words sobered the moods of everyone in the room. "And when you panic, you will end up dead." He gestured to Arwan. "Again."

"No, thanks." She walked off the mat. "I'm done for today." She pushed open the door and marched down the hall. The rhythm of footsteps behind her flared her anger. Only one person would be stupid enough to follow her. She fisted her hands. "Leave me alone."

"We need to talk."

"There's nothing to talk about."

The footsteps quickened until he caught up to her. "Zanya, please. I should have told you, and you have every right to be angry."

"Good, because I was going to be if I had a right or not."

He took her hand and tried to slow her down. She channeled a shock through her fingers, and he yanked back. She spun to face him. "Listen to me. I don't know when you decided I didn't need to know *that* side of you, but I gave you every opportunity to explain. Now it's too late. You told me you were half-underworlder and I was okay with that. Why didn't you tell me the rest?"

"I didn't…" He swallowed. "I didn't want to face it myself. I've spent my entire life denying who I am—pushing it away because my darkness only hurts people. It was the reason my mother died, and it's the reason…" He paused, searching her face.

She crossed her arms, tapping her fingers over her bicep. "The reason what? Because it better be good."

"The reason we will never be able to bond."

Her lips parted. "What?" Her seething anger was suddenly overwhelmed by a wave of unexpected grief. "And you knew? All this time?"

He nodded.

She sharpened her gaze. "It figures. You led me along anyway."

"I never led you anywhere I wasn't willing to go. I know we can't bond, but that doesn't mean we can't be together."

"Yes." She nodded. "Yes, it does." Her throat ached as she stepped back. "I'm meant to bond with someone, and that's clearly not you." Her glare intensified. "Not that I would have chosen to be with you, anyway. Not after this."

***

The next morning, there was a knock at Zanya's bedroom door. She grabbed her stone and sat up. "Who is it?"

"Mom."

Zanya rested her back against her headboard. It was almost ten o'clock in the morning, and her mother was probably there to drag her to the dojo for another full day of training. She rubbed her eyes and sighed. "Come in…I guess." She mumbled the last bit.

"I heard that." Eleuia butted the door open with her hip and stepped inside, a mug in each hand. Zanya was surprised to see her wearing normal clothes, her hair down in waves—like the first time they'd met. "How did you sleep?" The scent of fresh coffee made her stomach growl.

"Okay." Total lie. She gestured toward the mugs. "Is one of those for me?"

"It is." Her mom sat on the foot of her bed and handed her a cup. "Tara made it. I wasn't sure how you like it."

Zanya sipped the sweet, milky brew. "Oh my God. This is so good. And just in time." She squinted at the sun pouring through her window. "I bet Renato has been up for hours. He's probably waiting on me start training."

"Not today. We have special plans."

Zanya took another sip of her coffee. "What's going on?"

"You're going to meet some of the people we are traveling to the winter solstice with. Other Riyata I have gotten to know over the years. They heard about Sarian's death, and it was enough to make them come out of hiding. They want to meet the new guardian. Do you think you can handle socializing for a couple of hours?"

"I guess. How many people are coming?"

"Just a few close friends."

An hour later, Zanya descended the stairs to the empty kitchen. Murmurs leaked through the crack of the French doors that led to the veranda.

"Pretty weird, right?" Jayden walked into the kitchen and settled beside her.

"What's weird?" Besides how totally awkward it was to see him.

He nodded to the doors. "Your mom's creepy friends."

Zanya glanced at the veranda. "They're outside. Right now?"

"Yup." He pulled out a wooden diner chair and took a seat. "So." He propped his feet up on another chair in front of him. "Are we going to talk about what happened?"

Zanya walked around the counter and poured another cup of coffee, the earthy aroma steaming into the air. "Nope." She added some creamer, and the colors swirled together in her cup.

Jayden followed her with his gaze as she walked toward the French doors.

"My mom has guests and she asked me to introduce myself, so whatever you want to say is going to have to wait."

"Until when?"

She drew in a deep breath, readying herself to be socially presentable. "Never."

Zanya pushed open the door and walked outside.

Two olive-skinned teenage boys were throwing gusts of wind at each other in horseplay. They were windbenders, no doubt. They wore clothing that seemed to have come from the Middle East rather than Central America.

A woman with long blonde hair that fell straight and sleek down her back lingered beside the railing, playing with a flame between her fingers. She glanced up at Zanya, her eyes flickering like the flame she'd conjured out of thin air.

Her mother stood from the love seat and smiled. "Zanya. These are my friends." She pointed to the two boys. "Ahmed and Yousef are twin windbenders from the East." The boys dropped their hands, and the unnatural breezes suddenly died.

The tall one with darker hair rested his hand on his chest. "*Marhabah*. My name is Yousef." His gaze flashed at the shorter brother. "This is Ahmed."

Ahmed waved and then shot a gust of wind at Yousef, knocking him onto the sand. The boys picked up where they'd left off, throwing strong gusts at each other in fun.

"And this," Eleuia said, "is Eadith."

The tall blonde stepped forward and clenched her hand, extinguishing the flame into a plume of smoke. "It's a pleasure."

"Nice to meet you."

"Grima and Beigarth are on their way," Eleuia said.

"There are more?"

Her mother grinned. "Many more, but Grima and Beigarth are the only others traveling with us. You'll see more at the solstice celebration."

Zanya leaned against the cool rock wall. "Where exactly are we going?"

"The Tikal Temple, in three days."

"Is it close?"

"South, in Guatemala," Eleuia replied.

Zanya sipped her coffee. "So Tikal is where the bonding ceremony will be?"

"Yes," Eadith said. "It is where the lights of Aurora touch those destined to bond during the great celebration. Your mother says this will be your first solstice?"

"Um, yeah." She turned to her mother. "Arwan said—" She paused, then continued. "I heard about these lights before. But I don't get what they are, really."

"Renato would be able to explain it better. He's good at that kind of thing."

Deep, hearty laughs echoed from the beach. Zanya turned to see Hawa leading a man and a woman over the beach, toward the veranda. The man was dressed in thick wool clothes, and the woman had strawberry-red hair woven into a braid. Her pinkish skin glowed in the tropical sun.

"Here's Grima and Beigarth." Eleuia stepped closer to the railing. "They're originally from Germany, and settled in Ireland—Vikings, from the old country. They may take some getting used to."

"Vikings?" This was just getting better and better. "Not to sound rude, but when I saw Eadith and met the Arabs, I couldn't help but think—aren't all Riyata Maya descendants?"

"At some point in time, yes. I think their grandmother, six or seven generations back, was some kind of earth shifter. There are almost no full-bloods anymore. Now the cultures are so widely diverse. Most of the gifted Riyata don't look the slightest bit Mayan." She shrugged. "That's what happens when you're one-sixteenth Maya—or whatever they are."

"Renato told me Riyata and humans don't end up together very often, so how did they branch out so far?"

Pain flooded her mother's face, and her eyes darkened with grief. "That was the first thing I thought when I met your friend and the healer. He's in for a lot of heartache."

Zanya clenched her cup tightly between her hands.

"Don't go making them feel bad about being together. They'll figure it out."

Zanya examined her mother, who had gone quiet. "Is that why you never talk about my father?"

Her mother swallowed, then glanced down at her empty mug. "There's nothing to say. I selfishly fell in love with a mortal human." She circled the rim of her cup with her finger. "I didn't expect to lose you both so soon, but if I hadn't given you to your father, Sarian would have found us all, and there would have been no heir to protect the stone once you were gone. The obedience spell would have automatically been broken, and Sarian would have had decades longer to do his will." She glanced up at Zanya. "The world would have been lost to their kind."

Thick air lingered between them, only cleared when her mother cast her gaze to the beach. "Grima and Beigarth are cousins. I think you'll really warm up to them."

Zanya blinked, and Hawa was suddenly leaning

against the railing, while the Vikings trailed far behind.

Hawa watched Ahmed and Yousef roughhouse on the beach. "Arabs?"

Eleuia nodded.

"Thar's the wee lass," the man's deep voice bellowed from the beach.

Zanya drew in a sharp breath as she stared at Beigarth's thick finger, pointed straight at her. His wide smile was partially hidden behind thick, wiry facial hair that was the same color as his sister's bright red bow.

Zanya shifted closer to her mom. "What do they do?"

"They're petrifiers."

"That doesn't sound good."

"It's exactly how it sounds. They don't use their ability often because it's not reversible and obviously lethal. There aren't many of their kind left."

"I should be able to do it—petrify—right?"

Her mother's lips pursed, and the edges of her mouth turned down. "There are some abilities even I couldn't master as the guardian. Theirs was one of them. Petrifying is one of the most difficult to control, and it's more exhausting than any other ability. Worse, if you don't know how to control it, it's likely to backfire."

Zanya made an *O* with her lips. "Maybe that's why I haven't read much about it in any of Renato's books."

"There's still a lot for you to learn. But for today, let's get to know some of your new friends."

CHAPTER TWENTY-NINE

Arwan

Drina's house lay just over the hill. The cramps in Arwan's stomach increased with every step. His mind reeled with possibilities of what the page would say, most of them filling him with disappointment.

He rounded a twist in the path and stopped when he spotted Drina's hut in the distance. He slid his hand into his pocket and brushed his fingers against the rough edges of the textured paper. Maybe not knowing would be better. Then he could live the rest of his life believing his mother was an innocent victim who died still loving him. Destroying the page would give him that option, though it would mean spending forever in regret.

As if he needed another reason to hate himself.

He pressed forward until he reached the hut. "*Tia* Drina?"

"*Si.*" The old woman's voice sounded tired. "*Entra*, Arwan."

Of course she'd seen him coming. Drina's link to the magic of the Maya kept her well aware. He pushed through the flap into her modest home.

Drina sat on a woven mat beside a basin of clear liquid. Flower petals, sand, seashells, and herbs formed a circle around her.

"What are you doing?" Arwan asked.

She placed a handful of dried herbs in the water. "Preparing," she mumbled.

"For what, exactly?"

He hadn't seen a traditional Maya ritual done in many years. His curiosity must have annoyed her, because the old woman scowled. "You need answers?"

Arwan nodded.

She sprinkled wild jasmine flowers into the basin and then dropped in pebbles that instantly sank to the bottom. His muscles clenched when she extended a knife. "We need blood offering."

Arwan took the blade. He had just healed from slitting his own wrist, with a scar to remind him of the nightmare. "I was hoping not to make a habit out of this." He ground his teeth and dragged the blade over his forearm. Blood rose from the wound. He extended his arm over the bowl, allowing plump droplets to fall into it.

The scarlet dispersed into the water, tainting it a light pink.

Arwan applied pressure to the cut. He hadn't gone deep—just enough to draw blood. The wound would heal on its own, without a healer's touch. He watched the bowl, waiting. Whether there would be a written message, or perhaps some kind of image, he wasn't sure. After a moment, he looked at Drina. "What's going to happen?"

She frowned. "Magic takes time, boy. Not everything happen so quick. Have patience."

Arwan checked his cut. It had already stopped bleeding. He wiped his bloodstained hand on his pants and pulled the page from his pocket. She snatched it from him and unfolded it in her lap. Her wrinkled fingers pinched the page as she examined the markings. A deep sigh and the drop of her head made his chest tighten.

She gently placed the page into the basin. Water curled around the edges and crept on top, dragging it down to the rocks. The ink bled, and the glyphs smeared.

Arwan sucked in a breath and reached to pull it out, but Drina smacked his hand away. "Patience. Anyone can copy a page of t'e book, but only bloodletting can tell if it is true. If t'is is from Contessa, we make sure it is real before anyt'ing." She leaned over the basin, watching the dark ink merge with the bloodied water.

Drina rested her wrinkled hands on the rim of the bowl, and her graying black hair fell on either side of her face.

The space was silent and the air was still. Arwan shifted. "I want to know."

Her shoulders rose and fell with each breath. It seemed as if she was stalling, or perhaps she didn't want to be the person to say it aloud. If that were the case, he would confront it head-on.

He sat beside her. "Is it true? Did my mother kill herself because of me?"

The old woman nodded, and she swallowed. For the first time since Arwan had known her, Drina's eyes shimmered with tears. "T'at is what t'e page says." She reached into the bowl and cupped her hands under the page, rescuing it from its watery grave. As she waited for the rest of the water to roll off its surface, her eyes narrowed. "Wait, t'is is not right." She peered at it closer. "It does not say she killed herself, it says…she gave her life." She carefully splayed the wet page on a stone slab he often saw her knead bread on. "T'ere is a difference in t'e words. She gave her life—her immortality." She peered closer at the page. "T'is cannot be right."

"What?" He examined the paper even though he couldn't read it. "What does it say?"

"Your mot'er gave her longevity before she was sacrificed."

"What do you mean, '*sacrificed*'?" The word made his body temperature spike.

"Just what I said, boy. Sacrificed, by t'e gods of Tamoanchan."

"Sacrificed by the heaven gods?"

She stared up at him, her lips parted. "Yes, Arwan. T'e heaven deities, t'e gods of Tamoanchan, chose your mot'er to be given to the king of the dark realm. T'ey chose her, and she agreed."

If she'd been a victim, he could have gone on believed it had all been a great injustice. Something out of her control. Now he was forced to understand she'd actually *chosen* to consummate, and after she'd conceived him, she chose to leave.

***

The walk back to Renato's house went fast, but the familiarity of the jungle didn't bring him any peace. The trees became sparse as he neared the beach and the ground changed from the soft, mossy turf to loose sand. He broke through the tree line to see a group of people standing outside Renato's house.

He didn't recognize any of them. Something had to be wrong. He broke into a sprint, working to propel himself over the beach.

A tall, lanky blonde turned to face him. Her dark brows bowed under a glare, and her eyes flared as red as rubies. When she extended her hand, a flame bellowed toward him as if shot from a flamethrower. He ducked and rolled under the inferno, then quickly gained his footing and pushed forward.

Their house was under attack and he hadn't been there to fight. Why hadn't Marzena called him? Perhaps she was wounded, or worse. If anything had happened to Zanya, he'd never forgive himself.

A man with bright red hair and a thick beard stomped toward him over the sand, his lip curled in a snarl. Two men wearing turbans and robes stepped into sight.

Arwan sized them up as he charged forward. The woman was a fire conjurer, but he couldn't get a read on the other three. If he took out the husky older man first, maybe the others would fall back.

Using the man's weight against him, Arwan skidded at his ankles to strike him, sending the stranger head over heels. The man thudded to his back on the sand and let out a loud wheeze.

Fierce winds formed a roaring cyclone around him, carrying sand in its force. He strained to see beyond the barrier, but it was impossible, and jumping through it would hurt like hell. He ground his teeth and covered his eyes, then leaped through the sandstorm. Grains slashed at his skin, and warm blood dripped down his cheek and arms.

The blonde was waiting on the other side with a fireball in her cupped hands. It grew between her palms until it was a bright storm of flames, rolling and flickering with light.

"Hey!" Zanya hung halfway out the door to the kitchen, staring at them with wide eyes. "He's with us!"

The blonde slowly smothered the ball of fire until it was no more than a puff of black smoke that vanished into the air. She pursed her lips. "Next time consider announcing your arrival." She raised her chin, showcasing her fair skin and a gaze as sharp as steel. "Then we may not try to kill you." Blonde strands whipped around her. When she turned, her long coat carried in the air behind her.

Zanya stalked toward him, glaring almost as fiercely as the fire conjurer. Half of her hair was pulled up. The other half was draped over her shoulder. She looked stronger. More hardened. "Where the hell have you been?" Zanya snapped.

Her scornful tone slammed him back into reality. She hated him, even though the book was wrong about them being fated, and even if he didn't deserve her a damn bit.

"I had to see Drina."

Zanya paused. "Oh. Right." She crossed her arms over her chest, and the flush in her cheeks faded. "The page from the Popol Vuh." She gave a tiny shrug. "Renato told me."

The husky, red-haired man grumbled as he passed them.

Arwan raised an eyebrow. "Who are these people?"

"Friends of my mom. Other Riyata. Apparently we're not the only ones in a hundred mile radius."

"I thought we were the only ones on this continent." The two younger men in robes strode side by side, whispering in Arabic.

"What about the page? Did you get what you were looking for?" She brushed away strands of hair that had blown across her face from the sea breeze.

He suppressed the urge to do it for her and cradle her cheek in his hand…feel the warmth of her skin. He swallowed and averted his gaze.

"Listen. Just because we aren't…" She paused and shifted her weight. "It doesn't mean I don't care. I know how much it means to you to find out what really happened to your mother."

"She betrayed me," Arwan growled, unable to hold back the pain tearing through his heart.

Zanya's gaze softened. "I don't understand."

"It's not hard to understand." He locked eyes with her. "She gave herself up, knowing she'd be killed. She gave up her longevity so she didn't have to watch me grow up and see what I am. She became a willing sacrifice, and worse, a willing bride." The darkness inside of him flared. He narrowed his eyes. "She hated me, and she would have rather died than stay with me. *That's* what the book said, and that's the truth I will have to live with for the rest of my life."

CHAPTER THIRTY

Zanya

Renato's study was more crowded than ever. Zanya sat on the love seat beside Tara, and Peter squished them closer together when he took the seat on the other side.

The two petrifiers, Grima and Beigarth, stood by the fireplace at the back of the room, warming their hands. Zanya recognized their soft conversation by their deep accents, distinguishable from the combined chatter of the group.

The man seemed jolly, like Santa in Celtic wear. His hair was slightly frizzy, and his red beard was wild, except for the single braid on either side, keeping the facial hair at least slightly maintained. His sister was just as broad-shouldered, giving her the stereotypical Viking stature but with the features of an Irish maiden. Her pink-toned skin was dotted in freckles and was framed with thick strawberry-red hair. She seemed kind. Zanya sensed a warm energy from them both. Her stone liked them, too.

The Arab brothers, Ahmed and Yousef, looked

nothing alike, even though they were twins. Still, their lighthearted nature was a welcome change from the heavy air that lingered in the home. They spoke mostly Arabic and some broken English. Thankfully, Renato was fluent in Arabic and often chattered with them in their native tongue.

And Eadith, the blonde fire-thrower, carried herself like a French socialite. She stood with such pride and grace that the prospect of sparking a conversation with her was almost intimidating.

Regardless of her slight insecurity around the newcomers, they all seemed to welcome her with open arms. Sure, this was her house, but she had only been a part of this world for months, and they could have just as easily turned their backs and rejected her. Maybe her mother's presence put them at ease, but she appreciated their affable spirits regardless.

Renato cleared his throat as he sorted through a stack of manila envelopes. He wore a smile she hadn't seen for a quite some time. "Very well." He handed out envelopes to each person in the room, starting with Marzena, who stood silently to his right. It seemed like forever since she'd seen the dreamwalker. She had to remind herself that even though Marzena lived in the north wing of the home, she appreciated her privacy more than the average person.

"These are our travel itineraries."

When he handed one to Tara, her eyes lit up with excitement. "I'm going? Seriously?" She clasped the envelope against her chest and beamed up at Renato.

He chuckled and nodded. "Yes, *seriously.*" The word pushed out of his lips in an unnatural way. "The solstice would not be the same without you."

Jayden was the first to examine the tickets. "A train. Sweet."

"I was not sure if everyone had the necessary paperwork to fly, and Guatemala is not far."

"It's comin' up quick." Beigarth clenched his fist in front of him and flexed his arm. "I can feel it in me veins."

Renato smirked. "Our new friend is right. The winter solstice is around the corner, and this will be the first year we travel with a group since Ellie left." He took a moment, and then exhaled. His gaze rested gently on Zanya's mother. "It feels remarkable to be able to speak about you as being alive."

Her mother bowed her head in a playful gesture.

"This'll be the lass's first year." Grima's chubby cheeks pushed out in a broad smile. "She's a wee bit wet behind the ears, she is."

Heat rose in Zanya's face. "Yeah." She cleared her throat and turned to her uncle. "Mom told me you would explain more about the lights?"

Renato finished passing out the envelopes, leaving two on his desk. One had to be his, and the other must have been for Arwan, who was absent from the meeting.

"The lights of Aurora are more commonly known as the Aurora Borealis, or northern lights."

"I've seen pictures of them. But I thought you could only see them in really cold places like Alaska and Canada."

"A common misconception." Renato removed his pipe from his desk and lit it with a strike of a match. "The lights of Aurora are visible from anywhere in the Northern Hemisphere. In fact—" Plumes of smoke filled the air. "The Maya were the first to recognize the power behind the lights. Then, in 1621, a French scientist named Pierre Gassendi named the lights after the Roman goddess of dawn, Aurora. He was an eccentric fellow for a man of science, as I recall. And I was beside myself when I learned the lights had been named after a Roman goddess rather than a Mayan goddess."

Eleuia groaned. "Please don't get him started on that again. We'll never hear the end of it."

Zanya chuckled. "So, what do you know about the power of the lights?"

"Scientists long ago disclosed how the lights occur. When highly charged electrons from the solar winds collide with elements in our planet's atmosphere—like nitrogen and oxygen, for example—the interacting elements create the illuminations. The color depends on which gases meet."

"Okay, but I don't see how that applies to us."

"The one variable that scientists—or any other people on earth—have failed to consider is *how* the gases are pushed down."

Zanya raised her eyebrows. "Um." She wanted to be able to offer an intelligent answer, but she fell flat.

"The reason the gases are pushed down, the reason the winter solstice is so precious to us, and the reason bonds are able to be made, is because the gods of Tamoanchan descend from the heavens, moving through the atmosphere as they descend to earth, and grace us with an affirmation that yet another spring will be underway."

"But…" She squeezed out of her cramped seat and leaned against the armrest. "What you're saying is we're actually going to *see* the heaven gods—the gods of Tamoanchan?"

"No, not see them. No one has ever actually laid eye on the heaven deities. But when two Riyata choose to bond, the gods use the lights as a means to embrace the couple's commitment. That is how the bond is sealed."

She stiffened her lips and looked away. "Or the gods just decide *for* you that you *can't* bond." She couldn't hold back the bitterness edging her tone. She glanced up at her uncle. "You know. No free will and all that jazz."

"They do not decide for us. Usually we decide for ourselves, as everyone else has the right to. But just as a fish and a bird cannot live beside one another, some bloodlines are just not compatible. Two Riyata *are* fully compatible, and the gods pair them as a favor."

"But shouldn't two people be able to decide on their own if they want to be together?"

Her mother huffed. Zanya glanced over her shoulder, and her mom shrugged. "Sorry. It's just that you remind me of myself when I was your age."

"And exactly how long ago was that?"

Her mother's lips fell open. "Touché."

"Regardless," Renato continued, "the gods of

Tamoanchan have been around much longer than any of us, and it is with our best interest in mind that these rules are set in place."

The echo of footsteps on the wood floor caught Zanya's attention. She turned to see Arwan walk into the study and cross the room toward Renato.

"Ah. Just in time." Her uncle extended the envelope.

"What's this?"

"Travel plans," Hawa leaned against Renato's desk, using her envelope as a fan. "Solstice, remember?"

He silently examined the envelope in Renato's hand. "I don't know if I'll be going this year."

Renato quickly removed the pipe from his mouth. "Why wouldn't you attend?"

Arwan glanced at Zanya. She did her best not to show any visible signs of the anxiety bubbling in her chest. He dragged his gaze to her mother and then to the other faces in the room. "Of course I want to go. And I would…" He turned toward Eleuia. "But only if it's all right with you."

Eleuia stood in silence.

Arwan stepped forward, never breaking eye contact with her. "I will only attend if you allow me to travel as part of the group. With you, your daughter, and the rest of the Riyata. Otherwise, I'll stay behind. It's your first solstice since you've come home, and I won't impose on it if I'm not wanted."

The room fell silent.

Zanya's skin burned with anticipation. He'd been through so much. For him to stay behind while everyone attended the celebration would be like rubbing salt in his wounds. Maybe she couldn't be with him—*wouldn't* be with him—but that didn't mean he deserved to be excommunicated.

Her mother examined him. "You're serious."

When Arwan didn't respond, her lips slowly closed, and she looked at Zanya, who tensed under her sudden attention. Eleuia looked back at Arwan. "Fine. Come along, half-breed. It's not as though you'll be able to do anything anyway."

CHAPTER THIRTY-ONE

Zanya

Zanya shoved and pushed through the crowds in the train station. She gasped when someone shoulder-checked her, nearly knocking her off-balance. She glared back at the stranger, readying an energy ball that would zap him so hard it would burn the hairs off his ass.

Her mother grabbed her arm. "Keep walking." She pulled Zanya's forward. "I've seen that look before."

"I wasn't going to do anything," Zanya mumbled.

"Somehow I don't believe you."

"I'm sorry." Renato acted as a plow to clear a path for Marzena, who followed close behind him. "It is just days before Christmas celebrations, so even the train station here in Guatemala is rather busy."

"No kidding," Tara said, clinging to Peter's arm.

The train ride had been long. Thankfully she'd

had her own bunk with a travel-size pillow, a soft mattress, and thick velvet curtains that blocked out the light. With the rhythmic motion of the train, she was able to sleep through most of the trip. And when she wasn't asleep, she lay back in her bunk and played an imaginary violin, humming the notes while she glided the air-bow over the strings. When they returned home she would start playing again. She longed for the peace it gave her.

They hiked to the outskirts of the train station, where taxis and busses waited along the curb. "We have to take two cabs," Renato said. He flagged down a six-passenger transport van. When it pulled up, Renato opened the front passenger door and pointed to another van behind them. "There is another cab for the rest of you."

Zanya slipped into Renato's cab, taking the window seat. Tara and Peter sat in the far back. Hawa settled in beside them. Arwan sat in the seat next to Zanya.

Zanya curled into her seat and turned her attention to the commuters hustling past. Part of her wished the winter solstice would just pass and she could go back to feeling like herself again. Sure, her powers were stronger than ever, but her emotions were all over the place, and she could barely stand the constant longing that haunted her every waking moment.

The van creaked and rocked to the side when Beigarth took a seat beside Arwan. His freckled lips rose into a full smile. "Ye ready, lad?" He elbowed Arwan in the ribs.

He grunted from the blow and nodded. "Ready."

Beigarth clenched his fist in front of him and flexed his arm, as if the gesture related everything he wanted to say.

Thanks to the Beigarth's natural cheer, the weight that had settled in her gut had all but vanished. She turned back to the window and leaned on her bag, watching as more crowds hustled by.

Her focus shifted to Arwan's reflection in the glass. He was watching her.

The heat radiating from his skin made her uneasy. She secured her grip on her pack. It was just her luck to get stuck beside him the entire ride.

She rested her forehead against the cool glass, and her breath fogged the window.

Beigarth settled deeper in his seat, shifting Arwan even closer. His leg pressed against hers, and her stomach warmed with butterflies. It didn't take long for the warmth to morph into sharp pains. She gripped her belly.

"Are you okay?" His voice came out in a cool, smooth whisper.

She hated him for talking to her.

If he could only read her thoughts, he'd see how *not* okay she really was. She nodded, squeezing her eyes shut.

His hand rested on her forearm. "Zanya."

She balled her fist, and he quickly withdrew his touch.

"Please talk to me," he said softly. She could barely hear him over the multiple conversations filling the van's cabin. He leaned in closer. "Can I just say something?"

She fogged the glass again with a long exhale. "What?"

"I wanted to say I'm sorry."

She scoffed and rolled her eyes. "Too little, too late, don't you think?"

"Yes." His tone was solemn, which brought her anger down a notch. "I know I can't say anything to make up for the way I've treated you." He rested his other hand over the top of hers. This time she couldn't bring herself to pull away. "The truth is, even if I hadn't kept my secrets, I still don't deserve you." He removed his hand from hers, leaving her skin cold.

She clenched her eyes shut, fighting the raw ache in her throat. "You're such an asshole."

His deep sigh worsened the ache in her chest. "I hope you can enjoy the solstice. It's really something. Like nothing you've ever experienced."

Almost an hour later, they arrived at the entrance of the ruins. When the cab finally came to a stop, Zanya impatiently waited for the door to open and her turn to climb out of the taxi.

She and Arwan hadn't said a word to each other for the rest of the drive.

The shocks squeaked and the van rocked when Beigarth stepped outside. Arwan followed the petrifier, and Zanya sat in the taxi, waiting as the rest of them filed out, until only she, the cab driver, and Renato remained.

Her uncle turned in his seat. "Are you ready, Zanya?"

She gazed out the window at the growing crowd. "Is everyone here Riyata?"

"No. But those who are not Riyata are Maya descendants and locals, all of whom enjoy the holiday as much as we do."

"So how do we tell the difference between them and the Riyata?"

"Unfortunately, unless the lights reach down and bond them, or they introduce themselves, we won't."

"Oh." She gripped her bag and slid to the end of the bucket seat. Arwan stood just outside, talking to Beigarth. A sad smile found her lips, and she lowered her head.

"Zanya." Her uncle's soft voice made her look up. "Are you all right?"

She shrugged.

Renato turned to the driver. *"Excusanos un momento, por favor?"*

The cabby nodded, stepped out of the taxi, and shut the door behind him.

Renato removed his pipe from the inner pocket of his jacket and ran his finger over the surface, touching the intricate carvings. His expression softened, lost in thought. Her focus shifted to the images carved into the white bone.

Elephants and caribou formed a ring around the pipe's bowl, and small *M* shapes mimicked birds soaring in the sky.

Renato's hand was steady, but the way he breathed, quiet and controlled, made her chest tighten. "Have I ever told you how I acquired this pipe?"

She shook her head.

"This pipe was given to me by my closest friend,

Barout. After the Maya civilizations collapsed, many of us separated into clans and lived as nomads. Barout was part of my clan, as was your mother, and dozens of others. His sister also traveled with us." His gaze slowly drifted into the distance. "Her name was Ysalane."

Zanya sank back in the seat. The pain with which he spoke her name made it clear he had loved her. "Were you guys bonded?"

Renato shook his head. "Ysalane and I never had the chance to bond." He was silent for a long moment before he spoke again. "She passed before the solstice arrived that winter. Barout gave this pipe to me the night before he left. I have not seen or spoken to him since. The death of his sister tore the heart from his very chest." His Adam's apple bobbed. "And from mine."

She watched Arwan through the open door of the cab. "What was she like?"

"She had a beautiful voice and would often sing fables to keep our spirits high. And she loved the ocean. She wore earrings made of white seashells. They were small and spiraled. She wanted children—" His voice caught. "I miss her so very much. The void in my soul has never been filled."

Zanya pulled her knees to her chest and searched for something to say, but there was nothing. When someone was cut so deeply, time didn't always heal the pain.

She rested her chin on top of her knees and peered out the window at the stone temples. Once they'd been the pride of the Maya civilization; now they were only visited by tourists, Mayan descendants, and then the Riyata, who came just once a year for the winter solstice. While she admired the debilitated city, one fact stood out in her mind.

Growing up sucked.

When she was younger, it was easy to blame her heartache on everyone but herself. Her mother for abandoning her. Her father for probably ditching her mom long before she was born—before Zanya knew the truth. Her doctors for not believing she wasn't crazy. God, if he even existed. She'd been a victim of circumstances her entire life, and believing *that* made her feel better. A little less responsible for being so screwed up.

As she grew older, she learned she'd have to eventually stop pointing fingers and make the decision to move past the pain. She also realized she'd have to take control of her future and fight for something more than what life had handed her. It was the only option, aside from ruining any chance she had at a real life.

"I don't want you to live in regret, Zanya. Do not live like me. Arwan is a good man. I understand he wronged you, but regardless of what your mother may say, his heart is *not* black. It would be such a transgression of love if you robbed yourself of the opportunity to care for someone as much as I cared for Ysalane."

She smiled softly, and a stinging tear slid down her cheek. "Thanks, Renato." She shrugged. "But we're just not meant to be. Even if I could forgive him, we can never be together." She lowered her head. "It was all a mistake. One big, horrible mistake."

CHAPTER THIRTY-TWO

Arwan

The air was cool on the evening of the solstice. Arwan drew in a deep breath as he stood alone, admiring the abandoned hills in the lowland. His mind wandered through time, recalling the first winter solstice he'd attended as a young man, when the ruins were not ruins, but mighty temples at their greatest.

He would never forget the first time he stood in the lowlands at the base of the Temple of Tikal, staring at the top of the temple, where the shaman stood beside the ruler of the kingdom. The king and his soothsayer had been dressed in brightly colored clothing and jewelry made of turquoise, gold, and amber.

Large fires were scattered between temples, turning the dark skies orange and red. Attendees dressed for the occasion. Women wore chokers made of coral and decorated their hands and feet with henna, which made their olive skin stand out against the silky moonlight.

Offerings would be placed around the flames—sweet-berry wine, maize, and handmade glass beads served. There was no blood shed that day for sacrifices, as the winter solstice was about life, not death.

But it was the drums that made the solstice truly memorable. As a young man, he'd wandered between the temples, watching musicians gather in groups. They braced drums between their legs and beat their palms over stretched ox-hide, infusing the night with rhythm and life.

"Arwan. Look." Renato's voice pulled him back to his current place in time. He turned to the horizon, where the sun slowly dipped below the rigid mountains in the distance. "It will begin soon."

Renato turned to Zanya and pointed to where they would stand when the lights appeared. The higher they were, the better, which was why royalty had claimed their seats at the top of the ruin in the past. Now no one was allowed on the stone structures, as they had been deemed a world heritage site long ago.

The rest of the newcomers gathered together, excitedly chatting and taking amongst each other. Arwan stood on the outside of the circle and dropped his head. The darker half of him was silent—for now.

A man dragged a crate of food past him, and Arwan pulled off his thin jacket and rested it on the ground. Renato noticed and nodded, giving him permission to help with the preparations.

Arwan approached the group of men gathered

near the truck of supplies and lifted a wooden crate of corn into his arms. They would use maize as offerings tonight, just as their ancestors had done from the birth of their empire.

His muscles flexed under the weight as he carried the crate down the steep hill to the valley. He appreciated having something to do—anything other than being lost in his thoughts.

It took nearly two hours for him and the men to haul the last of the corn to the fire pits. By the time he placed the final crate on the ground, his skin was slick with sweat. He lifted his arm and wiped his forehead, then turned to the hillside, where an older woman stood alone with a heavy shawl draped over her shoulders.

Arwan smiled. The solstice celebrations wouldn't have been the same without Drina.

He hiked up the hillside toward the group. The air became cooler as he distanced himself from the glowing fires. When he reached the top of the hill, Drina was standing with her back facing him. He placed his hand on the old woman's shoulder. Without turning around, she reached across her chest and rested her hand over his.

"I'm glad you made it, Drina. I was hoping—"

She turned and smiled sadly. "I would not have left you to celebrate alone." She glanced at the rest of the group, clustered together just yards away.

"I would've been fine. But thank you."

She patted his cheek with her wrinkled hand and smiled. "Cualli and Balam are here." She turned toward the nearby forest. A pair of yellow eyes glowed from the thick of the tree branches. Drina tugged on his arm. "Go. Go enjoy t'e lights from t'e lowland of t'e valley wit' your people."

***

Zanya

"It is almost time." Renato turned to Eleuia. "Are you ready?"

Eleuia beamed, dressed for the occasion in a green, blue, orange, and cream patterned dress.

Zanya hadn't had the foresight to bring something special to wear for the event. She glanced down at her jeans and T-shirt paired with sandals.

Renato and her mother smiled at each other. "We have something for you. For your first solstice." Her mother revealed a package she had hidden behind her back.

Zanya examined the burlap tied with a thin piece of rope. "What is it?"

"We picked it up for you in town," her mother said. "Actually, Renato picked it out. He said you would wear it well."

Zanya took the gift and glanced up at her mother. "Should I open it?"

Renato chuckled. "I would hope so. And you may use the cab to change if you'd like. The driver is enjoying the festivities. You will have your privacy."

Zanya's breath stalled while she gently tugged the twine loose. The folds of burlap fell open to reveal fabric—deep blue patterned with gold and burgundy diamonds.

"It's a dress. And there's something else in there, for your stone." Eleuia slipped a leather bracelet out from between folds of the fabric. "I thought maybe you could use a place to keep it with you all the time, now that you've shrunk it down to a more portable size."

Zanya's lips parted. "But how…"

"Renato told me." Her mother grinned. "Very clever. I never thought of doing that."

Zanya dragged her fingers over the soft fabric. "It's beautiful. Thank you."

"Let me help you with this." Her mom rested the bracelet on Zanya's wrist and wound two braided straps around several times, then tied it in a knot. On the main strap of the bracelet was a pouch, just large enough to house her stone.

"Did you make this?"

Her mother smiled. "It's been a long time since I've done any leather sewing, but I think it came out pretty good." She brushed her fingers along Zanya's hand as she pulled away. "Now go change into your dress so I can see it on you."

As Renato had promised, the cab was empty. Inside, she quickly stripped and wrapped the dress around her body. The fabric brushed against the tops of her feet, and a golden rope hung around the waistline. A single shoulder strap went over only one shoulder, leaving the other one bare.

She pulled her stone out of her jeans pocket and held it between her fingers. It glowed and swirled with color, as if cooing with joy. She smiled. "It's pretty exciting, right?" The stone buzzed in affirmation. Her smile faded. "And you've got a new home. Compliments of Mom." Zanya tucked the stone in the pouch on the top of her bracelet and tied it shut. The stone's light pushed through, illuminating the edges of the pocket. "What do you think?" It hummed in a low tone, then fizzled out. "Oh, come on. You'll warm up to it." Her stone flashed with annoyance. Zanya chuckled and pushed open the taxi door.

She stepped out of the cab onto the cool, soft earth. Her mother waited with Renato, her hands perched on her hips. "Well then." She scanned Zanya head to toe. "You look…" She swallowed and pressed her fingers over her lips. "You look beautiful."

Zanya fiddled with the strap of her dress.

"Here." Her mother stepped behind her. "There's a button back here to keep the dress from coming loose. She pulled the fabric tighter and secured it in place. "There."

Zanya admired the patterned fabric, soft and flowing against her skin with the gentle breeze. "Thanks, you guys. It's beautiful."

"I couldn't have you attend your first solstice in jeans." He glanced over Zanya's shoulder. "Looks like someone else has taken notice."

Zanya turned to see Jayden staring at her with his arms crossed over his chest and a crooked grin. She turned back to her mother, suppressing a smile. "He's such a clown."

"A handsome clown." She stepped around Zanya. "We should join the others. It's almost time."

When they passed him, Jayden raised an eyebrow. "Wow."

She lifted her finger. "Enough, Jay."

"Hey, most women appreciate a compliment."

She dropped her hand and smiled. He was right. At least he wasn't being a *total* ass. She smoothed down the fabric with her palms. "Thanks."

Jay extended his arm. "Shall we?"

She snorted. "Suddenly you're a gentleman?"

"I had to try it sometime." He winked and looped her arm in his, and they walked toward the rest of the group.

The energy of the night sparked in the air, flickering around them, mixing with the twinkle of stars and fireflies.

Zanya spotted Drina lingering at the edge of the group. "I'll be right back." It would be rude not to greet Drina after everything she'd done.

The old woman's eyes lit up at her approach. She clapped her hands in front of her and skimmed her gaze over Zanya's attire. "*Hats'uts!*"

Zanya didn't need to know Mayan to understand the sparkle in her eyes—beautiful. "Thank you, Drina." She took the woman's hands. "It's so nice to see you here."

The old woman nodded. "You are going to remember t'is night forever." She rested her finger on Zanya's chest. "Is very special."

She squeezed Drina's other hand. "That's what everyone keeps telling me."

A tiny gasp escaped the woman's throat, and her eyes softened as she tilted her face toward the night sky. "T'ere." She gestured to the city of ruins, which was now basking in the glow of dozens of fires in the valley below. "You see how t'e sky shakes? Do you feel it? T'e gods will soon descend. I must go."

Before Zanya could respond, the woman hobbled off toward the valley. Zanya watched her crooked frame balance down the path until she reached the ground, where Arwan waited for her.

Zanya examined the perfect, clear sky. Her eyes widened when the atmosphere seemed to shift far beyond the point of the moon.

Wavering clouds of shimmering color formed in the distance.

A cheer roared from the crowd below, and flames from the fires cast flickering shadows over the celebrators dancing around them. Children ran along the outskirts of the valley, their faces and chests painted in bright colors as if they were tiny ancient warriors.

Zanya stepped forward, admiring the royal blue, emerald green, and deep purple streaks illuminating in the sky. The dancing lights were mesmerizing.

Energy surged through her, forcing her heart to race. But this time it wasn't her. It was her stone, reacting to the presence of the gods of Tamoanchan.

A warm hand took hers. She looked to see Tara beside her, her lips parted. A tear ran down her friend's cheek. Zanya squeezed her hand. She looked back down at Arwan, who stood beside the base of a temple. Drina's arm was interlocked with his. As much as the priestess wanted to seem cold and callous, it was clear she loved Arwan like a son. At least he had that.

She inhaled, fighting back the flood of emotion tearing through her. If only things would have turned out differently, this night could have meant so much more.

Cold skin grazed the outside of her other hand. Jayden's fingers slipped between hers, and he stood silently beside her. She tried to smile. She really did. But her heart ached so intensely, she couldn't stop the sob clawing up her throat.

Jayden rested his cool lips against her forehead. "I know," he whispered. His familiar voice brought a tiny shadow of comfort.

The chants grew louder as the lights reached toward the crowds. The first swirl of color wound around two Riyata, who stood on the other side of the valley with their hands interlocked.

Zanya sucked in a gasp while a soft white glow surrounded the lovers. Inside it, streaks of blue and green swayed and fluttered, bonding the two for life. Then there was a burst of light, as though a star had exploded, sending a rippling glow around the bonded pair.

Jayden squeezed her hand tighter. She glanced at him and then at Tara. Neither of them took their eyes off the scene in front of them.

Peter approached and took Tara's other hand. The four of them stood side by side, watching the lights of Aurora bond willing souls. Another streak of light touched a couple, then another. It was magical and heartbreaking all at the same time.

A cluster of purple and green swirled and wove above her. Zanya lifted her gaze, watching as it became denser. The lights pulsed with life. Her stone buzzed wildly, streaking adrenaline through her veins.

"What's going on?" Peter lifted his gaze to the gentle cyclone of colors above them.

Tara shook her head. "I don't know."

Zanya stared at the lights of Aurora slowly sinking down to the earth. She glanced to either side of her, then back up to the sky just as the lights engulfed them.

A cool wave of light washed over her skin. The hairs on her arms stood on end, and her chest quivered with every breath.

A burst of light exploded in the valley below, as if a star had fallen.

She gasped when the light in her chest burst to life with hues of white and blue, intertwining with the lights of Aurora, and creating an invisible bond that could never be broken.

The heartache and fear lifted, finally allowing her to embrace what was underneath. The desire she'd pushed down for so long rose up like an army, staking its claim over her heart.

As the lights softened and lifted, Zanya opened her eyes and peered through the colorful layers. A smile spread over her lips, and she let out a long exhale.

As the colors drifted upward, she stood breathless, smiling the first real smile in a long time.

Tara and Jayden had let go of her hand. They stood on either side of her, their eyes wide. Zanya swallowed, not sure what had just happened. She was…different. Excitement bubbled in her chest.

Her heart was open and free. The bonds that had shackled her with such deep regret had been broken, and all she wanted was Arwan.

***

Arwan

Arwan held his breath, his feet rooted to the ground. Drina fisted her hand and pressed it over smiling lips, staring at the sky.

He raised his gaze to the heavens. The wavering outline of a woman's face lingered in the lights. Arwan blinked and peered more closely at the familiar features. The image danced and wavered for a moment longer, then dispersed into the starlit night.

"What just happened?" Arwan said. He stilled, and for the first time since he could remember, the darker half of him was quiet. There was peace. "Tia Drina?" He turned to the old woman, who was pointing at the hillside. A soft laugh pushed between her lips.

Arwan's breath picked up. He scanned the hillside, and spotted Zanya, her light like a beacon.

A breeze ran over the land, lifting Zanya's dress and pushing strands of hair across her face.

He brushed his fingers together with the urge to touch her.

Drina smacked him on the back of the head. "Stupid boy. Go to her."

Arwan stepped forward, his chest rising and falling with every anxious breath. Something had happened. Something impossible.

He burst into a full sprint, darting between people and weaving up the trail leading to the peak of the hill.

When he reached the top, Zanya stepped forward with her lips gently parted, looking beautiful and surreal. He closed the distance between them and then slowed his pace as he drew close.

"What the hell is going on?" Eleuia snarled.

Arwan heard her rigid voice but never broke his focus on Zanya. He took her hands, and a current of energy sparked between their fingers. "How is this possible?"

She slid her fingers between his, shaking her head. "I have no idea."

A moonlit shadow swooped over the ground. Arwan lifted his gaze and watched as a great white owl soared above, her eyes glowing like two small gems.

Zanya rested her hand on his chest, her fingers splayed. She shifted closer.

The bond pulling him into her nearly ruined him.

"I'm not just going to stand by and watch my daughter bond with that *thing*." Eleuia charged toward them with a scowl.

Zanya spun and shielded Arwan. "Mom, please—"

"No!" Her body trembled. "This isn't even possible. He must have done something. Something dark."

"Ellie." Renato rested his hand on her shoulder.

She slapped it away. "Don't you try to stand up for him! He is an abomination, and as long as he's here, he'll do nothing but bring the middleworld down in smoke and fire."

"You don't know that, Mom." Zanya's tone had turned desperate.

Arwan gripped Zanya's hand tighter. She needed to know he was there. That he'd never falter.

Eleuia's eyes narrowed. "Then I won't allow it. Choose. Him, or us."

Zanya glanced at Arwan. "You can't be serious."

She squared her jaw. "It's your family," she said, gesturing to the group behind her. "Or the half-breed." Her glare shifted to Arwan. "Make your choice."

EPILOGUE

Contessa

Contessa smoothed down her hair, content to see her beauty and charm had been rejuvenated when she'd returned to the underworld. The souls of those men—those stupid, piddling, mortal men—did nothing for her. She would have to find another source of energy if she was going to continue to exhaust so much power.

Contessa waited, tapping her polished nails against the petrified chair in the king's greeting room. The once-majestic castle had deteriorated since she'd last visited the ninth realm of the underworld.

The king hadn't seen it yet—the first layer of the underworld. She'd passed it as she descended. It was still in ruins from Sarian's failed attempt to stake his claim. That was one of Sarian's most treacherous downfalls. He thought small.

The heat from the ninth layer of the underworld was fierce, scorching her cheeks. This time she took the opportunity to examine what she hoped would be the kingdom under *her* rule one day. Fire, death, and anger flourished and grew here as if the realm itself were alive.

Giant arched doors made of charred wood burst open, and a sweltering breeze crawled over her. Contessa blinked and squinted against the inferno. She stood from her seat and pulled her shoulders back, her chin tipped up. "Your Majesty." She curtsied.

"What news have you?" he demanded. His eyes flashed red and black.

She sauntered toward him, swaying to and fro, enjoying the decomposed mush of death and rot under her feet. "It seems the prince is reluctant to reclaim his throne. I gave him ample opportunity to come home."

"You delivered my message? You told him I still have hope he will accept his place as heir to my throne?" He watched her intently, homing in on any clue she was being untruthful.

Fortunately she was a very talented liar.

"I did, and rather than returning to his father, he returned to the group of Riyata instead." Her gaze shifted to the pair of hellhounds trotting into the room, their fur singed to expose boiled flesh. She used her power to demand they heel at her sides. When they obeyed, she ran the backs of her fingers between their ears, grinning at the king. "It seems your guards have taken a liking to me, my lord."

He watched the hounds pant, their tongues licking at their oversized jaws. "It seems they have."

She tilted her head. "I've come to wonder if they are the only ones who find my company…" She licked her lips. "Pleasing."

The king squared his jaw and his eyes darkened. "What kind of trickery are you playing, witch?"

She cringed at his final word and pressed her lips into a tight line. "I play no tricks. But if you prefer this to be all work and no play, I can certainly get straight to the point."

"Please do." He paced while listening, his hands linked behind his back. Getting into the king's head would be more difficult than she'd thought. It would take finesse.

"Your son rejects his rightful place," Contessa stated bluntly. "He has made that abundantly clear. Your general is dead, killed by the very person you hoped would take over your throne."

The king continued to pace with no change in his expression.

"As I retained the power of Sarian's mother after her death—"

"Do not attempt to cloud my knowledge of what really happened, dear witch." He stopped pacing and faced her. Her throat tightened under his gaze. "You slaughtered Aditya. She was one of my most trusted allies, and you ended her."

A fierce fire rose in Contessa's chest. "I did not simply end her. I *consumed* her," she snarled, clenching her fist in front of her, *possessing* her words. "I drove a blade through her chest, pierced her heart, and then ate it."

His eyes narrowed, and he stepped toward her, each foot pushing lava and fire from the ground.

Her chest jumped when he grabbed her arms. Her bones ached under his tight grip. "You are a force of the gods."

Her lips curled into a grin. "Are you flattering me, Your Majesty?"

He jerked her forward and hovered his lips above hers. "Perhaps." His gaze flickered to her mouth.

"You do not need a general any longer," Contessa whispered. "You do not need a prince, nor your guards, nor any other *pathetic* creature under your command." She cautiously rested her hands over his armor. Her skin burned on the heated steel. "What you are in desperate need of, Your Majesty, is a queen."

*****Sneak Peek*****

Find out what happens next in:

ANARCHY

Book Four of the Stone Legacy Series

CHAPTER ONE

The glittering lights of aurora wrapped around Zanya's body, spinning in a cyclone of ghostly blue, emerald green, and purple. The light in her chest beamed with life as tears streamed down her cheeks.

Jayden still hadn't figured out what exactly happened. The lights were meant to bond souls, both in this world and in the afterlife. If they were touching Zanya, it could only mean one thing.

The crowds near the base of the temples gathered around fires with offerings of jade and maize. They cheered and chanted, beating on drums and dancing like the aboriginal Mayans, who had carried out the tradition for thousands of years.

Jayden backed away from Zanya, nearly stumbling on protruding rocks buried in the grassy hill. Everyone in their group waited with wide eyes, their chests puffed out as if they were holding their breath.

Jayden fisted his hands, watching the woman he

would die for, wrapped in the arms of the guy she was never supposed to be with.

It should have been *him* holding her close.

It should have been *him* kissing her.

He swallowed against a dry throat. It didn't make any sense. Arwan was half underworlder. Bonding with Riyata was forbidden. Hell, it was impossible. The two bloodlines just weren't compatible.

Zanya's mother, Eleuia, shook with fury. "I mean it," she said in a demanding tone, her sharp eyes trained on Zanya. "Choose him," she jabbed her finger at Arwan, "or us. Because I won't allow that *thing* back in my house."

"For the gods' sake, Ellie," Renato pleaded.

"No!" She spun and glared at her brother. "You've done enough damage as it is. She is *my* daughter."

Jayden's gaze stayed trained on Zanya. She was so damn beautiful in that dress. He clenched his fists tighter.

"You can't be serious," Zanya said, shaking her head. "How can you ask me to do that?" Her chest rose and fell with every quickened breath, her fingers still interlocked with Arwan's.

She held him so close, as if letting him go would ruin her. For the first time, Jay believed it actually would. Any chance Jayden had with Zanya was lost.

A collection of cheers shook the air. Jayden's head jerked up. He'd almost forgotten where he was.

With the lights retreated into the sky, the winter solstice celebrations had begun. Newly bonded couples were hugged and congratulated, though their group was far out of the crowd's reach.

"How can you guys just stand there and let her do this?" Zanya's desperate tone brought his focus back to her. It took him locking eyes with her to realize she was speaking directly to him.

He parted his lips to talk, but couldn't speak. He couldn't—couldn't stand up for them. Not when everything he wanted was torn away. Not when he still loved her.

Zanya's gaze shifted to Tara, who walked toward the newly bonded pair. "Yeah, this is messed up." Tara reached Zanya's side and faced the rest of the group, then crossed her arms over her chest. "They don't have any control over this stuff," she said, gesturing toward the lights in the sky. "There's got to be something more going on here that you guys missed."

"Missed?" Eleuia's tone had turned deadly. She stepped toward Zanya, who shifted in front of Arwan as if she were protecting him. "I didn't spend all this time hidden and running, just to return to a piece of underworld garbage like him," she spat, glaring at Arwan. "He'll ruin our kind's only hope at a future. He is the reason I missed you growing up, Zanya. Why your dad isn't here anymore."

Zanya flinch and dropped her head. Waves of hair drifted in a warm breeze, a soft sheen in her eyes. "No, Mom." She pushed out her chin and pursed her lips. "My father died because you fell in love with someone you weren't supposed to." She looked at Arwan and took both of his hands.

Jayden's throat tightened and he swallowed hard.

His breath increased in speed, and the dread building in his gut only worsened while he tried desperately to collect his thoughts.

He raked his fingers through his hair. Shit. He had to get the hell out of there before he lost it.

Jayden caught a glimpse of Hawa studying him. She held his gaze for a split second before he looked away.

He couldn't stay if he had to watch Zanya be with someone else, and he'd be damned if he spent another second as anyone's doormat.

Jayden analyzed his surroundings. The city of Tikal was crowded with parked cars of every type for the celebrations. The taxi drivers had abandoned their cabs to participate in the solstice.

He slipped away from the group and peered in car windows, one at a time. If he left on foot it would take twice as long. He needed a ride.

He paused when he spotted a pair of keys dangling from the ignition of a taxi. *Bingo*. He slipped into the driver's seat and turned the key. The engine roared to life. He took a moment to draw in a deep breath. Leaving was the only answer. He had to look out for himself now. No one else would. He wrung the steering wheel so tightly his knuckles turned white.

When he glanced in the rearview mirror, he was able to see the others, still crowded in a tight group, none of them realizing he was gone. Zanya backed away from her mother, drawing even closer to Arwan.

Jayden ground his teeth. To hell with this.

Just as he shifted the car into drive, the passenger

door flew open and Hawa sat, then slammed the door behind her. "Where do you think you're off to?"

He exhaled sharply. "Get out."

"Uh, not happening. I saw how you looked back there. There's no way I'm letting you just take off alone."

He scoffed. "What do you care?"

"Who said I do?"

"Then get out," he barked.

Hawa bit the inside of her cheek, examining him. "Look. I know how bad it sucks to watch the person you care about be with someone else."

Jayden relaxed his grip on the steering wheel. He'd almost forgotten that she and Peter used to be together, and Hawa was forced to watch while he fell for Tara.

Hawa shrugged. "Plus, it'll be nice to get the hell out of the jungle for a while." She gestured to the carved path of crushed grass. "Well? Are we going or what?"

He hesitated, glanced once more in the rearview, and then slammed his foot on the gas. Grass and dirt spit out from the back tires.

He didn't look back.

A blur of green streaked past their windows as he sped out of the jungle. Anger bubbled inside of him, paired with a deep, unsetting humiliation. How could he be so stupid? He never would have gotten Zanya back. It was just his luck. Always the underdog. Always the loser.

The tension in his muscles wound tighter until he couldn't stand it anymore. Searing range exploded through him. He balled his fist and punched the center of the steering wheel as hard as he could. "That *wasn't* supposed to fucking happen!"

The car swerved and Hawa grabbed the wheel, preventing them from flying into the trees. "Whoa! Either pull over or calm the hell down before you get both of us killed!"

Jayden punched the steering wheel one more time, and then relieved some pressure from the gas pedal. The car slowed to a reasonable speed.

"You good?" Hawa slowly let go of the wheel.

He nodded and took back control of the car. Both of them were silent the rest of the drive out of the jungle. He needed the time to think, and thankfully Hawa wasn't one of those girls who couldn't shut up if her life depended on it.

He slowed when they reached a paved road, making the rest of the ride smoother.

"You *do* realize when we get in town, the cops will probably be looking for this taxi, right?" Hawa slouched in the passenger seat and kicked her heavy leather boots on the dashboard, bobbing her foot left to right. "Unless the owner of the cab is too wasted to realize it's been taken, at least until tomorrow morning. That'll buy us a couple of hours."

That was the best-case scenario. It would give him enough time to figure out what he was going to do next, because at the moment, all he knew for sure was that he wouldn't go back to Renato's house.

"So, where to, *el capitán*?"

The muscles in his shoulders tensed again. "I don't really know."

"Sweet." Hawa flipped on the FM radio and fiddled with the stations until Latin music thumped from the speakers. She leaned back again, mouthing the lyrics.

He glanced at her. "That's it? You don't care that I have no idea where the hell we're going?"

She shrugged. "Not really. I'm always in for a good adventure."

"I'm *not* going back to Renato's house."

She yawned and laid her head back on the seat. "Let's roll down the windows." Hawa used the hand crank to let the night air pour into the cab.

Since when did she want to be around him? Hawa gave off a *screw you* vibe every second of the day. Suddenly, she was up for a road trip? Maybe she'd decide to split when they arrived at the next town…or maybe not. He glanced at her again. Slouching in her seat, her eyes were closed and black hair whipped wildly around her.

He swallowed, his stomach twisting and bubbling. Why was he so freaked out about her being around?

Who cared?

Jayden blinked and shook his head as if trying to clear the thoughts out of his mind.

He did, apparently.

He had to keep his shit together. He stole a quick look at the gas gauge. Full tank. Good. He'd just drive through the night until they reached civilization. At least he didn't have to worry about getting tired anymore. His muscles relaxed. This whole kinda-dead thing had its advantages.

ACKNOWLEDGMENTS

A mother's support is always present and never ending. Thank you, Mom, for being the support I needed to finish this book.

To my husband: Thank you for stepping over way too many dirty socks while I sat in my office, typing this book. You saw my drive and passion, and realized some things had to be compromised. So you gave me a smile and said, "come on kids. Let's help mommy and clean the house." It was a short, seemingly ordinary moment to most. But for me, it meant so much.

About the Author

A long-time enthusiast of things that go bump in the night, Theresa began her writing career as a journalism intern—possibly the least creative writing field out there. After her first semester at a local newspaper, she washed her hands of press releases and features articles to delve into the whimsical world of young adult paranormal romance.

Since then, Theresa has gotten married, had three terrific kids, moved to central Ohio, and was repeatedly guilt tripped into adopting a menagerie of animals that are now members of the family. But don't be fooled by her domesticated appearance. Her greatest love is travel. Having stepped foot on over a dozen countries, and traveled to sixteen U.S. states—including an extended seven-year stay in Kodiak, Alaska—she is anything but settled down.

Wherever life brings her, she will continue to weave tales of adventure and love with the hope her stories will bring joy and inspiration to her readers.

Facebook:
https://www.Facebook.com/theresa.dalayne

Twitter:
https://www.twitter.com/theresadalayne

Goodreads:
https://www.goodreads.com/author/show/7847410.
Theresa_DaLayne

Website:
http://TheresaDaLayne.com/

Instagram:
http://www.instagram.com/authortheresadalayne